THE MURDER CLUB

THE MURDER CLUB

Agata Stanford

A JENEVACRIS PRESS PUBLICATION

THE MURDER CLUB

A Dorothy Parker Mystery / May 2013

Published by
Jenevacris Press
New York

———◆———

ISBN 978-0-9857803-1-9

Printed in the United States of America

www.dorothyparkermysteries.com

For Anatole Konstantin, engineer and inventor,
Benedetto Puccio, architect and artist,
and Martin Greer, money manager.

Also by Agata Stanford

The Dorothy Parker Mysteries Series:

The Broadway Murders
Chasing the Devil
Mystic Mah Jong
Death Rides the Midnight Owl
A Moveable Feast of Murder

Acknowledgments

Thanks to my sisters, Rosaria Konstantin and Mary Rose Greer, and my good friends, Loretta Grabowsky, Jeannette Sinibaldi, Shelley Flannery, and Eric Conover, as well as the School of Performing Arts Class of '67 for their constant encouragement.

Contents

Who's Who in the Cast of
Dorothy Parker Mysteries

The Algonquin Round Table was the famous assemblage of writers, artists, actors, musicians, newspaper and magazine reporters, columnists, and critics who met for luncheon at one P.M. most days, for a period of about ten years, starting in 1919, in the Rose Room of the Algonquin Hotel on West 44th Street in Manhattan. The unwritten test for membership was wit, brilliance, and likeability. It was an informal gathering ranging from ten to fifteen regulars, although many peripheral characters who arrived for lunch only once might later claim they were part of the "Vicious Circle," broadening the number to thirty, forty, and more. Once taken into the fold, one was expected to indulge in witty repartee and humorous observations during the meal, and then follow along to the Theatre, or a speakeasy, or Harlem for a night of jazz. Gertrude Stein dubbed the Round Tablers "The Lost Generation." The joyous, if sardonic, reply that rose with a laugh from Dorothy Parker was, *"Wheeee! We're lost!"*

Dorothy Parker set the style and attitude for modern women of America to emulate during the 1920s and 1930s. Through her pointed poetry, cutting theatrical reviews, brilliant commentary, bittersweet short stories, and much-quoted rejoinders, Mrs. Parker was the embodiment of the soulful pathos of the "Ain't We Got Fun" generation of the Roaring Twenties.

Robert Benchley: Writer, humorist, boulevardier, and bon vivant, editor of *Vanity Fair* and *Life Magazine,* and drama critic of *The New Yorker,* he may accidentally have been the very first standup comedian. His original and skewed sense of humor made him a star on Broadway, and later in the movies. What man didn't want to *be* Bob Benchley?

Alexander Woollcott was the most famous man in America—or so he said. As drama critic for the *New York Times,* he was the star-maker, discovering and promoting the careers of Helen Hayes, Katherine Cornell, Alfred Lunt and Lynn Fontanne, and the Marx Brothers, to name but a few. Larger than life and possessing a rapier wit, he was a force to be reckoned with. When someone asked a friend of his to describe Woollcott, the answer was, "Improbable."

Frank Pierce Adams (FPA) was a self-proclaimed modern-day Samuel Pepys, whose newspaper column, "The Conning Tower," was a widely read daily diary of how, where, and with whom he spent his days while gallivanting about New York City. Thanks to him, every witty retort, clever comment, and one-liner uttered by the Round Tablers at luncheon was in print the next day for millions of readers to chuckle over at the breakfast table.

Harold Ross wrote for *Stars and Stripes* during the War, where he first met fellow newspapermen Woollcott and Adams. The rumpled, "clipped woodchuck" (as described by Edna Ferber) was one of the most brilliant editors of his time. His magazine, *The New Yorker,* which he started in 1925, has enriched the lives of everyone who has ever had a subscription. His hypochondria was legendary, and his the-world-is-out-to-get-me outlook was often comical.

Jane Grant married Harold Ross but kept her maiden name, cut her hair shorter than her husband's, and viewed domesticity with disdain. A society columnist for the *New York Times*, Jane was the very chic model of modernity during the 1920s. Having worked hard for women's suffrage, Jane continued in her cause while serving meals and emptying ashtrays during all-night sessions of the Thanatopsis Literary and Inside Straight Club.

Heywood Broun began his career at numerous newspapers throughout the country before landing a spot on the *World*. Sportswriter and Harlem Renaissance jazz fiend, he was to become the social conscience of America during the 1920s and beyond through his column, "It Seems to Me . . . ." His insight and commentary made him a champion of the labor movement, as did his fight for justice during and after the seven years of the Sacco and Vanzetti trials and execution.

Edmund "Bunny" Wilson: Writer, editor, and critic of American literature, he first came to work at *Vanity Fair* after Mrs. Parker pulled his short story out from under the slush-pile and found it interesting.

Robert E. Sherwood came to work on the editorial staff at *Vanity Fair* alongside Parker and Benchley. The six-foot-six Sherwood was often tormented by the dwarfs performing—whatever it was they did—at the Hippodrome on his way to and from work at the magazine's 44th Street offices, but that didn't stop him from becoming one of the twentieth-century Theatre's greatest playwrights.

Marc Connelly began his career as a reporter but found his true calling as a playwright. Short and bald, he co-authored his first hit play with the tall and pompadoured *George S. Kaufman*.

Edna Ferber racked up Pulitzer Prizes by writing bestselling potboilers set against America's sweeping vistas, most notably, *So Big, Showboat, Cimarron,* and *Giant.* She, too, collaborated with George S. on several successful Broadway shows. A spinster, she was a formidable personality and wit and a much-coveted member of the Algonquin Round Table.

John Barrymore was a member of the Royal Family of the American Stage, which included *John Drew* and *Ethel* and *Lionel Barrymore*. John Barrymore was famous not only for his stage portrayals, but for his majestic profile, which was captured in all its splendor on celluloid.

The Marx Brothers: First there were five, then there were four, then there were three Marx Brothers — *awww, heck,* if you don't know who these crazy, zany men are, it's time to hit the video store or tune into Turner Classic Movies!

Also mentioned: *Neysa McMein*, artist and illustrator, whose studio door was open all hours of the day and night for anyone who wished to pay a call; *Grace Moore*, Broadway and opera star, and later a movie star; Broadway and radio star *Fanny Brice* — think Streisand in *Funny Girl*; *Noel Coward*, English star and playwright who took America by storm with his classy comedies and bright musical offerings; *Condé Nast*, publisher of numerous magazines including *Vogue*, *Vanity Fair*, and *House and Garden*; *Florenz Zeigfeld* — of "*Follies*" fame — big-time producer of the extravaganza stage revue; *The Lunts*, husband-and-wife stars of the London and Broadway stages, individually known as Alfred Lunt and Lynn Fontanne; *Tallulah Bankhead* — irreverent, though beautiful, southern-born actress with the foghorn drawl, who later made a successful transition from the stage to film—the life of any party, she often perked up the waning festivities performing cartwheels sans bloomers; **Irving Berlin**, **George Gershwin**, and **Jascha Heifetz**—famous for "God Bless America" and hundreds more hit songs; composer of *Rhapsody in Blue* and *Porgy and Bess* and many more great works; and the violin virtuoso, respectively.

THE MURDER CLUB

Chapter One

They were known as "The Murder Club." Six authors in search of the perfect murder plot for the new mystery novels they were writing. Never could they have dreamed of what would befall them starting this day, the eleventh of October, in the year of our Lord, nineteen-hundred-twenty-nine.

Who would want to see them dead?

On this glorious autumn afternoon a bunch of us went to see Gino Di Cenzo to wish him luck on the opening of his new place. The speakeasy's new location is on the parlor floor of a Midtown brownstone, and it was smart of Gino to reopen his establishment two doors down from the police station. Having police protection is highly desirable. So what if the cops drank free? For cops the juice flowed free at any one of the other half-dozen speaks on the block, and most of the Boys in Blue knew Gino Di Cenzo from the days before the country dried up as the proprietor of Di Cenzo's Italian Restaurant around the corner on the avenue.

Since the hypocrites voted the country dry while guzzling down the imported stuff in the back-rooms of Capitol Hill, new businesses have been created—the manufacturing of rotgut, rum-running, bootlegging—along with the mobsters who run these operations. The pretense is wearing thin; nobody cares anymore. The courts have been so overrun with arrests that there is no room on the dockets to deal with real crime, so now everyone turns a blind eye, except, occasionally, the gung-ho Fed with a quota to fill.

After the tragedy that closed Gino's business almost two years ago, his excellent food had been missed by the men in the Department as well as the neighborhood folks. Nobody, and I mean *nobody*, can make a sauce like Gino. And as for his saltimbocca, there is no contender. But Gino just couldn't bear the tragic loss of his wife and teenage son in the fire that took their lives as they slept in the rooms above the restaurant. It happened on the very night Gino was standing vigil over the hospital deathbed of his mother, Mama Santina (as she was known in the neighborhood), the matriarch whose recipes were the afternoon daydreams of many a New Yorker. Gino lost his family and business in one horrific night.

So the cops were sympathetic, of course, and positively understanding after Gino woke up one morning last winter on the second anniversary of the passing of his beloved family. As he told it, he'd dreamed a vision of Santa Lucia winging down toward him, her robes aflutter against the dark void from whence she'd flown, forcing open his eyes and yelling in an oddly familiar voice, "Get outta-da-bed, you lazy-good-f'nuttin'!"

The fact that the shout was oddly reminiscent of Mama Santina on the Sunday mornings of his youth, rallying him to mass, may have been disconcerting but was nevertheless an instant eye-opener. It wasn't Sunday, but he had to do *something*, and all he ever knew how to do was cook.

A restaurant was a big enterprise to start up again, but he figured he could at least cook for a few of his old customers in the apartment he was renting for twenty bucks a month. It was his cousin, Salvatore, newly arrived from Naples and eager to harvest off the streets of New York the reported gold therein, who convinced Gino to sell the wine and the gin he was distilling in the garage of an abandoned house in Brooklyn, sponsored by the Brooklyn Union Gas Company, whose gas lines he had cleverly diverted to supply the power for the production of the spirits.

When Gino opened his doors last week, it was only natural for Sgt. Joe Woollcott and his cronies at the precinct to stop in, and for Joe to tell his cousin, the famous New York drama critic, Alexander Woollcott, the news of the grand-reopening of Di Cenzo's, instructing Aleck to pass the news on to all his famous friends. That's why, the afternoon after the doors were officially, if clandestinely, opened to the public, along with Aleck's pressing desire for a crispy-creamy cannoli—or three—a bunch of us walked over the few blocks after lunching at the Algonquin to welcome the long-missed Italian back to the neighborhood. We toasted his success, and to the future absence of federal agents from his establishment.

We settled in at a table and the waiter took our orders: an orange juice for me—"imported"—and a "can of beans" for Mr. Benchley, Aleck, and Frank Pierce Adams. Harold Ross and Jane Grant ordered "kit-and-caboodles." I asked for a "domestic" bowl of water for Woodrow.

We were enjoying our various cocktails in coffee cups when the lights flickered. We all knew what that meant, and our suspicions were confirmed when we heard feet treading heavily on the floor above, followed by the Running of the Bulls through Pamplona on the stairs. By the time there sounded the determined banging on the door we had already drained our cups of alcoholic beverages. Decoy pots of coffee had been delivered to the half-dozen occupied tables and the dumbwaiter bar stocked with hard imported spirits sent down into a trap in the basement below.

"Gino Di Cenzo," prefaced a little woman who walked over from a table toward the proprietor, "I arrest you for violations of the Volstead Act—"

A burly fellow swung an axe through the entry door, and then eyed, threateningly, the big water tank behind the bar.

Woodrow, who had been snoozing under the table, perked up and positioned himself in a spread-legged defensive stance. He bared his teeth and growled.

"Stop!" cried Gino as the man lifted his axe. "It's just a fish tank! See the catfish?" He broke away from the federal agent to intercept the man. "Taste it yourself, God help you." He opened the top and ladled out a coffee cup full of water from the big tank behind the "soda-counter."

"Careful—don't gag."

"*Shit!*" shrieked the agent, spitting out the water, even more determined to smash the tank.

"Of course there's shit in it," I said. "Fish have to go to the bathroom somewhere!"

"Unsanitary," said Mr. Benchley. "I never drink water or swim in a pool on account of that very reason."

The arresting agent pulled off her wig, revealing a tweed-skirted fellow teetering in high heels who grabbed Gino from behind the bar. He shook his head at the axe-wielding brute standing twice his size to stave off the destruction, and then ordered the other agents to search the premises. In a few minutes they returned from the kitchen with a bottle of Marsala.

"Bought before the Act went into effect," explained Gino. "Sacramental wine!"

"This ain't a church!"

"To Sicilians, Marsala is sacramental wine!" piped in Aleck.

"For *cooking*, for cryin'outloud!" said Gino.

"What's going on?" bellowed a baritone voice entering from the hallway and announcing the arrival of New York City Police Captain Michael Delaney.

"Oh, *crap*, Morton," yelled the captain after a quick assessment. "Whadda you want to bother Di Cenzo for? Sit down, you sonovabitch, and your posse, too, and have a plate of spaghets. Gino! Bring out the spaghets and a couple loaves of bread—garlic bread, okay? You! Put that goddamn axe down before you break sumpthin'."

When Morton objected to the policeman's interference, the captain smiled wide, and in a comradely fashion slapped him on the back, unbalancing the high-heeled Morton and sending him face-first into Aleck's plate of Italian cheesecake. With a look of disgruntled resignation, Aleck offered the federal agent a fork.

"Well, if it isn't the famous Alexander Woollcott and his band of merry men!" laughed Delaney. "And ladies." He nodded as he helped Morgan up to a standing position.

"Tell your men to take a load off, Morton, and wipe that cream off your face. It's disconcertin', 'f you know what I mean."

Mr. Benchley handed the agent his dinner napkin.

"Coffee?" offered Jane Grant, raising the pot.

"Chic outfit, Mr. Morton," I said, *stirring* the pot. "But you gave yourself away when you didn't shave your legs."

Morton considered the situation hopeless—he would get little cooperation from the police in making an arrest. Nowadays, nobody cared to prosecute the little guys; they were after the big crooks. So he huffed and puffed in defeat, tore out the itchy breast padding, and called off his dogs. His three government stooges took a table near the kitchen and ordered lasagna.

Harold Ross looked at the discombobulated Morgan, pulled up a chair from a vacant table, and said, "Have a seat."

Frank Pierce Adams offered, "Have a nickel cigar."

"Finish your dessert," ordered Jane, placing the plate of mashed cheesecake in front of him and hovering over the little man like a mother over a child's dish of uneaten vegetables.

"He really should try the cannoli," said Ross to Jane, who, after assessing the disparity between the corpulent Woollcott and the morbidly skeletal

Morton, pilfered a pastry from off Aleck's vast array of treats.

"I don't know why I bother," said the scrawny agent. "I make ten arrests a day, and *none* of them hold up in court, if they even get before a judge, which ain't often."

"Well, Billy," said Captain Delaney, addressing Morton as if he were an old friend, which he was, the two men having fought side by side during the Spanish War, "it's a pointless task, a waste of departmental resources. We've got bigger fish to fry these days, what with sopping up blood after Frankie Yale, and there's Luciano, the sonovabitch, and his friend, Meyer Lansky, the turd, and the Black Hands, the White Hands, and the Red Bolshies bombing everything. . . ."

"A regular kaleidoscope of hoodlums," said Ross.

As the captain recited the ever-lengthening list of culprits in the New York City Police Department's war on crime—"Bugsy Segal, Arnold Rothstein"—I looked out through the curtained window at the street, my eyes traveling toward a familiar figure: The writer, Ernest Stringer, was weaving through the pedestrian traffic at a faster pace than the usual brisk New York stride. Ernest, best known as "Ersatz" to his friends, was in a hurry to get someplace.

And then there appeared a fellow who reminded me a little of another writer I knew slightly, Trevor Hunter, zigzagging closely behind in Ersatz's footsteps.

This must be what it is like to be a cat, perched in a windowsill, watching the comings and goings of life outside the window. I spied a new, shiny-blue Dodge slowing to a stop from which three pretty girls fluttered out to disappear under the canopy of the hat shop on the south side of the street; a Chinaman walked out of the Bradley Bank and Trust and rode off on his food-delivery tricycle parked in front of the Pagoda restaurant next door; a mother struggled with an armload of packages and three rambunctious kids; a sophisticated boulevardier in dove gray swung his walking stick with practiced finesse as he paraded along the sidewalk, his standard poodle taking the lead. A teenage newsie hawked the afternoon editions, shouting the headlines; two men argued animatedly in front of the barbershop Indian, who I imagined assumed the role of silent referee. Two police officers escorted a burly mobster out from the police station and into a squad car. Reporters crowded in around them, cameras angled to capture the event for their evening papers.

And then the clang and whine of a fire engine sounded along Eighth Avenue, its horn blast repeatedly warning to clear a way through the traffic. A sudden end to the racket came as it turned just off the corner onto the street below; men were leaping down from the truck and searching for signs of a conflagration after a firebox alarm had been pulled. The reporters quit the precinct house for the newly arrived drama.

Watching the world outside the window was better than listening to Delaney drawl on about the less salubrious elements of our fair city. Jane asked me a question, but before I could turn in reply, this cat spied something more engaging than the proverbial mouse making a dash for the cheese.

"I think the bank across the street is being robbed," I said.

Mr. Benchley leaned over my shoulder and peeked out the window. "Why, so it appears, Mrs. Parker. But isn't it past banking hours?"

"What are you talking about?" said Captain Delaney, cutting short his recitation with a chuckle of disbelief. His attention was on the plate of steaming spaghetti and meatballs Gino was placing before him. "What makes you think that?"

"The man with the machine gun backing out through the doors, I'd say."

"By gosh, Mrs. Parker, you're right!" nodded Mr. Benchley, lighting my cigarette.

Captain Delaney pushed his great girth between us to peer out toward the scene on the street below.

"I don't fuckin' believe—McCarthy! Jones! Get down there. They're making off—Holy *shit!*"

This was no time to raise an alarm about the captain's language, I told Mr. Benchley, who was often critical of my own. The cops thundered out of Gino's and down the flight of stairs leading to the street. The big axe-wielding federal lug who had been leashed by his master and was now straining at the bit followed suit on the nod of his superior, Morton, who remained at the table stuffing his face with pastry. The rest of us crowded at the windows to watch as the bank robbers got in their getaway car, tires screeching as they stuttered off. The car stalled for a second, and with a loud backfire sent a puff of black exhaust into the air and onlookers to seek cover. The bank dick, staggering out, blood dripping down his forehead, yelled a warning that sent more people scattering for safety, some hitting the sidewalk, some running for cover behind parked automobiles at the sight of his drawn weapon. He fired at the robbers, which triggered a return hail of bullets from the getaway car, ricocheting with a pinging tattoo on a metal restaurant sign, piercing a stack of afternoon-edition newspapers into a confetti celebration over the newsstand, and splintering the wooden slates of a delivery wagon and sending forth a cascade of toothpicks and chicken feathers onto the street. One bullet hit its mark in the security guard's shoulder, the sting of pain and surprise knocking the gun out of his hand before he slumped to the ground.

Screams of panic propelled the wave of pandemonium in the wake of the getaway car's exhaust fumes. The short route to Seventh Avenue was blocked by traffic, so the robbers took to the sidewalk, riding the curb like a rail, sending screaming pedestrians to fly for cover against buildings and into doorways, skimming a mailbox and then a firebox, and knocking a fire hydrant a-kilter. The hydrant keeled over like a dead man, and after a breath-holding moment, followed by a portentous rumbling from the depths of the earth, it exploded. The gusher rose thirty feet into the air, obscuring our view just as the car disappeared around the corner.

The icy spray prompted more shrieks of cold surprise before people scattered away from the soaking deluge. A dozen of New York's Finest stormed out from the precinct house, weapons drawn as they ran toward the bank in a better-late-than-never, if ineffectual, show of strength.

As the drama outside dampened and the springtime sunshine cast a rainbow over the spray, I thought: *Only in New York does one rise in the morning to a day of exciting possibilities.* As I watched the shimmering effects of sunlight on the mist rising from the geyser, I thought of how my friend, Scott Fitzgerald, said it right: "New York has all the iridescence of the beginning of the world." Yes, great things begin here.

As I turned away from the street scene, my eyes landed on Captain Delaney's untouched plate. I stabbed a fork into one of Gino's fabulous meatballs. Big, black, soulful, needy eyes looked up at me. Woodrow Wilson had the power to shame me or con me. There was no use trying to ignore those liquid peepers boring a hole through my resolve. I tossed him a meatball.

Chapter Two

The crush of reporters blocked my view of the disembarking passengers from the *S.S. Mauretania*, docked at New York Harbor's Pier 54. Flashbulbs brightened a steel-gray day as the newsmen shouted the usual queries:

How's it feel to be back in the States, Mr. Fairbanks?

Are you looking forward to presenting your new theories to the Society, Mr. Einstein?

All New York is talking about you and your new play opening tomorrow, Mr. Coward.

Miss West, it's said that the King of England is your greatest fan. . . .

And then I heard the rich, bell-like voice floating over the tops of fedoras and bowlers — the reason for my gang's sojourn down to the docks: *Miss Soleil, your new book is a bestseller! Are you moving back to New York permanently?*

I turned to smile at Mr. Benchley, who was dutifully holding Woodrow in his arms to spare my pup getting trampled in the crowd. Aleck waved and bellowed out a contralto singsong, "Yoo-hoo!" to get Soledad's attention. She spotted us and nodded as she replied to the reporter from the *Daily News*, "I'm a homing pigeon, don'tcha know? And New York is forever my nest," she said with dramatic gestures.

"Oh, *brother!*" said Jane Grant at the hyperbole. "Just what New York City needs: another pigeon."

"Behave yourself," said her husband Ross. "She was taking poetic license."

"Well, someone should revoke it!"

"I thought you liked Soledad," I said.

Jane rolled her eyes.

"I absolutely adore the woman," Ross replied at the sight of the flamboyant mystery writer cutting through the crowd toward us. "Look at her! She doesn't walk, she floats! She's no pigeon; she's a swan!"

"Oh, brother," said Jane, not a little jealous, especially when Ross dove through the crowd to meet the beautiful woman.

"*Darlings!*" Soledad gushed. There followed cheek-kisses and hugs all around.

Aleck was beside himself, for he, too, adored Soledad Soleil from the moment I introduced them to each other in Paris a few years ago. Mr. Benchley and Ernest Hemingway and I got to know her during our crossing to France on the *S.S. Roosevelt*. But that is another story.

She gave me a squeeze and we squealed with delight, like bouncing schoolgirls. I couldn't help but giggle with joy at our reunion. It had been a year since we'd been together in New York, and it was grand that she would be taking up permanent residence here. I took a long look at my friend, who smelled of Shalimar and rice powder. And now she had succeeded in seducing the sun out from behind the clouds to shine on her sleek, dark waves. Her powder-blue ensemble—dress, duster, and matching chapeau—brought out the vivid blue of her eyes, and she was dripping rows of pearls. Her glossy-red smile dazzled. If I didn't love her so much, I'd be furiously jealous of her, like Jane.

The smile compressed, her voice dropped an octave, and her eyelids narrowed as she leaned in to whisper in my ear in a conspiratorial tone, "I could use a stiff one."

"Alas, what girl couldn't?" I replied, picking up on the double entendre.

She fluffed off my remark with, "*Pshaw!* You've a dirty mind, Dory darling."

"I wash and press it every morning, but by noon—well, you know how it is."

She turned her appeal on Aleck, who handed her a fabulous bouquet of lilacs and pink roses.

"Don't look at *him!*" I said, referring to Aleck's dubious nature, and we all laughed because no one has ever been quite sure about our friend, who likes to dress up as literary and historical heroines whenever he has the chance. He flashed me a withering glare.

Ross opened his mouth to speak, but Jane cut him down with an elbow to his gut.

Mr. Benchley opened his mouth to speak, but uttered only a gasp when I said, "You hound, you!"

"What?" he replied, feigning injury, while reaching into his coat pocket and removing his flask to offer a swig to Soledad. "Nothing wrong with being a hound, now, is there, Woodrow, old boy?" he said, nuzzling and scratching my pup behind the ears.

"All right, Bob, I'll settle for a drink, then," said Soledad.

After Soledad's trunks were sent on to the Plaza, we hustled her into a taxi, destination the Algonquin Hotel for lunch with the rest of the gang: George S. Kaufman, Heywood Broun, Frank Pierce Adams (a.k.a. FPA), me, Mr. Benchley, Aleck, Jane, Ross, and, arriving in a huff, playwright Marc Connelly, who squeezed a chair between Aleck and FPA.

As he took his place, Frank ran his hand lovingly over Marc's bald head.

"As soft as my wife's behind," he said.

Marc followed the gesture with his own hand. "So it is, so it is."

Frank chuckled good-naturedly. After all, a good comeback was always expected, and I knew he'd have wanted to include it in his column tomorrow, but for the editorial censor. There was no doubt that Soledad would be the main focus of his Samuel Pepys–styled column in tomorrow morning's paper, which was syndicated across the country.

"Marc," said George to his sometime-collaborator, "I understand your new play is full of single entendres."

"You know, it's just not the same without Harpo," said Soledad, when she asked about the Marx Brothers. "Everything is so . . . pleasantly subdued."

"We are basking in the funereal quiet, if you don't mind," remarked Ross.

"The boys have no time for lunch these days," said Aleck, presiding over the table like a mother superior. "They are too busy playing in *Animal Crackers* at night, just down the street at the Forty-fourth Street Theater—we'll see the show tomorrow, if you're free Soledad—and during the day they rush out to the Astoria Studios to make a talkie motion picture of their last show, *The Cocoanuts*.

"George wrote *Animal Crackers*, you know," I said.

George S. Kaufman raised his dark pompadour, which canopied his plate of ham and beans, at the sound of Soledad's exclamation. He replied with sullen resignation.

"Yes, yes, I wrote the book of their show, yes, with Morrie Ryskind. Let me rephrase that: Morrie and I wrote *a* play. But the brothers perform a different play every night, some *thing* of their own concoction. Our plot and their story may converge at times—the sets are the same, the songs don't vary—but as in every actor's nightmare, where the poor fellow cannot remember his lines, I wander around backstage unable to find a word I've written in the script. I didn't learn my lesson the first time."

"George wrote the book for *The Cocoanuts*, too, the Broadway show they are now filming," interjected Jane.

Big, lumpy, disheveled Heywood Broun, political and social columnist, sports writer, theatre critic, and all-around raconteur—the term *sorry-sack* comes to mind—chuckled and said: "George took the bowdlerization of his book very hard—lots of head-banging during rehearsals and while watching from the wings on opening night."

"At rehearsals, the only author that's better than an absent one is a dead one," said George. "Still, the Brothers manage to bring down the house every night at eight, and I get full credit, so who's complaining?"

"I'm not!" said Broun. "I saw *The Cocoanuts* thirty-three times, didn't I? And the boys always kill me. Fact is, Georgie-boy has absolutely nothing to do with the show."

"They kill you every time, do they?" said George. "Why, oh, why, doesn't it stick?"

"Broun's a zombie," said Ross.

"Ah, the undead!" said Soledad. "What a wonderful protagonist for a book!"

"Truth is, Sollie," said Ross. "George may not be bright, and he may not be dead between the ears, like Broun over there, but he isn't stupid enough to get in the Brothers' way, that's all."

"Thank you, Ross," said George. "I think?"

"Yes," said Broun, waxing dramatic, "when I leave this crazy world, I want written as my epitaph: *'Killed by getting in the way of some scene-shifters at a Marx Brothers' show.'*"

"What this country needs are more zany creatures like the Marx Brothers!" Mr. Benchley announced like a politician.

"God forbid!" I said. "Isn't there a big enough infestation of fools in Congress?"

"I'll tell you what this country needs," said FPA, his small and compact figure garbed in an excellently tailored cloth as always. He is the driving force behind the national fame of our little luncheon club, the *bon mots* of which he would recount in print in his daily column, *The Conning Tower*.

He pushed back from the table and then leaned back in his chair for the first step in his ritual cigar lighting. "There are plenty of good five-cent cigars in this country." He flicked his lighter. "The trouble is they cost a quarter." He puffed hard and then regarded the stinker he had just lit. "What the country needs is a good five-cent nickel."

"What the country needs," began Aleck as he slathered butter onto yet another popover, "is the stinkless cigar!"

"Who's the pretty one over there?" asked Soledad, admiring a rugged-looking man in a trench coat talking with Frank Case, the hotel manager. Frank pointed in our direction.

"Beats me," I replied.

"The brute!" she said with a scowl. "Look! He's headed our way!"

"I'm sorry to interrupt your lunch—" he began in a polite tone. His voice was a warm, rich baritone, with just the hint of a smile simmering deep within.

His jaw was strong, a prominent feature. His eyes were a clear-blue sky set against a snowy field, with serious, straight, wheat-colored brows. This was the countenance of Adam, or of a less-than-perfect Adonis for the little scar above his lip that marked his humanity. Embodied was the driving sexuality of Tristan, the might of Apollo, and the appeal of Dionysus I fancied, and if I weren't careful, I would see him in my dreams. But this appealing package all wrapped up in a trench coat was a man you didn't want to mess with, unless it left one's sheets a jumble.

"The Statue of David," whispered Soledad, as if she were reading my mind.

"You've undressed him already?"

"Mr. Benchley, stand aside!" she giggled in my ear.

Aleck gazed starry-eyed at the new arrival, if one can gaze starry-eyed through thick spectacles. But, that is how best to describe Aleck's admiration for the fellow standing over us, other than to say that Aleck suddenly stopped shoveling apple pie into his face, and it takes a lot to stop the momentum of his steam-shovel dining style.

If the rather unattractive jokers at the table wished they were seated under it for a time, they put up a good bluff. After all, these men were the greats of the newspaper and entertainment industries, so even if they were suddenly self-conscious in the light of this Greek God standing before them, they could hold their own for brains if not beauty and brawn. I looked at Ross: a sullen scowl with a Fuller Brush haircut. I glanced at the unkempt, matronly Broun, and turned to the gangly, large-beaked, black-haired buzzard that was George. I appraised the shiny, freckled, bald dome of a chubby Marc Connelly, and the rodent in the fancy suit, FPA, with his rattail comb-over, and decided that none of them, not even my debonair Mr. Robert Benchley, could hold a match, much less a candle, to this Adonis, this Billy Bud, this Titian-patrician.

"*Do* sit down and join us, young man," said an ingratiating Woollcott, signaling our waiter, Luigi, to fetch a chair. "Move over, will you, Connelly!" he ordered roughly.

The playwright did as he was told with grudging speed. He knew enough to move fast, for Aleck could easily, by his massive girth alone, shove him over if he chose.

Wedged between a decidedly pissed-off playwright and a groveling gourmand, the fellow declined the offer of coffee and got right down to business. "I'm Detective Nate Sparrow of the New York City Police Department, Eighteenth Precinct."

"It's only a friendly poker game, Detective—" interrupted Aleck, thinking that the visit by one of New York's Finest (and he was fine, all right!) was because of the complaints of other residents of the Gonk about the weekend poker games held in the second-floor suite of the hotel. After Jane had finally thrown the card players out of her dining room and told them to go to hell, the boys begged Frank Case to let them return to the hotel for their two-day games, promising to behave, never again to stamp out cigarettes on the carpets or spill booze on the upholstery, and to tip, not stiff, the waiters who served and cleaned up after them.

"Yesterday afternoon, I was told, several of you witnessed a bank robbery—"

I raised my hand. He nodded, and I said, "I do—I mean, I did!"

What? Was I still a kid in Miss Dana's School? Did I answer the question correctly?

The gang frowned at me; they didn't appear to appreciate a smarty-pants. It's not the way to make friends in the classroom.

"Captain Delaney was with you, Mrs. Parker, at Gino Di Cenzo's restaurant, and he said there were others—"

"Yes, several of us were there enjoying our just desserts," said Aleck, in a tone that suggested we'd attended, and very much enjoyed, a performance of *The Nutcracker.* "Gino's pastries are fantabulous!"

Why couldn't he talk like a human being? Who was he trying to impress, as if I didn't know! Was I going blind? Were Aleck's eyeglasses fogging up?

"Mr. Woollcott, the menu of the restaurant is not up for review . . ."

Sparrow flashed Aleck a wary grin, a normal reaction, I'd say, to an encounter with the lunatic fringe. The smile vanished promptly as the detective unfolded a sheet of paper and read off the names.

"Dorothy Parker, Robert Benchley, Alexander Woollcott—"

"Here!"

"Here!"

"Present!"

"Yes, all right . . . Franklin Pierce Adams—the columnist, right?"

"At'cha service!"

"Harold and Jane Ross."

"That's Harold Ross and I'm Jane *Grant*," corrected in my girlfriend, who had adamantly clung to her maiden name.

"Is there anyone I left out?"

We all looked at each other.

"All right, I need to ask you all a few questions."

"We had nothing to do with—I mean, we didn't see anything that Delaney—Captain Delaney, that is—didn't see for himself," said Ross, sounding guilty for just having witnessed the crime.

"Please let me be the judge of that, sir."

Nice manners, a gentle-but-firm technique. With a couple of deft strokes, Detective Nate Sparrow sent Ross to the principal's office and Aleck back to the second grade.

Well, I thought, *this is a new experience: a homicide detective who is nobody's fool!* And believe me, over the past few years I've encountered quite a few fools in the police department.

I should be fair. Mr. Benchley and I have been caught up in several cases of murder and general mayhem, and we haven't always played by the conventional rules. My friends and I have provided our own variety of mayhem to our method of cracking cases. Thanks to our connections in the newspaper business, and the daring, if imbecilic gall of the Marx Brothers, Mr. Benchley and I have brought to justice a number of dangerous criminals. But, often we've needed the assistance of Sergeant Joe Woollcott, up at the Eighteenth, Aleck's cousin from the normal side of the family. He was the spitting image of Aleck, but in a uniform of blue serge instead of a red-satin-lined opera cloak. Sergeant Joe is our *inside man*—meaning we are privy to autopsy and ballistic reports and can call on him for backup when in a pinch. And we often find ourselves in a pinch, usually between a rock and a hard place, for a good old cliché that fits the bill. Without Joe's help, lots of bad boys—and girls—would have gotten away with murder. Now, sitting before us, looking all gorgeous and efficient and generally— gorgeous—was a homicide detective *with smarts.*

No fooling around with this guy. But, I knew in my heart-of-hearts I would figure out some way of fooling around with this guy.

"Oh," said Heywood, "You want to talk about what went down yesterday afternoon! It was front-page news in all the evening editions — seren-dipitously for all those reporters hungry for a scoop covering the arrest of Big Dick Dietrich at the police station. Their cameras not only captured the Big Man but were blessed with a false fire alarm and the bank heist, too!"

Heywood's obvious joy at the luck of his news-paper pals in light of the havoc wreaked on one little side street yesterday received a blank stare from Detective Sparrow, causing our friend to quickly exchange the toothy grin on his face for a more sober expression.

"You want to interrogate the witnesses, of course. I wasn't there, so, having nothing to offer, do you want me to leave while you interrogate?"

"This is not an *interrogation*, Mr. Broun. No one here is suspected of any crime, so I'd like all of you to stay, for reasons I will, in time, explain."

Nice move. Heywood sent to the corner wear-ing the dunce cap.

"Mrs. Parker, I believe it was you who alerted Captain Delaney that the bank was being robbed?"

"Oh! Am I the 'key' witness? How exciting!"

"Oh," said Soledad with a trill in her voice. "This is what detectives do first, you see: They in-terview the witnesses, get a dozen contrary versions of what happened, and then dismiss the eyewitness accounts altogether."

"Please tell me exactly what you saw out the window, Mrs. Parker."

"Yes. I was looking out of the window onto the street, thinking about what it's like to be a cat, and how my friend, Scott, waxed poetic about our city, and—"

"Mrs. Parker?" The detective interrupted my reverie.

"Oh, yes . . . I watched people walking along . . . I watched the officers taking Big Dick Dietrich—say that name three times for a tongue twister!—and then the fire engine pulled off the corner of Eighth Avenue, blocking the way. And then I saw a gentleman with a machine gun coming out of the bank."

"I wouldn't call a man carrying a machine gun a gentleman," interrupted Mr. Benchley.

"He was very well dressed, I'd say Burberry, and he carried a briefcase."

"So does Mayor Jimmy Walker, and I don't care what you say, the man ain't no gentleman!" said Jane.

"Ladies!"

"Sorry, Detective. Let me say, then, *the guy* was wielding a machine gun."

"Yes?"

"And then I told the Chief that the bank was being robbed, and everybody came to watch out the window—except for the Chief and his lieutenant, I think, or was he a sergeant?"

"Corporal?" asked Jane.

"Don't be absurd!" interjected Ross. "There are no corporals in the police department."

"You're thinking navy. Corporals are in the navy," said George with a straight face.

"Whatever he was," I said, "he was in a policeman's uniform. Anyway, the Chief and the policeman left, but not the Fed, a gentleman named Morton—"

"That was no gentleman, Dorothy," said Frank. "He was wearing a skirt."

"All right, all right! The Fed in the skirt! He sent his flunky to help the Chief and his corporal, and then he sat down and ate the Chief's dinner."

"And most of my cheesecake, don't forget!" said Aleck.

"No gentleman, he!" said Mr. Benchley.

"Can we get back to what you witnessed outside the window?"

"Yes, Detective. Well . . . the bagman came out of the bank—"

"The bagman? You mean another man joined the gunman?"

"Oh! You mean the man with the gun isn't called a bagman?"

"A gunman is a gunman, Mrs. Parker," corrected Mr. Benchley, "and a bagman is a bagman."

"I see."

"What does a bagman do?" asked Jane.

"He's like a redcap; he carries your bags," said George.

"Of money," added Frank with a chuckle.

"Well, the first fellow was carrying a briefcase— Mark Cross, so I thought—"

"Did you see its serial number?" asked Mr. Benchley. I shot him a look.

"Dottie, how many men came out of the bank?" asked George.

"There were three," said Frank.

"I only saw two," said Jane.

"Are we counting the driver of the getaway car?" asked Ross.

"But he didn't come out of the bank," said Jane. "He was in the car, so he couldn't be a bank robber, you see."

Detective Sparrow had heard enough.

"Will everyone please allow *me* to conduct this interroga—interview?"

The children had been properly reprimanded. Chastened, we folded our hands on our desks and awaited the next lesson.

The detective nodded at me and said, "Proceed, please, your account?"

"Yes. Well . . . then the gentle—the man with the—the gunman—waved the gun around and shouted something. The window was closed, so I don't know what—"

"That's all right; what he said just then isn't important right now."

"Unless he gave his name and address," said Marc.

"Then what did you see?"

"People scattering, machine-gun bullets flying around, and the gunman and the bagman jumped into the getaway car and drove wildly, onto the sidewalk; policemen were running out of the station firing shots at the car, and people were screaming, and then a fireplug exploded!"

"Does anyone have anything to add?"

Everybody shook their heads, including George, Marc, Heywood, and Soledad, which was odd, because they hadn't even been at the scene of the crime.

"All right, Mrs. Parker," said Sparrow, nodding his head. "That's pretty much what other eyewitnesses saw, except for the details of the gunman's wardrobe."

"Do you want the license plate number of the getaway car?"

I didn't know why Detective Sparrow appeared so surprised. "You got the plate number?"

"Yes," I said, diving into my purse, "all but the last number. My pencil broke."

I pushed aside a Coty lipstick, a rouge-stained handkerchief, a box of matches, a pack of Lucky Strikes, and several business cards from people I'd probably never call on and which were all stuck together around a wad of melted after-dinner mints I'd thrown in there some time ago. Unable to locate the paper I'd scribbled the number on, I dumped the contents onto the table.

"Need a shovel?"

"Shut up, Ross. It's in here somewhere," I said, while Mr. Benchley took his butter-knife and began separating out the toothpicks from gum wrappers and broken pencils from hatpins and scrap paper from half-a-dozen bobby pins before lining them all up along the cloth like little dead soldiers.

"I'm fascinated by archeology," said Mr. Benchley. "We should come across some pottery shards, soon, or, if lucky, the Tomb of Tutankhamun."

"Didn't I tell you to be quiet?" I reprimanded.

"No, my dear, you told Ross."

"Wait! I didn't carry this purse yesterday." A groan swept like a virus around the table. "But I remember it—the number." A collective cheer.

"It was NY237."

Detective Nate Sparrow smiled his approval—or was it amusement?—and chuckled quietly as he shook his head. "Well, we can certainly try to find the car, although it was probably stolen for the heist. I must commend you on your presence of mind, Mrs. Parker."

"My mind is always present."

"Not always; sometimes it takes little excursions," said Mr. Benchley.

"Why, last Thursday evening, for instance," said Heywood, "it took a flight of fancy—"

"Yes, thank you, Mr. Broun," interrupted Detective Sparrow, "but it is not only the bank robbery that I wanted to discuss with those of you who were there. There was another incident that occurred at the same time, and I'm hoping that one or more of you might have seen something to shed light on what happened."

Silence overtook our table. I could hear Heywood's inhalation, Frank's cigar-smoke exhalation, and Soledad's little gasp.

"Two people were wounded by the gunman when he sprayed fire over the street," he began.

"I've a feeling there's a twist in this little plot," whispered Soledad.

"A third man was shot and killed."

"So we have a bank robbery with a murder charge," said Aleck.

"Two separate crimes, I'm afraid."

The officiating, and often tiresomely officious, Aleck, ordered, "Explain yourself, Detective!"

"A man by the name of Ernest Stringer was shot."

"Ersatz!" I blurted. "Ersatz Stringer!"

"I believe it is *Ernest* Stringer."

"That's his nickname," explained Aleck.

"But I saw him!" I said. "He was walking along the street right before I noticed the gunman coming out of the bank."

"This is what I was hoping to hear—that one of you saw the crime."

"Who the hell is Ersatz Stringer?" asked Soledad.

Before I could reply, Detective Sparrow said, "He was a writer."

"At one time he was a second-string show critic!" corrected Aleck.

"What an unfortunate name!" laughed Soledad. "But I suppose it was fitting. Do you suppose he was killed by a disgruntled performer or playwright for giving a bad review?"

"If that were the norm," said George, "someone would have murdered Aleck long ago, and Marc over there would be the number-one suspect."

"I suppose Ersatz was in the wrong place at the wrong time, Sollie," I added, "and got hit by a stray bullet."

"I think you misunderstand me. Mr. Stringer was not killed by a bullet from a machine gun, nor from any fired by the men of our department on the scene."

"Oh, so you think he got in the way of some cowboy, some vigilante passerby who shot him while trying to take down the bank robbers?" asked Ross.

Sometimes astute, Aleck said, "But that's *not* what you believe."

"The bullet that hit Mr. Stringer was not the cause of his death, according to the medical examiner."

"So you believe he was murdered deliberately?" asked Marc.

"Have you ever heard of a murder committed that was not deliberate, you imbecile?" said Ross.

"That is what happened," said the detective.

I pictured in my mind's eye the scene I had witnessed barely twenty-four hours ago. Ersatz Stringer cutting a path through the pedestrian traffic. I had recognized the odd hat he always wore—a green fedora with a feather.

"I caught sight of that mangy green hat he always wore, with the feather. The kind you might see men wearing in the Swiss Alps."

"A Französin Hut, is its proper name," corrected Mr. Benchley.

"Whatever *Frickosin' hat* it was, he always wore it."

"Mrs. Parker, from what direction was he approaching?"

"He was walking from Eighth Avenue. Walking fast."

"Did you see if he was with anyone?"

"He was alone, at first I thought he was, weaving through people walking along the sidewalk, like he was late for an appointment or something. Oh, and then I saw a fellow I thought looked familiar, but I can't be certain it was he. He looked like Trevor Hunter, but I can't be sure of that. He *limped like Trevor does*, so maybe that made me think of Trevor. Ersatz and Trevor knew each other, were friends, if I recall. Trevor's a writer, too. The man who looked like Trevor had his collar up and his hat covered his eyes and shadowed his face. He looked like he was in a hurry as well, a couple of paces behind Ersatz, filling in the path Ersatz cut through the crowd, maybe trying to keep up with him. Oh, my! You don't suppose Trevor killed Ersatz? Now, remember, Detective, I said I can't be sure it was Trevor Hunter walking behind him!"

"We just want to know what you saw, whether Mr. Stringer was with anyone in the moments before he was killed. No one is accusing anyone of a crime as yet."

"It's the term, *as yet*, that I'm afraid of!" said Ross.

"It just means we have to talk with the person who may have been the last person to see Mr. Stringer alive."

"Other than Dorothy, you mean," said Aleck.

"Did anyone else here, who was watching from Di Cenzo's, see Mr. Stringer, or any other activity that was unusual—other than the bank heist?"

Everyone who had been present shook their heads, except for Smarty Pants Parker: "I didn't know it until I saw the boy on the bike with my own eyes: The Golden Pagoda Chinese restaurant now delivers!"

"Since when?" asked Heywood, with a frown and an accusatory tone of disbelief.

"Since—how the hell do I know?" I threw back. "I saw the kid loading packages into the basket and then he rode off. The restaurant is right next-door to the bank; how could I miss it?"

"Mrs. Parker; sir," said Sparrow, eyeing me and Broun, the headmaster breaking up a schoolyard brawl. "Please. I've come to you today for your help."

Oh, brother, I thought, *this poor fellow had no idea what he was walking into when he approached our gang of misfits.* It was a good thing that Harpo was absent today, or the man would leave here completely discombobulated.

"I don't know how else we might assist you, Detective," said Aleck. "Those of us who were watching from Di Cenzo's saw pretty much the same thing—the bank robbers making their getaway. And Mrs. Parker was the only one of us who caught a glimpse of Ernest Stringer—"

"But I didn't see for sure if it actually *was* Trevor Hunter who was on his tail, and I certainly won't say I saw Trevor kill Ersatz—I mean, Ernest Stringer."

"Well, you see, it was your cousin Joe, Mr. Woollcott, who suggested I come to talk to all of you today, to solicit your help in finding out who may have had reason to kill Mr. Stringer. As he was a journalist, a serious writer, and theatre critic, an author of some renown—"

My friends sitting around the table were too polite or reluctant to speak ill of the dead—although that never stopped them before—to contradict the Detective's glowing assessment of the late Ernest or Ersatz Stringer's literary accomplishments. And so, instead, Ross snorted, Heywood brayed like a donkey, Marc sniffed the air like a bloodhound, Frank puffed like bellows on his cigar, George sighed in resignation, and Mr. Benchley let loose a nervous, if girlish, giggle, which indeed spoke their dissent in volumes. Jane, Soledad, and I turned to Aleck, who cleared his throat with an exaggerated rumble.

"Ah, yes, my dear, *simple* cousin Joe," nodded Aleck, drawling his words like a seemingly benevolent and patient Almighty, his hands steepled while pro-claiming from his heavenly perch. "Joe might be under the *delusion* that all who aspire to the literary arts are in fact equal in talent and skill, and therefore, it is assumed, must fraternize within the same professional circles, which, I must inform you, is far from the truth—"

"The man was a hack," interrupted Ross, cutting to the chase.

Unable to resist, George turned to his fellow playwright and sometime-collaborator, Marc Connelly. "You looked at Connelly when you said that, Ross," said George.

Marc flipped George the bird.

Mr. Benchley interrupted the adolescent she-nanigans. "Detective, there were a dozen or so re-porters and photographers wielding their cameras, so everything that happened must be documented."

"That's right, the papers didn't print everything the cameras captured, you know," said Frank.

"That is so, Mr. Adams, and the editors have been most cooperative in the sharing of all they have. We believe that the false fire alarm was meant to divert attention away from the bank. But there aren't any pictures documenting the moment of the robbers' getaway or the immediate surrounds at the time of Mr. Stringer's death, only photos of the general chaos that followed—people running, the hydrant spraying.

"Well, thank you, gentlemen, ladies," said Detective Sparrow, "that's all for now. I will leave you to enjoy the rest of your lunch. Oh, and one more thing: I'd appreciate the details of Mr. Stringer's death being kept under wraps and out of the papers for the next twenty-four hours. Let's let the murderer think we are fooled. For now let it be believed that he was killed from a bullet fired by the bank robbers."

"You do realize you have been discussing this whole thing with a bunch of newspaper men?" chuckled Aleck. "It's asking a lot."

"If there is honor among thieves, Mr. Woollcott, I trust there is honor among reporters. Twenty-four hours, please."

"Ha!" Aleck laughed. "We will forgive the comparison, as there is truth in that!"

"Detective Sparrow," said Soledad, "if the bullet didn't kill him, what did?"

"He'd been poisoned."

"Shot *and* poisoned? I'd say that wasn't murder, that was overkill," said Frank.

When Sparrow left, Marc said, "Why didn't he grill you witnesses better?"

"I'm certainly glad he didn't!" said Mr. Benchley. "Never give the police roasting instructions. You know how it works with them: They grill you, unmercifully, and then when they're done with you they turn up the heat and you get fried to a crisp in the electric chair."

"It appears to me," said Soledad, "that you may not have fraternized with the late Mr. Stringer, but you've provided Detective Sparrow a substantial amount of information in just a very few observations."

"You think so?"

"Yes, Dory, darling. Tell me more about this Ersatz character."

"Ernest Stringer," began Aleck, "'Ersatz' to everyone in publishing circles—obtained his less-than-flattering moniker while working as a third-string drama critic for the *Sun* back in 'seventeen, from whence he was sent off to review the lesser shows on the vaudeville and Yiddish stage that any first-string critic wouldn't even consider wasting his time on, let alone column space. Another pot of coffee, Luigi."

"In 'twenty-two," added Jane, "he wrote and got published a trashy novel, *Blaze*, about a teenage girl who left a trail of dead bodies in her wake as she climbed her way up the ladder in the world's oldest profession—"

"Society matron," chuckled Frank.

"Yes, and because of the sensational nature of the story—sex, booze, greed, sex, murder, and, uh, sex—it was banned in Boston—"

"—which made it an instant bestseller," said Frank.

"It was a crummy book," said Heywood, "but it had sex, lots of it."

"*Sex, sex, sex, sex*," said Aleck, shaking his head.

"Yes, it did," I nodded, "and sometimes sex, halfway-decent sex, is distracting enough to overlook bad writing—"

"—and the fact that he snorts when he laughs or has a forest growing out of his ears—" said Jane.

"I certainly do *not* have hair growing out of my—" objected Mr. Benchley, sticking an index finger in his ear. "My nose, perhaps . . ."

I threw my friend a withering stare. "Jane was talking about Ross, dolt!"

"Oh, yes, now that you point it out, he does have hair—*by God!* She's right! It's a veritable Kansas wheat crop!"

Ross turned on Mr. Benchley with offended response: "Didn't Dottie tell you to shut up?"

"She told *you*, Ross."

"I told you *both*, you nincompoops!" I said, and then tried to return to answering Soledad's question: Who was Ernest Springer?

"Ernest Springer has spent the past six—no, seven or more—years trying to write another best-seller," I said. "I don't know much more than that, or why someone would want to poison him."

SS Mauretania

Chapter Three

Jumping from a five-story building will probably kill you. If you want a guarantee, there are lots of taller buildings around Manhattan. But the taller the building, the longer the trip to the street, during which time you may have second thoughts, and as there's no turning back, well, then, where would you be? I wouldn't suggest jumping off of any building over eight stories. Why suffer second thoughts?

I entertained these morbid daydreams as Woodrow and I strolled through Bryant Park after lunch.

For years I have struggled with the recurring and pressing desire to end my life, and I have come to see that I have no real talent, outside of the dramatic gesture, for making the decisive "leap" into oblivion. I always wake up back where I started.

So, as Woodrow and I circled around his favorite sniffing spots, memories of a rainy night nearly a half-dozen years ago came rushing back to me, when any ambiguity over my future existence became decidedly bent toward survival, even in this imperfect world. My eyes fell upon a stalwart presence.

Across from the park, bordering 40th Street, towered the Gothic Art Deco behemoth known as the American Radiator Building. Back in 'twenty-four, I had found refuge there from a determined killer. The building is an astounding twenty-three stories. At the time, that seemed huge to me. Looking around the landscape of Manhattan today, it is a dwarf among giants.

There's a new monster growing up a short, three-block walk from Bryant Park on the corner of 42nd and Lexington, called the Chrysler Building. Now that it is near completion, I have to say it is strikingly beautiful, with its radiating terraced arches and sunbursts, the marvelous sheen of silvery "stainless steel." Its automobile-like grillwork is stunning.

Rumor has it that Walter P. Chrysler told his architect, William Van Alen, that he wanted the building not just to scrape the sky but to pierce it. *Ha!*

There has been a frantic race among the moguls of industry to literally top each other with their "skyscrapers." These warring factions are certainly changing the landscape of our city as a result of their skyscraper wars. The bigger the ego, the bigger the structure. It's a "mine-is-bigger-than-yours" mentality. Case in point: Chrysler insisted that the design of his building include an extravagant apartment on the highest floor. After all, he was paying for the place from his own pocket, for cryin'outloud, so he should get his money's worth, right? And in this apartment, he told Van Alen, there must be the most luxurious bathroom, from where, according to rumor, "he could take a dump on Henry Ford and the rest of the world."

Now, downtown, Chrysler's competitor in the phallus-building contest, the Bank of Manhattan and Trust, has just completed its erection of 40 Wall Street, soaring toward the heavens at 927 feet. This exceeds the final expectation of Van Alen's design by just a couple of feet. Men and their measuring sticks.

The landscape of my city is ever-changing. A friend, on his third visit from France, when asked when he would return to New York, replied, "Let me know when it's finished."

When I was born, in the last century, there was nary an automobile to be seen; north of Columbus Circle the west side of the Central Park was still mostly a mudscape of shantytowns flanking the pathway to the Dakota apartments, and ten blocks beyond, the Museum of Natural History. We've filled in all the spaces; the only way left is up. I suppose the skyscrapers of today reflect our national exuberance for building the biggest and best.

Now, after ten years of increasing prosperity, I wonder at what height will the sky be the limit before the ceiling is reached? It's been a decade of glitter, and I can't help wondering how much longer it will

last. Everything is moving so fast that the pessimist in
me just knows the party has to end sometime. We're
all getting too old and tired of staying up all night. I
can smell change coming in the air, the way you smell
rain right before the storm. My group of friends are
scattering further away from the city and for longer
periods of time. Hollywood has beckoned many of
them, including my Mr. Benchley, who often travels
west on motion picture assignments. Yes, I can smell
the change in the air. I suppose I'm a little afraid that
I'll be caught in the deluge without an umbrella.

———•———

Ernest Stringer's obituary was published in all
the afternoon editions, and having seen the notice,
Edna Ferber telephoned Aleck to ask if he was planning to attend the wake or the funeral service. After
all, Aleck knew Ernest from before the War, when he
was Drama Critic for the *Sun* and Ernest was his un-
derling, more an office boy, really, fetching and typing
and generally doing Aleck's bidding. He later filled
in as second-string reviewer. And so it was decided
between them that they would pay their respects to
the deceased later that evening, after cocktails at my
rooms at the Algonquin.

I had invited the usual suspects for drinks, as
well as mutual friends of Soledad's who were anxious
to see her again after an absence of nearly two years
from the States. My two rooms were crammed with

dozens of people and there was an overflow into the hallway, my door kept open to the traffic of fifty or more partygoers at any given time during the two hours. Aleck insisted on providing the hors d'oeuvres, which he catered from the Colony, along with two cases of champagne sent by his bootlegger. Jane and Ross brought a gallon-jug of gin, homemade, from their bathroom distillery, and there were bottles of imported scotch and Canadian rye provided by several of the more affluent guests. Besides Mr. Benchley, Aleck and Edna, Marc, and Frank, whom we had lunched with only a couple of hours before—Heywood Broun was off to Madison Square Garden to cover a prizefight and George Kaufman was at home and at work on a new show—most of the other guests welcoming Soledad back to the States were book publishing people.

At around seven o'clock the party was winding down, and Soledad made a grand exit to go off to her suite at the Plaza. Her publisher, Josh Latham, a silver-gray fox in his mid-fifties with a scholarly Yale-Oxford twist marking an otherwise-well-groomed sophistication, escorted her out on the premise of discussing her next book. We were to meet for supper at the Central Park Casino at ten o'clock.

So when Harpo arrived dressed in a leather flyer's jacket and helmet, its flaps dangling, soon after Soledad's departure, and peeking over a huge bush of spring blooms that must have rendered Holland barren, he was beyond consolation.

"I had the taxi stop specifically on Park Avenue for these flowers!" he cried. "You have no idea the trouble I went through to get them."

"Yes," said Mr. Benchley, "I can see you pulled up each one yourself, if the roots are any indication."

"Well, it does account for the bare meridian along Park between Forty-ninth and Fiftieth," said Chico, following him in.

"Where else can you find such beautiful tulips this time of year?" asked Harpo.

"Certainly not the florist's," said Jane.

"I didn't think about that," he replied, dirt drizzling out from the bottom of the newspaper-wrapped offering; a bulb loosened from its tangled root and fell to the floor.

"I'm sure you didn't think; it wouldn't be like you to think!" scolded Jane at her nemesis. "And what's with the aeroplane pilot's getup?"

"I've taken to the skies, don't you know?"

"Yeah," said Chico, "he's a regular penguin! You should see him soar!"

"I told you, penguins don't fly, for cryin'out-loud!" said Harpo.

Harpo's sudden appearance was often a harbinger of trouble—or a big cleanup—like the time he had arrived at the weekend card game of the

Thanatopsis Literary and Inside Straight Club, when it was still held at Jane and Ross's. He'd just returned from Aleck's retreat on Lake Bomoseen with a fish he had caught three days earlier. After presenting Jane with the stinking thing in a bag, she told him to throw the wretched fish in the trash can outside the back door, adamantly refusing to fry it up for him to eat while he played cards with the boys. "I'm not your servant!" she hollered, and when he tried putting the bag into the refrigerator, she told him "not on your life," so instead he placed it into Jane's dining-room sideboard, meaning to retrieve it after the game was over—two nights later. The summer heat wave didn't help much, and of course, he'd forgotten about the fish—I couldn't understand how, except that the stench mingled with the smell of salami sandwiches, spilled beer, cigars, and sweaty men. In the meantime, the rotting fish attracted the feline population of a twenty-block radius to scratch and screech at Jane's back door.

"Where is my little Liebchen?" moaned Harpo. "Where is my buttercup staying? I'll go to her right now."

"Your Liebchen is meeting with her publisher, and your buttercup is residing at the Plaza," said Mr. Benchley.

"Dear boy," said Aleck with avuncular magnanimity as he patted Harpo's shoulder, "try not to be too enthusiastic; you know where it sometimes leads you."

"Yeah, and we want Sollie to remain in town," said Ross with a sour face. "So don't scare her off."

Although Soledad held Harpo in high esteem, there were times when his over- rambunctious adoration tested her otherwise sweet nature. Case in point: Paris. After climbing the frontage of Notre Dame Cathedral, Quasimodo-style, in an attempt to rescue me—it's a long story—Harpo scaled the Eiffel Tower after being warned by the Paris police not to do so. Once atop the Tour d'Eiffel he refused to climb down; he had informed the press before the climb—photographers had arrived, some with motion-picture equipment, to document the startling sight of the Marx Brother's assent (or sudden descent)—that he would not climb down until the woman he loved, the famous mystery writer, Soledad Soleil, arrived on the scene to receive his proposal of marriage. Soledad, who had driven off a few hours earlier to visit Cole and Linda Porter in Antibes, became the focus of a nationwide hunt. Her car was first sighted in Dijon. By the time she went through Lyon, she'd acquired a posse. But it was a roadblock set up in Avignon that stopped her flight. Upon her refusal to return to Paris—"I love Harpo like a brother, forgive the pun, but he must be out of his mind!"—Soledad was branded by the press and most of France as the heartless hussy who had broken the heart of the romantic Frère Quasimodo. It was the arrival of the beautiful Josephine Baker at the tower's base that encouraged Harpo's descent and eased his broken heart, for God's sake!

Harpo dashed out of my apartment, Chico on his tail.

"I just don't understand all the fuss," said Jane when they'd gone.

"Soledad is a beautiful woman," I replied, "and you know how Harpo is attracted to women who are taller than he is."

"Well, there's Margaret Dumont."

"She won't have him," replied Mr. Benchley.

"Soledad is not only beautiful, but she is *de-lishous-ly—*"

"Button it, Ross!" said Jane, cutting off her husband's dewy-eyed reflections.

"Yes, old sport, it's best to keep it buttoned," agreed Mr. Benchley, hand to his trousers.

"In both places," said Jane, turning her back on the men.

"What did I say?" asked Ross, clueless, frustrated.

"You said too much," said Frank, chuckling. "You are an exacting editor, Ross—for your magazine—but you haven't a clue about how to edit your own words."

"That's right," said Mr. Benchley. "Take Frank's good advice—he's been married three times."

How to explain the union of Ross and Jane? An incongruous mating of Neanderthal man and Suffragette? Beauty and the Beast?

This unlikely couple met during the War when Jane, who'd been a society columnist for the *New York Times*, was aiding the war effort through her work with the Red Cross. She had known Aleck Woollcott from her days at the *Times*. Aleck was soon to meet Harold Ross, a reporter who had worked on a string of small-town papers before enlisting and was now a fellow writer for *Stars and Stripes*. The verbal exchanges between the slob and the dandy have continued over a dozen years and serve as an expression of their mutual love–hate relationship.

It was Alexander Woollcott who introduced Jane to the irascible Harold Ross while in Paris in 'eighteen, and it was Aleck who insisted on choosing Jane's wedding band at Tiffany's after she and Ross announced their engagement upon their return to New York after the war. And it was Aleck who replied to the clerk's request for the ring's inscription: "No inscription; she may want to use it again."

Soon, after the glow of romance had faded and gray reality had set in, it was apparent that Jane and Ross were polar opposites at cross-purposes. Although he liked her enterprising spirit, Ross hadn't considered that marriage would not replace Jane's career. He had become too lovesick to see much beyond her beauty and cleverness.

Not that Ross is an easygoing man or a delight to live with; no one could ever say that. He is often brusque. Jane, too, was blinded by whatever it is that gets splashed into the eyes of the unsuspecting when they fall in love. It's not true that, upon first seeing Ross, small children hide behind their mothers, but on first sighting, one's eyes do widen. And yet this hypochondriac—he is always convinced his head colds are precursors of terminal illness—is a trustworthy, loyal friend. Everything Ross does lately annoys Jane, and his admiration of Soledad Soleil has not helped calm things between them. I think Jane and Ross have been going through a rough patch in their marriage for the past ten years.

"Jane," said Edna Ferber, "don't bother, dear; Soledad wouldn't look twice at him. It's a wonder you ever did."

Edna Ferber is one of those people who is always cheerful, and it annoys the hell out of me. This unfortunately homely spinster is an astoundingly fortunate bestselling author, and *that* annoys the hell out of me. To be honest, if I didn't find sitting down at my typewriter to produce even one page of a short story so mentally grueling, I might be more charitable toward this prolific, Pulitzer Prize–winning author of sprawling American family sagas, she who cranks out page after page of narrative from her typewriter with the facility of a jolly laundress feeding bed sheets through a clothes wringer. That enthusiasm *really* annoys the hell out of me.

But, Edna is never mean-spirited; she is a good sport, never flaunts her success, is generous with her friends, has a sharp wit, and never throws one's shortcomings in one's face. So my annoyance with Edna is really born of my annoyance with my own lack of self-discipline. It's not really her fault that her presence makes me twitch and sets my teeth on edge.

"Shall we leave now for the wake?" Edna asked Aleck, and then turned to see whether there was anyone else interested in tagging along.

"Oh, there's nothing I enjoy more than spending a dour hour staring at a corpse," I replied.

"I thought you *liked* Basil Rathbone in *The Captive*," said Mr. Benchley.

"Isn't that why he was arrested?" I replied, knowing full well that the real reason *all* the members of the cast of *The Captive* were jailed was because the play was deemed immoral: The wife of Basil's character leaves him for another *woman*. Just shocking!

"Well, since I've nothing else to do, it might be a pleasant change to join you."

"We'll see lots of old friends, perhaps," said Frank.

"Perhaps they'll serve refreshments." I said.

I fed Woodrow the remains of the party's pâté and several chunks of imported Blue. He turned his nose up at the pickled herring, but enjoyed the cheese puffs. Mr. Benchley filled his water bowl. Before exiting the lobby, I asked our bellboy, Jimmy, to take Woodrow for spin around the block. We piled into a taxi and headed downtown to Greenwich Village.

Greenwich Village is a part of Manhattan that developed "off the grid." The Village has long been a place off the grid in other ways. It has been a retreat of sorts, going back to the early nineteenth century. People stayed and made new homes here after a yellow fever epidemic had them fleeing to the cleaner air north of the swamplands of the lower settlements. For years, this has been a community where artists gather to live lives of aesthetic sensibility, away from the rigid constraints of the Victorian society that has permeated the upper regions of Manhattan.

In this part of the city wound a patchwork of randomly set streets, because three centuries ago, long before the grid of Manhattan was laid north of here, Dutch settlers built their cabins wherever they chose to on old Indian tobacco fields. Washington Square was a potter's field, and 20,000 bodies still remain buried beneath the park. This Greenwich Village was the site of a Royalist Post before the Revolution. After the Revolution, Newgate Prison was built on what was later to become West 10th Street, near the Christopher Street Pier. Up to the north and west lay the tract of King's Farm and smaller, newly plowed farm parcels. Meadows, forests, craggy hills, lakes, marshlands, and streams that flowed pristinely through the landscape would give way to the expansion north to 14th Street and beyond, to the private farms along De Heere

Straat, later called the Bloomingdale Road, and still later, Broadway.

I am constantly aware of the old and the new as I travel by foot or taxi around my hometown. Now, after centuries of expansion north of the Battery, there is nary a grassy plot left in most neighborhoods and the city is moving upward into the sky. But there are pockets of Manhattan that have retained the relics of olden times and where little has changed from the days of my early childhood. Although I embrace our modern times, there is a part of me, a sentimental spot in my heart, that cherishes this little bit of the past when so much of the city north of Greenwich Village has been razed, leveled, and replaced. In Greenwich Village, the shop signage may change, but the small-town charm remains.

A display of shabby Bohemia greeted us as we entered Romany Marie's Café on Waverley Place, where a gathering of friends of the dead author and the morbidly curious had come to pay their respects to his memory.

Most of the mourners were a shabby bunch dressed up in their shabby best. There was an effort by some to express their respect for the dead man by the addition of brightly colored ascots and paisley scarves, which in stark contrast only served to call attention to the frayed lapels and cuffs of tattered tweeds and worn worsted suits; many of the men were unshaven and wore the pallor of poverty. By contrast, there were several gentlemen who were obviously better off, wearing business suits, a few sporting evening attire.

The female contingency came from a variety of classes: There were the drab, colorless faces of women dressed in sorry, shapeless shifts of faded cloth that hung from boney shoulders over emaciated bodies, cheap strings of inconsequential beads for decoration around their necks, perhaps a ribbon holding back dull, unruly hair, or a shabby hat. By contrast, these urchins faded into the background for the vibrant and embroidered silk fringed shawls of gypsy-styled rich girls and chicly coifed matrons in svelte black crepe. It was a heterogeneous sampling of New York's artistic life from uptown and downtown.

The room was thick with smoke from tobacco and the woodstove, on which was steaming a fragrant pot, and there was the musty smell of marijuana mingled in, which made me heady and my eyes burn. In a corner a violinist played a sad Hungarian lament. The conversations were subdued, and a waiter passed around a tray of *café noir à la Turque* spiked with brandy. Aleck beamed when he spied an assortment of pastries being brought out from the kitchen, and as he was unable to mentally will the waiter to bring the tray directly to him, he made a beeline across the room to secure a hefty selection for himself.

Ross looked sullen, obviously disapproving of the whole setup. Frank fogged up the room even more as he lit up another stinker. Mr. Benchley collapsed his top hat and assessed the room with mild amusement. Jane said, "What a dive; I love it!"

I had never frequented the Village cafés much, and in the cab Edna told us all about this place. This watering hole is where Marie Marchand fed a meal each day to the starving alcoholic Eugene O'Neill when he was first trying to write a play, back during the winters of 'sixteen and 'seventeen; it is where Buckminster Fuller played with the idea of designing a silo-like dome structure called a Dymaxion house, and collaborating with Isamu Noguchi, the model of the Dymaxion car—whatever that is. It is where painter John French Sloan liked to retire at the end of the day—he painted a lovely portrait of Marie a few years ago—and where Vincent—Edna St.—knocked off the quatrain, "My Candle," later retitled "First Fig."

"This reminds me of the cafés in Paris," I said, looking around. "Except that the place is all silvery." Candlelight shimmered along the silver-painted walls and tin ceiling like a reflection from water.

"Bucky Fuller decorated it for Marie," said Edna, "in exchange for meals. But the patrons all hated his original design. He called it 'Dymaxion' style."

"What the hell does that mean, Die-*what?*"

"'Dymaxion.'"

"You want to tell me what that means? It can't be in a dictionary."

"Don't look at me," said Mr. Benchley. "It's probably one of those words that people make up to describe some abstract idea."

"Anyway, the place was glaringly bright," continued Edna, "with aluminum tables shaped like aeroplanes that wobbled and spilled your coffee in your lap. The regulars, who were wise to the defects of the poorly designed canvas-sling chairs, used to watch and wait for them to collapse under startled newcomers—I understand there was wagering going on as to how many bottoms hit the floor each day. And there were odd, suspended cone-shaped lamps killing the soft candlelight everyone had grown used to. All that's left now are the silver-painted walls. But despite the decorating debacle, Marie is still feeding Bucky one free meal a day as payment for his décor design. There's Marie, the woman standing near the woodstove."

"The gypsy?"

"Well, she just dresses in the Romanian tradition, to honor her mother."

"Or she's too broke to buy a new dress," said Jane.

"She has quite a distinctive face," I said upon seeing the dark, broad-jawed middle-aged woman. Hers was a determined face, but not an unkind one. Her expression changed from one of frowning, concentrated attention to the man addressing her into an easy smile when Edna caught her eye. Dimples creased her wide mouth and her black eyes sparkled, giving her face a merry quality.

Marie Marchand took Edna's hand in greeting and introductions were made all around. "Yes, Marie," said Edna, "it has been many years since—back when you had the place on Christopher Street."

"Ah, yes," said Marie, "You were friends with that young man—what was his name? You used to come in together."

"That was long ago. He was the brother of a friend of mine come to New York from Missouri to be a writer. He lived down the street. He died in the War."

"Oh, I am sorry," said Marie, her face compassionate, saddened as if she knew the young man well and it was a personal loss. "So many died. . . . You knew Ernest Stringer?"

"I knew Ernest Stringer, yes," said Edna. "And Aleck knew him from when Ernest worked at the *Sun*. The publishing business is a small world, Marie; we were all acquainted with Ernest in varying degrees."

"There is his brother, Everett," said Marie, indicating a table across the room where a group had gathered around a morose-looking fellow who had an uncanny resemblance to the dead author. "He is with Ernest's friends from the Murder Club."

"What?" I said, "the Murder Club? What's that all about?"

"A writers' group," explained Edna. "They get together every so often to discuss their novels' plot lines. They run various scenarios by one another; they work out the details of their murder-mystery plots."

"Is that a wise thing to do?" I asked. "You know writers are notorious for stealing each other's ideas."

"It's true," agreed Mr. Benchley. "Why, I had an idea for a story about a parsimonious old geezer who is visited by three ghosts on Christmas Eve, and that British rascal stole it out from under me!"

"There's a little larceny in every soul," said FPA, the man whose column brazenly mimicked a daily installment in Samuel Pepys' journal.

"I had a brainstorm the other day, a story about a bunch of pie-eyed Americans bar-hopping through Paris and talking bull in Spain," said Mr. Benchley. Then, conspiratorially, "Don't tell anybody!"

I turned to see Detective Nate Sparrow entering the café. He caught my eye and touched a forefinger to his lips. It was obvious he wished to remain incognito so that he could observe the people in the room.

"Why, there's—" began Mr. Benchley, before I cut him off with an elbow to his ribs. Jane, Ross, and FPA got the message. Aleck was busy exchanging his empty coffee cup for a new one. As Edna had not been to luncheon today, she had not met the detective. She noticed none of our gesturing, because she continued talking about the whereabouts of old friends with Romany Marie.

"I want to know more about this Murder Club," I said when there was an opening in the conversation.

"What do you want to know?" said Edna.

"I don't know. It sounds intriguing. How can I join?"

"You are a writer of mysteries, Mrs. Parker?" asked Marie with a look of surprise. "I know, already, you are a great poetess."

"You are very kind."

"Not kind, truthful. *Enough Rope* was a great success. I would be so pleased if you would come one evening to recite your poems."

"Thank you."

"Are you a nihilist or an existentialist?"

"I drift from pillar to post, I suppose," I replied, "although I hope to be pleasantly surprised when I find out."

When Marie had moved on to greet new arrivals, I asked Edna to tell me more about the group of men who were members of the Murder Club. "You are intrigued, aren't you?" said Edna, looking at me with suspicion. "What are you up to?"

We quickly brought her up to date about the luncheon interview with Detective Sparrow regarding the murder of Ernest Stringer.

"Dorothy may have witnessed the whole thing," said Jane.

"Aleck told me last night that you all watched the bank heist getaway, but he said nothing about Ersatz—"

"We didn't know Ersatz had been killed until this afternoon at lunch, Edna," said Ross.

Edna's questioning gaze prompted me to explain that I had caught sight of Ersatz walking along the street just before the bank robbers started firing their guns, and just before I alerted the others of the goings-on outside Di Cenzo's window.

"You were the last person to see him alive!" exclaimed Edna.

"Not the last," I said.

"What do you mean?"

"The person who poisoned him—"

"*What!* Are you saying his death wasn't the result of a stray bullet?"

"Edna, it is not common knowledge yet," chided Frank. "We took an oath—"

"Don't be all dramatic, Frank," said Ross. "We just promised Detective Sparrow over there to keep the details under our hats 'til tomorrow. He wants the murderer to believe that the police think it was a gunshot killed Ersatz."

"He's a cop? My God! He *is* a looker!" said Edna after seeing the tall, reddish-blond man talking with Everett Stringer and the members of the Murder Club.

"Down, girl!" I said. "You mean to tell me that Anthony Young, Daniel Cousins, Mark Wendt, and Stephen Shaw over there get together and swap murder plots?"

"Who are these people you are talking about?" asked Aleck, rejoining our little conference.

Edna told them all she knew about Ersatz Stringer's fellow mystery writers: "The old-maid type is Anthony Young, Aleck."

Anthony Young is a mystery writer who met with a small success when he sent a manuscript of his first mystery novel into Boni & Liveright five years ago. My friend and publisher, Horace Liveright, agreed to publish Tony's first mystery featuring as the novel's amateur detective a frumpy, dried-up, effeminate history professor who solves crimes by means of applying historical references to catch murderers. One's first impression upon meeting Tony is that he stepped out of one of his own novels, for he, too, is a frumpy, effeminate history professor. Notwithstanding, the fifth entry in his Professor Montague Fairchild series, *A Time to Reap*, is enjoying a third printing.

"And the fellow with the unruly mop? The one sitting down?" asked Jane.

"That's Daniel Cousins, and it is a good thing that he is sitting down."

Daniel Cousins has wild, wavy black hair and heavy facial features. There is a handsome ruggedness about him. But there is also an air of melancholy expressed from big, sad brown eyes. He also has the biggest feet I've ever seen in my life. Besides what they say about the prowess indicated, it is something other than romantic considerations that makes one suck in air when Daniel enters a room—that he manages to progress forward without tripping on the rug and crashing into the hostess's buffet table is nothing less than miraculous. To watch him on the street, one marvels that he does not catch his toe in every raised crack in the sidewalk. He was made for the circus, and more than one wise-ass has presented him with a red-ball nose and polka-dot trousers. Daniel authored one quiet little novel, six years ago. It's been said that he has shouted plagiarism at one time or another.

"Who's the tall boy, looks like a Ballet Russe dancer?" asked FPA.

"Mark Wendt," I replied.

Wendt has a string of Wild West novels that are very popular among the quasi-literate. This past year he had published a mystery whose murder-solving sleuth is the antithesis of himself. His alter-ego talks tough in two-syllable statements, smokes cigars, wears spats, pinstripes, and Cartier diamond studs, knocks back Napoleon brandy, blackens his hair, and brags about his conquests, both with women and in rum running. Mark is a fragile-boned, introverted man of thirty-something years, who looks to have survived rickets as a child, and who now lives precariously from behind his typewriter and through his accidental sleuth, mobster Mr. Tomato. This latest prize is so outrageously improbable that, upon discovering a copy on her husband's bedside table, it evoked snickers of laughter when a senator's wife read aloud certain purple passages as entertainment at a ladies' tea. As it is made of the nonsensical stuff of male fantasy, Wendt has created another surefire success with the boys.

"That's Stephen Shaw standing next to Mark," said Ross. "What a jackass."

"From what I hear, you've got that right," I agreed. "So, that's what he looks like; I never saw him before. He has a wily, unsavory appearance."

"Odious," said Edna.

Shaw writes thrillers now, in a new way that deals with political and social unrest. Before taking on this new genre, he wore the mantle of Muckraker. A real rabble-rouser, rather than beating down prejudice and corruption as Upton Sinclair has tried to do through his brilliant exposés, Shaw merely manages to incite bigotry. His books are carelessly researched, and more than once he has been sued for defamation. Jews are crafty villains, women are unfaithful, disloyal sluts, and the Negro is the cause of all that ails America. He purports to support Labor; he is a communist who rails against anarchism and socialism even though they are all waging the same fight for the worker. Beefy, brawny, pock-faced, Shaw is a wily, ginger-haired devil with a big mouth stamped with a smirk that brings to mind a scheming Iago. If it weren't for his cunning, I'd think him a fool. People like Shaw often have nasty agendas. But you don't always know what they are.

"I don't see Trevor Hunter," I said, searching the room for his distinctive features.

What strikes one upon first meeting Hunter are his eyebrows. Positioned far below a high dome, they are strikingly black and silky, as if Russian sable pelts were plastered above his lashless gray eyes. A nervous twitch on his sallow left cheek occasionally sets the left brow aquiver, which is unsettling to say the least, for it gives the impression that one furry critter is not quite dead and is struggling to escape. *Everything* about the man is unsettling. My prejudice is solely founded on appearance. He is the author of intellectual real-life crime novels.

"Perhaps Trevor has already been here, or will come in later to pay his respects," said Edna.

"I don't know him very well," I admitted, "but his crime books are quite well done. One was bought for the movies, I heard."

A ragged, black-haired woman staggered in from the street. All eyes turned toward her as she entered the café and leaned against the door jamb for support as she took in the room. The violin music stopped abruptly with a screeching note. I followed her gaze across the room to Everett Stringer, who looked aghast at the sight of her. The scholarly, yet foppish, Anthony Young dashed to her side, put his arm around her waist and walked her to where Romany Marie sat at a table. Marie quickly ordered a waiter to bring a cup of coffee to the woman, and within a minute a plate of food was set before her. There was much cajoling by Marie to get the woman to eat and drink, and much coddling by Young in a show of comfort, but her distress was so profound that she sat there dumb and dead-eyed to their efforts.

Marie gestured to the musician, so he quickly set about playing an upbeat melody. Another young man picked up a tambourine and began to play a gypsy dance rhythm. The incongruity of the music to the mood of the room was offsetting and false; suddenly the grieving woman shot up from her chair—her arms plastered at her sides, her form rigid—and let out an earthshaking scream.

Detective Sparrow caught her as she fell into a faint. He picked her up and carried her to the door. Mr. Benchley held it open for him and the three left the café. I followed them out, and caught up as Mr. Benchley was opening the door of the detective's car. Quickly, on a whim, I entered the automobile from the street side, unbeknownst to my friend, who watched in horror as Detective Sparrow drove off and I waved from the backseat.

"Where are you taking us?" I asked, startling the detective. He hadn't seen me enter the car.

"Mrs. Parker!" he exclaimed. The maiden in distress was out cold in the passenger seat.

"Who is she? I suspect she is Ersatz's wife?"

"You shouldn't be here."

"You're right, of course; I didn't mean to stay, I was only—"

We turned a corner and then Sparrow pulled to the curb. He turned to look at me.

"Why are you stopping? You want me to get out? I just wanted to help!"

"I do want you to get out; and since you're here, I can use your help."

I looked questioningly into the handsome face.

"This is where she lives, Mrs. Parker."

"Oh! All right, I see," I said, glad not to be tossed out at the curb.

I got out and followed as Sparrow carried the woman from the car to the door next to a shoemaker's storefront. I opened it and led the way up the stairs to the apartment he indicated on the second floor.

The door was unlocked. I found the light switch. I walked into a space that was cramped with piles of books on every surface. The chairs were worn, soiled-shiny and frayed. On the walls were hung dozens of paintings in the cubist style, and although quite competently rendered, most employed a monochromatic palate reminiscent of dried dung. A desk held a Royal typewriter and a confusion of papers, manuscripts, and books. A knocked-over bottle of India ink, the black pool still wet and viscous like blood, was dripping onto the faded rag rug, barely missing a direct hit on a pair of men's slippers, their seams split at the instep, the leather of the right slipper ages ago splattered with some unidentifiable condiment and dusted with cigarette ash.

Piles of cigarette butts filled half-a-dozen ash-trays, and ash had settled into every crevice and dusted every surface. I opened a door to the bedroom, turned on a table lamp, and saw that the room had a sense of order, if only in that it was spare and uncluttered with furniture. Sparrow followed me in and placed the distressed woman onto the bed. I removed her shoes and covered her with the counterpane.

"Go put a kettle on—see if there's any tea or coffee," he instructed me, while pulling up to her bedside a wooden chair from near the window.

I did his bidding, finding a can of tea in the kitchenette cupboard and filling the kettle with water before setting it on the scarred enamel stovetop.

Dirty plates and cups and a frying pan were stacked in the sink, grease and egg congealed on the surfaces from a breakfast past. I struck a match to light the burner, lit a cigarette on the flame, too, and then returned to the sitting room to bide my time while waiting for the water to boil.

My glance fell on the desk, the big, black Royal dominating the space, and I looked to see what Ersatz had been working on. I flipped over a stack of typed pages and riffled through the manuscript, one hundred and sixty-two pages of a book entitled *The Body in the Basement*. Two carbon copies of the book were positioned facedown and cross-hatched to the left of the typewriter—typical stacking at the end of a day's work. But there was a dusting of street soot and cigarette ash atop the manuscript and the carbons and along the exposed wood of the desk, indicating that no work had progressed for some time.

Ersatz's notebooks were stacked nearby, and I smacked the dust off one and fanned through it. They contained book notes, plot ideas, typical fragments all writers accrue for future use or jot down when ideas strike—news clippings sparking interest, bits of dialogue overheard in a café, or the random image popping into one's head. I wondered whether the notebook he was working from held clues as to the reason for his murder.

I was interrupted when I heard Detective Sparrow's voice through the open bedroom door. But I couldn't discern the conversation.

There was a knock on the door, and when I answered it there stood a spritely, elderly woman in a bright-green housecoat and slippers looking at me with concern in her eyes. "Is Cherish—I heard commotion—is she all right?"

"I don't know," I said. She hesitated at the threshold and I moved aside to let her enter. "We brought her home, the detective and I; she's in a bad way. May I ask—?"

"I am Charlotte Vega," she said. "I live next door. I have been worried. She would not come to the door today, though I know she was here; I could hear her crying. What can I do?"

"She needs a doctor. Do you know one who will come?"

"I will call my doctor. Yes, I will call Dr. Hayes. He lives close by. He will come. Yes!"

I gestured to the telephone and Mrs. Vega went to dial the number, looking over the disarray of the room. From the look on her face I suspected that she had never entered the apartment before, or if she had, that it was in worse condition than she remembered.

"He will come right away," she said while standing at the entry of the kitchenette. I poured boiling water over a teabag.

Mrs. Vega followed me out as I carried the cup into the bedroom, and she waited in the sitting-room for my return. She didn't have long to wait, because Sparrow took the cup from me and then gestured for me to quit the bedroom.

I found Mrs. Vega picking up a coat from off the floor and hanging it on the rack by the door. She'd already stanched the ink-spill with a rag. She held a metal wastebasket into which she dumped the over-flowing butts from the ashtrays. When she turned to me I recognized the look of the manic housekeeper. There was nothing she wanted to do more than to take a carpet sweeper to the rugs and a dust cloth to every-thing else. If she could have hosed down the place to make fast work of it, that would have been gratifying. I smiled and she shook her head with dismay.

"It was not always like this."

"There is almost no food in the kitchen," I said.

"*Oh!*" she cried, finding her purpose. And then with a conspiratorial tone she said, "I will bring some soup and I have a loaf and butter and cheese and a nice piece of boiled beef—"

"How lovely," I replied, wondering if she was just an old busybody that the woman in the bedroom didn't want to have snooping around. I didn't really care at the moment. She seemed genuinely kind and considerate.

"Yes," she said, her words suspended as her eyes scanned the room. I could see her thinking about what to attack first, until there were footsteps on the landing and she turned to open the door. "Doctor," she whispered, and the man allowed himself to be guided to the sick patient. Mrs. Vega nodded at me and then departed on her errand. Detective Sparrow came out to wait while Cherish was ministered to. He looked around the room and then at me.

"Good you got a doctor."

"It was the neighbor, Mrs. Vega, who called him."

"Good," he said, distracted, as he perused the objects in the room. Then he said, "I don't understand it; Stringer had a bestseller. Why live like this?"

"It's a mess, but I think—"

"That's not what I mean," he said briskly, cutting me off. "Stringer had more than five thousand dollars in the bank. Why live in a dump?"

"*Wowie! Shit!* From that book he wrote? He wrote it seven years ago! Is that what his publisher told you?"

"No. I haven't spoken with his publisher. His bank statement."

"Oh . . ."

"Have you read it?"

"His book? No," I said.

"You should."

"Whenever anyone suggests a book, I choose another."

He smiled. And it was a really nice smile. It did nice things for his face. Crinkled up his eyes; dimpled his cheeks. He had good teeth, too. If he were a horse, I'd buy him. "Looks like he was halfway through writing a new novel," I said.

There was a knock at the door, and I opened it, expecting Mrs. Vega's return, but there before me stood Mr. Benchley.

"Well?" he said, batting his eyelids, eyebrows slanted and forming an inverted V, his lips pursed—his injured-ego look.

"Well, what?"

"You don't look at all surprised to see me."

"What do you want, a fanfare?"

"It would be appropriate. Considering how I tracked you down through deduction."

"You followed my crumbs?"

"You left no droppings."

"That's because I left Woodrow at home," I said. "Marie told you where Mrs. Stringer lived. You figured we took her home. Big deal; no fanfare."

"All right. Yes—a lucky guess on your part. But she isn't Mrs. Stringer. She is Cherish Winter, Ersatz's common-law wife. Aren't you going to ask me in?"

I held the door open for him.

"Good evening, Detective."

"Good evening, Mr. Benchley."

"Now, Detective Sparrow," I said, "what I told you about seeing Trevor Hunter yesterday afternoon—"

"You're going to say you are not certain it was him, I remember."

"Yes, well, have you spoken with Trevor?"

"Not yet."

"Well, I'm sure he'll have an explanation if it was he I had seen—or an alibi if it wasn't. He's never struck me as the type who would poison anybody."

"That's true, my dear," said Mr. Benchley. "He'd be more likely to *stab* a fellow in the back! Remember what he did to old Gregory Hanson!"

"Mr. Benchley?"

My friend hemmed and hawed for a moment, having stuck his foot in it. "Just a slight disagreement awhile back between friends; marital problems."

Sparrow stared blankly, waiting for Mr. Benchley to elaborate. When he didn't, I said, "Trevor Hunter stole another man's gal."

"I'm sure he couldn't have poisoned anybody," said Mr. Benchley. "After all, from what I gather, Ersatz—I mean, Ernest, well, the two men were friends."

"So were Arthur and Lancelot," noted the detective.

"Are we done singing, 'Somebody Stole My Gal?'" I asked.

Detective Sparrow cleared his throat and said, "We've yet to speak with Mr. Hunter. There is the possibility that it was Hunter you saw. After talking with you this afternoon we attempted to find him. He wasn't at his home, and I expected to see him tonight at Romany Marie's, but he didn't show up. His friends don't know where he is and haven't heard from him."

"It's still early; he might stop in there," I said.

"Yes. I plan to go back and wait to see if he shows up. After I speak with Mrs. Stringer."

The doctor came out of the bedroom, shutting the door behind him. "She's had a terrible shock. I've given her something to make her sleep."

"But I need to talk with her."

"Not tonight. Tomorrow."

The doctor, a round, butterball figure of forty years, said to me, "Someone should be close by when she awakes."

We were supposed to meet Soledad at the Central Park Casino in little more than an hour. I was about to tell Mr. Benchley to make my apologies to her, when in walked Mrs. Vega, carrying a tray full of food. She spoke with Dr. Hayes, and volunteered to stay the night.

After the detective left, Mr. Benchley and I helped Mrs. Vega cart various items from her apartment—a bucket of cleaning products—Babbo, furniture polish, a sponge, a mop, and Julius, the name she had given to her trusty carpet sweeper. She would set to work on cleaning the apartment, she said, so that when Cherish awoke she would feel better just to see things were in order.

"What a time she's had, poor thing! These past weeks have been hard."

"Then, you were close to the couple?" I surmised.

"Well, we were not what you'd call *close*, really. Not like when the Marinos lived in this apartment. They used to come to my place for bridge on Thursday nights, before he died. Jerry and I—that was my husband, Jerry—we would be with the Marinos on New

Year's—we were good friends. Then Helen—Mrs. Marino—she went to live with her daughter when her husband died. Cherish and Ernie came here, let me see, two, no, three years ago it was. . . . Neighbors. Neighbors look out for neighbors. . . .

"It is sad. When they came here they seemed happy. I thought they were newlyweds. I didn't know—I thought they were, well, you know, *married*. But her letters came to Miss Cherish Winter, not Mrs. Stringer." She grimaced and tossed her hands, "It is the modern way, I suppose; a new generation."

"You said they *were* happy," I said, "but things were not going well for them these past few weeks?"

She leaned on the mop handle. "Things were not so good. Ernie used to smile and chat for a few minutes when we'd pass on the stairs, and after my Jerry passed away, Ernie would help to carry the groceries up if he saw me, or take down the trash. Sometimes, he would knock on my door with a book he thought I might like to read, or a box from the bakery. He liked my Jerry. But these past few weeks, Ernie didn't look so good. He was pale, getting thin; I could see his belt tightened a notch. They was arguing all the time—well, it was her voice I'd hear, mostly. I could hear through the wall, and when the windows are open, you can hear like they was in the room with you."

I was about to ask what the arguments were all about when Mrs. Vega said: "And then, the other day, when I came in from the grocer's, I hear Ernest and another man yelling at each other. Cherish was not at home. I had just seen her at the post office half an hour before."

"Which day was this?"

"The day before yesterday—the day Ernest was killed!"

"Do you remember what time it was?"

"Of course. It was just before one o'clock. I know this because I got home just in time to listen to my radio program. I don't like to miss my radio program. My husband, Jerry, he bought the radio for Christmas two years ago. He liked to hear the music programs in the evening. He is gone, now, almost a year . . ."

"I'm sorry," I said.

"Oh, yes, thank you. I miss him. We were married thirty-six years."

I wanted to hear more about what she had heard the day of the murder, but propriety demanded I wait a few breaths before leaping in.

"Did you hear what they were arguing about, Mrs. Vega?"

"It made no sense to me, what they said. Ernie kept saying he wouldn't do it."

"Do what?"

"I don't know—whatever it was the other man wanted him to do."

"The other man. . . . And then?"

"And he was shouting."

"Who was?"

"'I don't know who said it, but one of them said, 'You'll be sorry when they find out!'"

Mrs. Vega was getting animated now, reliving what she'd heard. "Yes, that's what he said, one of the men. Oh, it went on and on, and it got so loud and I heard scuffling around, like they was fighting, and a thud on the wall."

"Did they mention anybody else—did you hear them say anybody's names or—"

"I think . . . I think somebody said something about the police. Oh, and it must have been Ernie who yelled, 'Get out of my house! If I see you here again, I'll kill you!'"

"And then?"

"And then it was quiet."

"So, there was nothing else?"

"Oh, yes! One of them said, 'What are you going to do?'"

"About . . . ?"

"I don't know. I heard the door slam, the apartment door, and then footsteps down the stairs."

"So, you heard an argument between Ernest and another man. But, you don't know who the man was?"

"He was dressed in his costume."

"You *saw* him?"

"Yes, when I heard him on the stairs, I looked out the window, and saw him come out on the street."

"Did you recognize him? Had you ever seen him before?"

"Oh, yes."

"A friend of Ernest's?

"They didn't sound so friendly, let me tell you."

"But you recognized the man?"

"Well, he looked like William Gillette."

"William Gillette? The actor?

She nodded. "William Gillette. We, Jerry and me, before the War, we saw him one time on the stage."

"He was dressed as Sherlock Holmes!"

"Yes! Sherlock Holmes."

William Gillette as he appeared in his legendary role of Sherlock Holmes

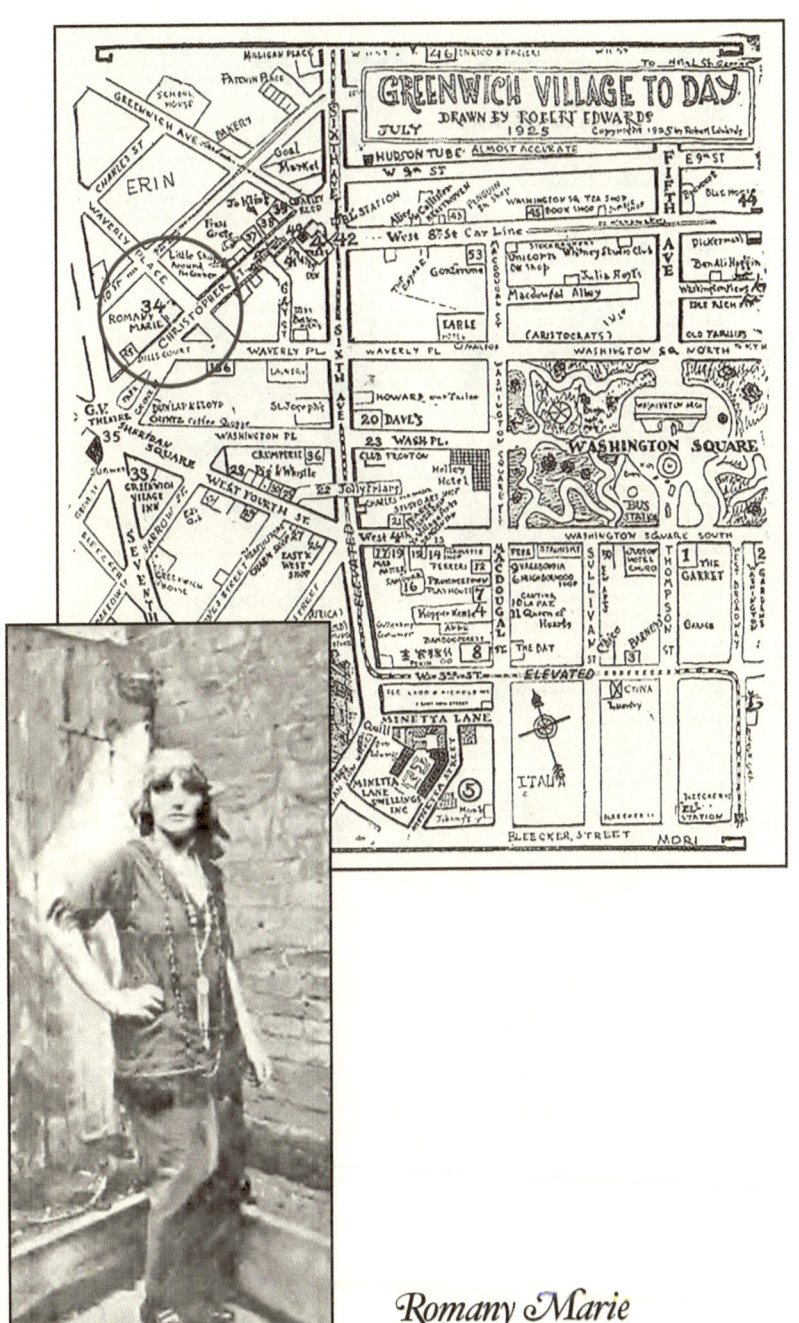

Romany Marie

Bucky Fuller's Dymaxion Car

Romany Marie's Cafe

Chapter Four

The Central Park Casino is known as "Jimmy Walker's place." That's the Honorable James J. Walker, mayor of my fair city.

Everybody from William K. Vanderbilt to Robert Lehman to Adolf Zukor to Florenz Ziegfeld had a hand in making the Casino the hottest nightspot in town. It's been said that Arnold Rothstein, the "cultured mobster" who fixed the 'nineteen World Series, is the main investor. Joseph Urban, the set designer for the Metropolitan Opera, created a spectacular space. At this dazzling nightclub on the east side of Central Park near 70th Street, Gentleman Jimmy arrives nightly in his chauffeur-driven Doozie, his mistress, Ziegfeld chorus girl Betty Compton hanging sveltely on his arm. When the doorman spots him, he signals the orchestra leader to play the one hit Walker wrote back in 'ought-five, when he was an aspiring songwriter, "Will You Still Love Me in December (As You Did in May?)." The place is all decked out in maroon-and-green fabric, with great big stars and balloons dangling from the ceiling between magnificent crystal chandeliers. Eddie Duchin on grand piano sets the dance beat. And the food! The maître d'hôtel is René Black, "Master of 40 Sauces," and Louis Rothschild's former chef is the man behind the menu. Fiorello La Guardia, who lost the mayoral election to Walker, sourly dubs the nightclub the "whoopee joint in the park." It sure as hell is!

The place was hopping when Mr. Benchley and I arrived a little bit after ten o'clock. Spirits were high as was the foot-stomping on the packed dance floor as a hundred pairs of feet shuffled out the Charleston, causing the walls to reverberate; the balloons swayed and we would have heard the chandelier crystals tinkling if it wasn't for the blaring syncopation of the horn section. The place was a party of laughter and pulsing motion, like being inside of a beating heart, blood rushing through its chambers.

The maître d' brought us to the table where Soledad was sandwiched between her publisher, Joshua Latham, and Aleck. FPA and Edna were about to take a turn on the dance floor where Jane and Ross were already lost in the crush.

Latham lit Soledad's cigarette, which was tapped into the end of a long cigarette holder that bobbed around precariously and threatened to put out his eye, if not to ignite the elaborate blue feather headdress perched atop her head. Although I had changed into my party clothes—a green-silk sheath embellished with a sprinkling of rhinestone geometrics down the skirt's sides and circling the hem—I paled next to Soledad, wearing a shimmering blue-and-green peacock-patterned gown, with a low, scooped neckline. Her back was bare down to her waist. Clipped into her hair was an elaborate tiara, a peacock with its bejeweled feathers fanned out. From the crown extended foot-long, curled feathers that waved about in the breeze. At times like these, I both admire and envy her élan. The thing about Soledad is that there is nothing pretentious about her, even if her extravagance suggests it. She is glamorous without effort, and would be so should she wear a burlap sack. When she enters a room she dominates it with style and substance, grace and intelligence, humor and kindness, and both men *and* women (eventually) gladly surrender to her charm. I suppose that's why I love her. When she levels those big blue eyes on me I feel the safety and acceptance of a sister.

"Aleck and Edna told us about your venture into the Avant Garde," said Soledad.

"Well," I replied, "what poses as one, anyway. More gypsy camp, I'd say."

"Tell us what happened after the dashing policeman carried you away?"

"He carried away the fainted Cherish Winter, Ersatz's woman."

"And of course our Nosey Parker, here—the phrase coined after our very own Mrs. Parker—insinuated herself into the affair," said Mr. Benchley.

"I did no such thing!"

"Sparrow is a man worthy of a thousand insinuations, Bob," said Aleck.

"Be that as it may—"

"Bob was beside himself, you understand," said Aleck.

Jane, returning to the table with her winded husband, flopped down into her chair. "Ross, you are not having a heart attack. It's plain old exercise, dancing is; that's why you're flushed."

"She doesn't care if I live or die," said the hypochondriac.

"Of course I do. If you're dead, I won't have to file for divorce."

I could sense an oncoming escalation of their hostilities, so I jumped in with: "I helped Detective Sparrow settle the poor grieving woman, and a doctor was called in to sedate her. Then I spoke with the neighbor, a Mrs. Vega, who gave me an earful."

I told them what she told me, and Joshua Latham chuckled. "The Sherlock Holmes outfit. Yes, that's Trevor Hunter's costume. He wears it when he lectures to ladies' groups and men's clubs on the art of Conan Doyle."

"Before you arrived Josh was telling us about these Murder Club people," said Soledad.

After giving the waiter our orders, we all turned to Joshua to fill us in.

"They are a strange bunch, that's for sure!"

"Why, that's what they say about *our* little luncheon club," said Mr. Benchley.

"Yes, but you all have a modicum of talent—" said Josh.

"I beg your pardon!" objected Aleck.

"As the good editor I am, and wishing to remain in your good graces, let me rephrase that: You are all top-drawer—how's that?"

"You are redeemed!"

"Thank you, Alexander. They, the members of the Murder Club, are middling at best."

"Cruel, but true," said Mr. Benchley.

Ross said, "You know, a couple years ago I turned down several *awful* short pieces submitted by Shaw to my magazine. You know, the rabble-rouser fellow—Stephen Shaw? He couldn't corroborate his claims. He stormed into my office. He chewed me out and told me I'd be sorry."

"Nothing that Jane doesn't say to you every day, Ross," said Aleck, enjoying the taunt.

"True, but she doesn't generally say she's going to burn down the place."

"Not until I get my things out of the house," said Jane with a wily grin.

Josh ignored the needling. "These fellows first met a couple of years ago. They were all represented by Niles Pickering."

"The publisher who died—what—two years ago?" asked Soledad.

"Yes, he had a heart attack at his desk."

"He was always hoping to score a bestselling author," said Mr. Benchley. "Nice fellow, by the way, forced to publish commercial novels to keep afloat after several literary flops."

"Ernest Springer was the closest he'd ever come to a bestselling author, but after that first book seven years ago, Stringer dried up. As for Stephen Shaw, he caused the company litigation trouble. Trevor Hunter, well, he was a distracted author, always writing, never completing anything worthwhile other than a couple of true-crime stories. And then there's Daniel Cousins, well, his career didn't pan out. Anthony Young—a moderate success with his history-professor-sleuth novels—I don't know why he's involved with the other fellows. Mark Wendt, who writes those fantasies for the adolescent male, the cowboy books—"

"Oh, yes, Ross reads those," said Jane. "And I've seen grown men on the subway reading them, too."

"That's because the women in his stories are not only beautiful, they never nag their men," said Ross.

I cut in: "Six club members all signed with Pickering Publishing. . . . Who took over the business when he died?"

"Nobody did."

"So, the fellows were out on their own and banded together?" I said.

"I don't know about that. Wendt got a new publisher; as you say, there's an adolescent male audience. Anthony Young, too. Cousins hasn't produced anything for a long time. But he tripped over his feet," Josh chuckled, "and landed over at the *Saturday Evening Post*. He's writing ad copy. It's a paycheck. Trevor Hunter is singularly strange. Born to money; considers himself a genius; fiddles around with his varied intellectual pursuits, but hasn't written anything really original."

"Edna thinks that all of the men are talented."

"Yes, Dorothy, Edna mentioned that. Talent," Joshua said, then paused to consider his words. "Lots of people have talent, but one needs focus, to find one's voice in order to produce something worth reading."

Before I could consider my own issue with completing—hell!—even *attempting* to write a novel, Mr. Benchley said: "Shaw? Tell us more about this character, Stephen Shaw, Josh."

"Nobody in his right mind will touch Shaw."

"That goes without saying," cut in Ross.

"Mobsters threatened Niles Pickering after Shaw's exposé on the world of sanitation."

"And Pickering died!" I said.

"Natural causes."

Edna and FPA returned from the dance floor: Edna limping, Frank, a broken cigar dangling from his lips. "She's trying to kill me," said Frank.

"I told you to quit stomping on my feet, you little—"

"Children!" thundered Aleck before turning to me with, "Is there a full moon?"

"Why the hell do you ask me?" I replied.

"Looks like there is murder in everybody's heart tonight," said Soledad.

"The dance floor is the Argonne all over again!" said Frank.

"Here, have some caviar, Frank," said Soledad, heaping a spoonful of the Beluga eggs onto a cracker and offering it like a mother feeding a child. He tossed the cigar and opened his mouth.

"Let's play 'aeroplane,'" said Ross in a baby's voice.

"Ross, have an oyster," said Soledad with a coddling tone to the other grump. "They are amazing."

"I'm allergic."

Less graciously, "Pickle?"

"Gives me gas."

"Why am I not surprised?" said Soledad, eyes wide and flashing amusement across the table to me.

The music stopped suddenly and then, with a fanfare, the orchestra played "Will You Still Love Me in December," heralding the arrival of Jimmy Walker. Walker's mistress, Betty Compton (his wife was vacationing in Florida), hung on his arm. The dancers parted, as the couple, dressed in their finest evening clothes, walked through them like royalty to their table. He was sleek and dapper, a sparkle flashing off his diamond tie pin, and she, blonde and shining in silver lamé, dripping jewels and draped in white marabou feathers.

When the fashion show was over and the orchestra began playing "My Blue Heaven," Mr. Benchley asked me for a dance. "What the hell," I said, rising. "What do I have to lose?"

"You lost your virtue years ago," said Frank.

Mr. Benchley drew back my chair and then offered his arm to escort me to the dance floor. "So what do you think?" I asked, after we squeezed into a square-foot of dance floor.

"About what?"

"About what Josh was saying about these Murder Club people."

"An unsavory assortment."

"Like a box of cheap chocolate creams?"

"Of nuts."

We shuffled about within our allotted space, Mr. Benchley smiling vaguely and very much somewhere else in his mind. I was not used to this detachment from my friend, and after a few swings around the room I needed to fill in the weighty silence that had settled in between us and reengage him.

"After hearing what Mrs. Vega had to say about the argument she overheard, it appears there was no love lost between Trevor Hunter and Ersatz. I'm now pretty sure it *was* Hunter I saw following him down the street."

"How sure? Ninety-nine percent sure, or sixty-five percent? Three-to-one, five-to-two, or is it a longshot, twelve-to-one? Half-empty or half-full?"

"*One hundred percent.* I just didn't want to condemn a man without knowing the facts. Especially since I recognized him before I knew anything about this Murder Club and his connection to Ersatz. I wonder what they were arguing about?"

"I suppose we will never know . . . but perhaps Hunter was moving in on Cherish Winter. After all, he's done it in the past."

"Cherish might be able to tell us."

"Us?"

He stopped short to stare at me with big eyes, causing a couple to plow into us and bringing about a chain reaction of collisions and exclamations before we were forced to resume our foxtrot. "Oh, Dorothy, Dorothy, my dear demented child!" he said, pulling me stiffly around the dance floor. He laughed low and derisively. "I know your little tricks, my dear. I know what you have in mind, and I must object!"

"What did I say? What tricks?"

He hissed, "Don't play coy with me."

"*Moi?*"

"*Vous! Vous êtes une trickster!*"

"I simply said that Cherish might know the reason for the men's disagreement. How is that a trick, and what's with the quasi-French?"

"You started it!"

"Well, pardon my French!"

It was like arm wrestling, the way Mr. Benchley shuffled me around. He was angry. With me. And it was real, not like his sometimes-feigned indignation that served as comic relief during emotional confrontations. I kept quiet, allowing myself to be guided around the small space. *Why fuel the fire,* I thought? He'll simmer down, and then we might discuss things more rationally.

But suddenly Mr. Benchley's fire flared and he said, "Cherish might have been privy, sure, but the only way for you to know what she knows is to meddle into the affair."

"Who's *meddling?*" I replied, quite reasonably, and without emotion. "But out of curiosity, wouldn't you like to know? I thought we might ask her about it."

A sudden jerk and we stopped short. "*We?*" he said in a tenor's register, flames lashing up through the skylight roof. He drew away to stare at me with consternation and again there was a five-car pileup. "Is that the royal *we*, or the *we* that means you are about to drag me along for the ride?"

"When do I ever leave you at home?" I said with a smile.

"You have lost your mind!"

"After my virtue, what else was left?"

"Your life, *my* life!"

"And how is a little talk with Ersatz's girl going to put your precious life in danger?"

"That is *exactly* the kind of thing you always say right before people start shooting bullets at us!"

"Mister," said a man over his shoulder after knocking into Mr. Benchley, back-to-back, "this is a dance floor, not a bus stop!"

"Doesn't the Number Five stop here?" I asked.

"What's that supposed to mean?"

"Oh, stick it in your hat," I said.

"Oh, yeah?"

"Stuff it!" I mumbled.

"Take the talk somewhere else, or get crackin'."

"Don't get her mad, Mister," warned Mr. Benchley. "She bites."

"Harold!" said the girl "Harold" was dancing with, "Don't get involved. Can't you see they're quackers?"

Harold pushed his partner deep into the crowd as I led the way to our table.

"*Quackers!* Can you believe the nerve?" I said.

"Well, your harebrained idea of interfering in this murder—"

"*Harebrained! Quackers!* You're driving me crazy!"

"I rest my case."

"*Phooey!*"

"A full moon!" nodded Aleck upon our disgruntled appearance.

"Aw, can it, you old maid!" said Mr. Benchley with uncharacteristic vehemence.

It was the sort of feckless comeback that I would toss out when I couldn't think of an appropriate putdown, but to hear Mr. Benchley address Aleck—or any human being—so brazenly was upsetting enough to cut off any rising retorts from our party. Aleck fell back silent, astonished; Ross fiddled with his napkin, and everyone else just froze.

Mr. Benchley smoothed his moustache and ran a finger through his collar, pulled at his cuffs and then grabbed from the pickle dish and violently bit into a celery stick, an obvious substitute for biting off Aleck's head. He was red-faced and furious as he removed his flask from his coat, unscrewed it, emptied his water-glass into the floral centerpiece, held it up to receive the contents of the flask, but instead of pouring gulped directly from the container until it was dry. Flask emptied, he screwed its lid in place and returned it to his inside coat pocket. Then, with deliberation, he took out his cigarette case, chose one, snapped the case shut, produced his lighter, flicked it to flame, and then another snap. He finally reached for his money clip and drew out several bills, all the while avoiding our stunned expressions.

This was a rare sight for those of us at the table who knew him so well. The silence was pregnant with wonder for what he would do next.

Suddenly, he shot up from his seat, dropped the cash near his plate, and nodded. "Goodnight," he said, before turning to stalk out of the room.

Gentleman Jim's "whoopie joint in the park"

Chapter Five

After a fitful sleep, I awoke at dawn.

I was troubled about Mr. Benchley. His uncharacteristic behavior of last night upset me. A wave of affection swept through my heart for the man who was the most important, most constant influence in my life. He always made me laugh. He always pulled me up and out of the mire of my dark moods when I began to sink into depression. He was my leveler. He never told me what to do, although at times I wished he would. Truth is, in the past I wouldn't have listened to his protests, anyway, once I set my mind to something. Mr. Benchley knew that about me. And yet, he was always there for me, ready to catch me before I fell flat on my face. Yes, I knew he was the best friend I could ever hope to have in my otherwise lonely life, and his concern was real.

I understood, too, that I was often bored with my life; I had not accomplished the things I'd set out to do a decade ago. And it is true that whenever there is a crime to solve, a murder puzzle to complete, a culprit to catch, I feel wonderfully exhilarated. It must be the thrill of the hunt, for I am carried away for a time from the petty concerns that depress me.

And so, I'd had trouble sleeping.

I slapped water on my mascara-smeared face, dabbed rouge on my sallow cheeks, dressed haphazardly, and picked up the "nuggets" that Woodrow had deposited on the sitting-room carpet. The little critter who bounced up on my bed every morning was nowhere to be seen. I dragged him out from under the pile of clothes on my closet floor.

"I'd put you in the doghouse, but Mr. Benchley already put me in it."

As I leashed him, he looked up at me with soulful regret for his indiscretion, which melted my heart, as he knew it would.

Woodrow, my precious Boston terrier, has been my companion for nearly a decade. I have found consolation in his presence. He is my other best friend, a heartbeat in my otherwise lonely room. Woodrow doesn't talk back very often, nor does he say "I told you so" when things go wrong. He's never turned on me, like some Mr. Benchleys I know. . . .

Woodrow is getting on in years. His eyes tear when it is cold out, the black fur on his chin is graying, and he has less pep in his New York stride. He needs a footrest these days to make the leap onto my bed. I patted him on the head, and he licked my hand. He knows how special he is to me. I don't let just anybody lick my hand.

It was a soft autumn morning, the sunlight defusing the mist and spreading a hazy edge along the buildings of Greenwich Village. Woodrow and I got out of the cab and entered the door leading to the apartments above the shoemaker's shop. I knocked on the door and Mrs. Vega bid us enter, and after fussing over Woodrow Wilson, she insisted that I sit down at the little table where she had set out breakfast dishes. As she fetched a cup and saucer from the kitchen I looked around the room. All the surfaces were sparkling, the floor was polished, the tabletops wiped clear of grime and cigarette ash, the hundreds of scattered books and magazines and periodicals stacked neatly, and the small carpets beaten and swept. I had the distinct impression that sometime during the night Mrs. Vega had taken on the perilous task of standing on the window ledge to wash the grime off the glass—there weren't even any dust motes dancing in the rectangles of light.

"She is much better this morning," Mrs. Vega said as she returned from the kitchen with the steaming percolator in one hand and a cup and saucer in the other. I hadn't eaten a thing last night since my cocktail party, and never touched my dinner at the Casino, so the smell of coffee, the sizzling bacon, and

the yeasty aroma of baking bread made my mouth
water. I must have groaned with pleasure as I sipped
the brew, because when I looked up I saw she was
smiling with satisfaction.

"You are a miracle worker," I said, indicating
the room, the coffee, everything. "I want to take you
home with me forever," I purred.

"Cherish is in the bath," she said, and before
she could say more, out from the bedroom she came,
wrapped in an old terry robe, her dark hair wet and
combed back from her face. Her questioning look
made me rise from the chair to introduce myself. I
extended my hand, and the one I received was firm
and rough. I gleaned from the dark ridges lining her
nails and embedded in the cuticles that she was an
artist who worked with oils.

"I'm Dorothy, Dorothy Parker," I said gently, "I
am so sorry about Ers—Ernest's passing."

"Thank you," she said weakly. "Mrs. Vega—"
She stopped midsentence as she took in the room
around us.

Mrs. Vega was at her side and shuttled her over
to the table, guiding her to the chair across from me,
where she poured out a cup of coffee and handed
Cherish the pitcher of cream. Then she disappeared
into the kitchen, Woodrow at her apron strings.

For a long moment the woman across from me
sat staring at her coffee cup, and I could see she was
still in a haze from the sedative and the life-shattering

events of the past two days. I sipped from my cup, and she lifted hers to her lips in unconscious imitation. When Mrs. Vega returned with plates of bacon, fried eggs, and biscuits hot from the oven, Cherish looked up with humble gratitude at her neighbor. She touched Mrs. Vega's arm with a gesture of thanks as the older woman placed a block of butter near her plate.

"Eat, my child," said the older woman, her eyes moist with affection and concern.

"Won't you sit; I see all that you've done," said Cherish, taking it all in.

"Yes, yes, in a minute. I just want to see to my Josie, and I'll be right back," said Mrs. Vega. "My cat," she said to me.

Cherish just stared out of the window behind me, and I didn't know what to say, so we sat in silence for a time, I watching the eggs congeal, she lost in thought.

Finally, hunger won out over me and to break her trance I broke a piece of the crisply fried bacon and fed it to Woodrow. Then I scooped an egg, strips of bacon, and a biscuit onto a plate and handed it across the table to her. She turned her wide-eyed gaze on me, and after a moment, when she recovered her place in this world, she accepted it.

I sensed that she was too wounded to indulge in small-talk or to answer any of the questions I wanted to pose, so I tore off a section of biscuit, buttered it, and sipped from my cup, waiting for her to initiate the conversation. I didn't expect to hear her say: "I never believed it would come to this . . ."

I had to proceed with care. I had to allow her to say what she was thinking without too much prodding or she might shut down, so I simply nodded. She turned soulful, aching eyes toward me. "But, I didn't understand. . . . I never really understood why he was behaving so strangely. I thought he was . . . delusional. It can happen, you know, when things don't work out the way you want them to."

"He was troubled?"

"Yes. And I thought it was all in his mind. What other reason would he know such despair that he would take poison and end his life?"

I was stunned. She obviously believed that the poison was self-administered. Could it have been? But Detective Sparrow didn't think it was suicide or he wouldn't be chasing suspects to build a murder case.

"Had he any disagreements with anyone that were upsetting?"

She looked out over my shoulder toward the window. "The sunlight is strong," she said.

"Do you want me to draw the —"

"No!" she said, and as I began to rise she reached across the table and touched my sleeve. She smiled. "There are no shades to pull down and, it appears, no curtains."

"Mrs. Vega must have taken them down to do the windows. Wish she'd come to my place, it needs a good scrub."

"It's nice, really. I haven't seen daylight in this apartment for more than a month. Ernest wanted the curtains kept closed all the time."

"I'll bet they'll be laundered and pressed to within an inch of their fibers and rehung by the time it gets dark," I said lightly.

"She is a wonder. Ernest liked her and her husband, Jerry, when he was alive, very much. They doted on him like a son—the Vegas never had children. I found it sweet, but lately, Ernest, well, Ernest was moody, and I'm afraid he could be quite curt, a bit rude to the sweet old thing." She blurted out, "He was afraid all the time!"

The last statement stunned me, because it was so pointedly out of context. I decided it was time to come right out with it: "What was Ernest afraid of, Cherish?"

"I don't know. For weeks he . . . seemed to be afraid . . . of *something*."

"He didn't talk about it at all?"

"No, and when I asked him what the trouble was, he'd tell me to leave him alone, there was nothing wrong, nothing to tell, or he'd say it was the new book he was writing."

"Oh, last night I saw a manuscript on the desk."

"The mystery he had started writing. Not that one. Something else. He was writing something else, something he wouldn't let me see. And he carried it around with him. Took it with him when he went out."

I looked around the room, and in spite of Mrs. Vega's handiwork, it was the apartment of struggling artists. I wondered if Miss Winter was aware of the amount of money in her boyfriend's bank account. So I decided to broach the possibility that she didn't know by asking, "Money problems?"

"When wasn't there?" she replied, wrapping the robe higher around her neck. The raised chenille design was worn out in places like a rutted highway. We smiled at each other. We had that one problem in common: money.

"But, we were no worse off lately than usual. I mean, I sold a painting last month and a gallery, actually Romany Marie, is going to exhibit some of my paintings."

So she didn't know. And I could tell she wasn't lying. This woman was too worn out, too weak, and too steady with her reply to be feigning ignorance. "I see, forgive me for asking, only—"

With unexpected energy she blurted out: "Who keeps the shades closed all day and peeks out at the street a dozen times an hour? Who refuses to answer the telephone? Who looks over his shoulder when walking down the street? Who doesn't want to see any of his old friends anymore? A *paranoid*, that's who—a man who is afraid!"

Or, I thought, *a man who owes somebody—or a lot of people—money.* Hell, I was always avoiding the Gonk's manager, Frank Case, when my rent was a couple of months late, taking the stairs rather than the elevator so I wouldn't have to pass the front desk. I had a variety of inane voices I would use when the telephone rang and I guessed it was a bill collector on the line. I'd say, "Mrs. Parker is out of the country."

Even though he had more than five thousand bucks in the bank, it was still possible that Ersatz's fear had something to do with money. Maybe it wasn't *his* money in the bank! Maybe he had stolen the money and feared being caught! But then, why deposit stolen money in a bank? The police would surely find it if he was suspected of theft. I wondered in which bank the cash was deposited. And the timing of his death—just as a bank he was about to walk past is robbed! Could he have had some connection to the heist? Was that the gist of the argument Mrs. Vega had overheard? Had it been Ersatz's afternoon visitor, Trevor Hunter, who threatened to kill him if he didn't do "something," or threatened to go to the police? Or was it the other way around? Did Ersatz threaten Hunter with a visit to the police? Wild scenarios raced through my head, but I would never voice them to a grieving widow.

"When did this behavior start?"

"Not long ago, a few weeks."

"Can you think back to that time and remember anything specific that happened, anything unusual that might have frightened him?"

"I couldn't tell you."

He wasn't ill, was he?"

"What? Oh, no. I mean, no, I don't think so. Ernest never got sick." After a few moments of reaching into past memories, Cherish frowned and shook her head.

"Something must have happened to set him off," I said.

I doubted she had been told that I was the last person, other than his murderer, to see Ernest alive. Since Cherish had risen from bed this morning, I doubted that Mrs. Vega had had the chance, or the inclination, to mention the argument she had overheard between Ernest and Trevor Hunter on the day of Ernest's death. My omission of this knowledge during our talk gave me the advantage. If Cherish knew what I had seen and been told, she might prematurely leap to the wrong conclusions, or the knowledge might color her words and thoughts to somehow distort or cover up some recent occurrence that might explain Ernest's distress and ultimate murder. Still, in my mind, Trevor Hunter was the likely culprit.

"Tell me about his friends."

"Ernest didn't have many friends, just people he knew. Acquaintances, really."

"What about his Murder Club friends?"

"Oh, they weren't really friends—colleagues, but not even that. They were just other writers, artists, and you know how they are."

"Self-involved . . ."

"If one criticizes another's work, it's because he's jealous; sometimes that's true, sometimes not, and you never know who wants to help you or who's out to get you. Whom can you trust? So, why get together? I never really understood why they got together."

Yes, why did *they get together?*

I thought about the relationship between Picasso and Braque. The two men feed off each other's imagination, each deliberately producing similar work after discussing subject and execution. In their case, neither was mentor or student; they were in direct competition with each other and yet they thrived on their self-imposed artistic challenges. "Ernest must have gotten something useful from his association with these men," I said.

"I suppose. . . . He said they helped devise scenarios for each other's books. I suppose they did help each other, for a while, anyway."

"But not of late?"

"He stopped going to their get-togethers."

"How did he get involved with them?"

"They once shared the same publisher."

"Oh, yes, that's right."

Mrs. Vega entered the apartment carrying a large laundry basket stacked high with folded linens. I rose from my chair and bid her sit down at my place. I poured out a cup of coffee and offered to fry a couple of eggs, but she said that all she wanted with the coffee was a biscuit with jam. Our little domestic scene was interrupted by a knock on the door. I opened it to find Detective Sparrow.

"Why, hello!" I said.

And then Mr. Benchley came into view, peeking out from behind him.

"Oh, it's you."

"You *who?*" said Mr. Benchley.

"*Yoo-hoo* yourself."

"I'm not sure how to take that."

"In the worst way."

"Mrs. Parker," nodded Detective Sparrow.

"Detective."

"Miss Winter, Mrs. Vega."

"Well, now that we all know who's who—" said Mr. Benchley.

Detective Sparrow looked at me with a questioning scowl, so I smiled and he quickly rearranged his features into a much more pleasant aspect. I moved aside to let him enter. He nodded at the women at the table, but remained a long moment at the threshold. I could see his mind taking in the domestic scene.

"Coffee?" I said.

"Yes, thanks," said Mr. Benchley.

"What?" said the detective, distracted. Having decided on his approach, he nodded. "Yes. I take mine black."

Mrs. Vega went to the kitchen and returned with cups. Cherish rose from her place at the table and offered the detective a seat in one of the two stuffed chairs that formed the sitting area of the room.

"I've got to ask you a few questions," he said, and Cherish nodded weakly. She would not be better for a long time, I thought, taking in the image of her thin, frail body, the limp hair, nearly dry from washing and plastered along her skull. Her brown eyes were moist pools, dark-circled and bloodshot. Her paint-stained fingers fluttered nervously as she fussed to tighten the wrapper around her chest and hold it securely, protectively, at her waist; with the other hand she tightly gripped the closure at her neck. Detective Sparrow's presence appeared to unnerve her, tossing her back to the dreadful, stark reality of the past couple of days. She suddenly noticed that she was not properly dressed to receive gentlemen, so she asked to be excused.

When she disappeared into the bedroom, Detective Sparrow asked Mrs. Vega about the woman's state of mind this morning as Mr. Benchley circled the room, cup and saucer in hand, taking a sip every so often. The arrival of my best friend irked me, but I wanted to get violent when he said to the blushing Mrs. Vega, "This is the best cup of coffee I've ever had," followed by, "Mrs. Parker didn't brew this, she *couldn't* have; if you'd ever tasted what she tries to pass off as java, well . . . so it must be the hand of the delightful Mrs. Vega?" he said, taking her hand.

I wanted to throw up, but swallowed and rolled my eyes instead.

"Call me Charlotte, Mr. Benchley."

"And I'm Bob."

"Bob's your uncle," I said under my breath.

"What's that?" he said turning to me, knowing full well what I had said.

When he kissed her hand I could almost feel the oily residue dripping down through my hair.

Detective Sparrow, satisfied that he could interview Cherish, scolded us for having disturbed the room, which he had planned to search for possible clues that might prove a motive for murder. Mrs. Vega was properly repentant but, woman of spunk that she was, after hearing his criticism, defended her actions by stating that nothing but dirt had been disturbed, and that every slip of paper was accounted for and stacked in neat piles, so it would be far easier to review. Of course, she failed to understand that in a murder investigation even the seemingly random placement of objects could reveal much information leading up to the fatal event.

"You washed the dishes, I was told."

"Well, yes—"

"Mr. Stringer died by ingesting poison. There might have been traces on the plates or glasses, and the cigarette butts might have given a clue to who may have recently been here—"

"Detective," I interrupted, "If he was poisoned here, wouldn't the murderer have cleaned up after himself?"

"Yes, but—"

"I made my point."

Cherish returned dressed in a dark-blue sheath that had seen much wear. Detective Sparrow wasted no time.

"Who do you think killed your husband?"

"I can't think who."

"Did he have any enemies?"

"I don't know," she said. "He never spoke of any; he was only concerned with his work."

"When was the last time you saw your husband?"

"The morning of the day he was . . . he died. I left him here to go to my studio at around nine o'clock."

"Where is the studio?"

"The attic room upstairs, I share the space with another artist."

"You were in your studio all day?"

"Yes. But—well, I went grocery shopping around twelve-thirty and then went back to work."

"And the artist who shares the space? He can attest to that?"

"Well, yes! I mean, uh, no. Roberto is paint-ing—he got a commission to do a mural—he stopped in to fetch some supplies, and he was just leaving when I arrived, so . . ."

"Roberto . . . ?"

"Roberto Cellini."

"I'll need to speak with him."

"Yes. Why, though? Do you think that I had anything to do—"

"No, Miss Winter. I am asking anyone who knew Mr. Stringer these questions. I am only trying to piece together, to find out where everyone was that afternoon, if you saw or heard anything that might lead us to whoever had opportunity to kill Mr. Stringer."

"Yes, yes, all right," she replied, impatiently rubbing her brow. "So, you think he was *murdered?* That he didn't commit—?"

"It doesn't appear that he took his own life."

"Detective, I have an awful headache."

"Yes, I understand, Miss Winter. But one more question, please."

She stared at the floor, waiting.

"Did Mr. Stringer usually carry a small spray-bottle of saline solution with him?"

"What?"

"One was found in his pocket."

"Oh, you mean for his allergies. Yes. He suffered hay fever, and whatever else was in the air."

"How often did he use it, the spray, I mean?"

"What?" she replied, distracted.

"Was he using the spray occasionally, or—"

"Oh, yes, I see. He carried it everywhere he went, especially through the spring and autumn, he used it often."

"Indoors as well?"

"Oh, yes. Constantly."

"Thank you, Miss Winter."

"C.R. Winter?" said Mr. Benchley, turning from the desk where he had stood sipping his coffee, his back to us. Above the desk and a little to the side he indicated one of the cubist-style paintings, this one a creature with five eyes wearing a top hat—or two men and a Cyclops fighting over a hat, I couldn't swear which. It dawned on him suddenly and he said, "I know your work! I've seen it. On the wall at Leo

Stein's—you know, Gertrude's brother," that last he directed at me.

"Yes," she said, with an air of disinterest. "He has one of my paintings."

She had returned to her place at the table, leaning in on her elbows, and now she rubbed her brow as if to rid herself of pain—or perhaps to clear away the grueling emotional effects of answering questions that seemed pointless. "Detective, I'm so . . . can we continue this at another time?"

"Yes, Miss Winter, but soon," replied the detective, as Cherish rose to her feet and swayed slightly. "Would you mind very much if I looked over your hus—Mr. Stringer's desk? Perhaps we might find something that—"

"Yes, yes, do what you want. It's all over there," she said dismissively, as she hurried out of the room. Charlotte Vega followed her into the bedroom, with words to the effect of fetching some aspirin tablets.

"You'd think she'd want to know how Ernest was poisoned," I said. "By the way?"

"Strychnine."

"I see. But, where, how?"

"When the coroner discovered the telltale signs of poisoning, he tested the contents of Ernest's pockets. Stringer was carrying a pack of Lucky Strikes and a spray-bottle of saline solution."

"Strychnine! And he administered it himself!" said Mr. Benchley.

"How long would it take to, uh, have an effect?" I asked.

"Depends on how much he used. A few minutes to an hour, perhaps."

"There's more to the events of the day Ernest was killed," I said to Detective Sparrow, "Mrs. Vega can tell you."

"Oh? I'll have a talk with her."

"Detective, you said that Ernest had five thousand dollars in the bank. When was it deposited?"

"Last week."

"In which bank?"

I watched as just the hint of a smile crossed his lips when he realized where I was going with my questions. The sunlight on his head shimmered gold in his taffy-colored hair. "The bank that was hit, the robbery that you witnessed. It was deposited there."

"So perhaps he was about to make a withdrawal?"

"The bank had just closed, Mrs. Parker," said Mr. Benchley, "just minutes before the bank robbers made their exit."

"Perhaps he had already made a withdrawal, and that's why he was killed—to rob the money off of him!"

"He was heading *toward* the bank, Mrs. Parker," said my onetime friend.

"Yes. I suppose. . . ."

Detective Sparrow intervened: "There was no record of a withdrawal from his account that day, so it's moot."

"He was going to the police! Ernest was the one who said that before he threw Sherlock Holmes out of the apartment."

"What are you—?" said the detective to my rather disjointed statement. I quickly recapped the conversation I'd had with Mrs. Vega and the comments made by Cherish about Ernest's state of mind.

Detective Sparrow was not happy—at least, the expression on his face was not one of admiration toward me. "I'd like it if, in the future, you didn't meddle in my investigation. It's bad enough that this apartment had been disturbed, and now you've been interviewing the principals in this case."

Mr. Benchley stepped forward in my defense. "Detective Sparrow, I find it unkind to accuse Mrs. Parker of deliberate obstruction. Did she not assist you last evening in bringing Miss Winter home?"

"Yes, yes, but—"

"It's not Mrs. Parker's fault that people shed their inhibitions around her, thereby divulging a plethora of information because they feel they can trust her."

I could have fought this battle on my own using a quick jab with an icepick retort, but I let my wayward friend do it as penance for his behavior of last evening.

"Rest assured," he continued, "she will not involve herself in your case, again."

I dropped my self-satisfied little grin for a scowl at the last remark.

"That would be best," agreed Detective Sparrow.

After spitting a satisfying obscenity to each of the men, I quickly retrieved my purse and leashed Woodrow and walked determinedly out of the apartment. Before closing the door behind me, I turned to say: "There's a missing manuscript."

It felt good to witness their perplexed expressions as I slammed the door.

Greenwich Village Street

Artists

Chapter Six

The next morning I expected to see Jimmy the bellboy come to give Woodrow a walk around the block when I answered the door in my favorite, if battered, old kimono with my hair curled up in bobby pins.

I had stayed in the evening before, having ordered a sandwich from the hotel kitchen, not really wanting to see my old gang at lunch or supper. Soledad was spending the evening with Aleck and Edna and Heywood, going to see the Marx Brothers' show down the street. So I had stayed home and stayed up late into the night, trying to finish a short story I had promised to get to Ross for publication in *The New Yorker* three weeks ago. My typewriter ribbon had reached the end of the line before the last paragraph—one of the many excuses I've used when tardy with copy to a publisher.

But this time, when I was duly employed in the task of storytelling, I really couldn't find a spare, causing me to wonder if it wasn't merely I who was my own worst enemy but the so-called gods working their tricks against me, too. I penciled in my final paragraphs to complete the story, and then, depressed, drank down the dregs from a bottle of Canadian Club and fell asleep on the sofa listening to the sweet melodic strains of Rudy Vallee singing "I'm Just a Vagabond Lover" on the radio that my onetime friend, Mr. Robert Benchley, the rat, had presented to me for Christmas of 1925.

What sensible woman would ever allow a man she wanted to drag to the altar to see her as I now appeared before an awestricken Detective Sparrow?

In my pathetic condition I nearly shut the door on his nose to prevent the image from burning a hole in his brain. But I sucked in my gut, as well as my chagrin, raised my chin to meet the approximate location of his pectorals, and bid him enter. As Woodrow was immediately all over him, I kept my head down and told Detective Sparrow to have a seat while I finished dressing, and scurried off to my bedroom.

After tearing out the pins from my hair, throwing on a new green dress I'd bought for a day out with Soledad so I wouldn't look too shabby walking the town beside her, and applying enough powder, rouge, lipstick, and mascara to brighten the dull aspects of my face, and a few spritzes of Coty's Chypre, I adjusted my stocking seams, slipped on pumps and a couple of strands of pearls, and assessed the results. A few quick and rather brutal swipes through my bedspring head of curls, in an attempt to uncoil the results of too much setting lotion, prompted me to jam on a brimmed hat to cover the fiasco that was my hair. I took a deep breath and returned to the sitting room to find the detective sitting with the morning edition of the *World* in his lap and staring at the Renoir hanging above my desk.

"Looks like a Renoir."

"It is."

I didn't bother to tell him that it had been left to me in the will of the famous Broadway producer, Reginald Ignatius Pierce, whose murder, and those of several others, Mr. Benchley and I, with the help of our friends, had solved back in 'twenty-four. It was a famous case, coined by the newspaper reporters as *The Broadway Murders*.

"The girl in the painting looks like you."

"Yes."

"Right down to the funny hat."

Was he saying that the hat in the painting was funny, or that the hat I was wearing was? Either way, I didn't like his attitude. "You have no sense of the current style, detective."

"That makes two of us."

I wanted to spit out something crushing, but nothing popped into my mind. I wanted to rip the hat from off my head, a very stylish number—I thought—one I had purchased at the Chapeau Boutique on Madison. Suddenly, I felt foolish wearing it in the apartment. But I controlled the urge to doff it when I remembered the state of my hair. I walked over to the table by the door to fetch my purse and Woodrow's leash, but the leash wasn't to be found. Neither was Woodrow.

"Your bellhop came for your dog while you were dressing."

"Yes, of course . . ."

I went to the desk and picked up the pages of my story, just going about my business as if he wasn't there, pulling out a manila envelope and jamming the pages into it, all the while ignoring the devastatingly handsome, god-awful man sitting across the room like he owned the place. With nothing left to do but leave the apartment, I turned and said: "Well, you haven't come to see me off for the day, so what do you want?"

"I came by to apologize for yesterday."

I raised a haughty brow. That was all he would get.

"And to ask for your help."

"Back up," I said, giving him a level stare. He wasn't going to get off that easily. "You said you came to apologize."

"Yes."

I held my ground, waiting.

"I apologize."

"For . . . ?"

"For being . . ."

"A brute, a lout —"

"Let me help you out: I was rude, accusatory, and yes, a lout, but that's how I am."

"So, you don't *try* to be offensive, you're just stupid?"

He let out a hooting laugh, the kind that makes one feel small and ineffectual. "I deserve that!"

"Yes, you do," I said, noncommittally, and then checked my purse for the necessaries: change-purse, lipstick, handkerchief. . . . I wasn't registering any of it.

"Now, don't get all hoity-toity on me, please."

"You haven't *begun* to see my hoity, Mister, much less my toity. Adding *please* at the end of a remark like that—well, Freud has a name for people like you."

"I'm sure he does."

I kept my eyes focused inside the purse, and removed my room key, waiting for him to pick up my cue and leave.

"You were right, you know. I talked with Mrs. Vega and she told me about the argument she overheard between Stringer and Hunter."

Putting the newspaper down on the coffee table and getting to his feet, he walked toward me. I snapped the purse shut, opened the door, and, pulling on my gloves, waited for him to leave.

"We didn't find any manuscript, any papers at all on Stringer."

"Well, there is—*was* one, according to Miss Winter. And he never left it out; he took it with him everywhere."

I fitted my key into the lock. He hovered at the threshold, forcing me to wait for him to exit. "We need your help."

"*We?*"

"The department. We're scrambling to bring down a big—well, let me say, there's what you'd call 'syndicates' terrorizing our city right now, and we don't have the manpower. We're up to our ears in—"

"Yes? What are you up to your ears in?

"All right, *I* need your help. I can't work three cases at once. There's the bank job you saw go down. There are thugs like Terranova, Luciano, Masseria, and Morello throwing their weight around the neighborhoods. The murder of a writer isn't a priority right now. So, I asked around the station and I'm told you and your friends get results—sometimes through unorthodox methods—but results."

"You want my help? Have you checked with Robert Benchley? Has he given his permission, his blessing?"

"Mrs. Parker," he began, and then took a deep breath, indicating both impatience and irritation, before continuing, "I am asking you to help me find a murderer."

"Arrest Trevor Hunter. He's your man. And since he killed Stringer, he probably took the manuscript from off the body. Go out and arrest him."

"I can't."

"Why, did he skip town?"

"No, he has an alibi."

"But, the Sherlock Holmes getup!"

"Was he wearing a deerstalker when you saw him trailing Stringer?"

"Well, no, he was wearing a fedora."

"He was with Anthony Young at one o'clock when Mrs. Vega heard the argument at the Stringer apartment. Perhaps someone wanted to point the finger at Hunter and wore a deerstalker. Any haberdasher has one. Thing is, the saline solution could have been doctored with strychnine at any time, not necessarily by the one o'clock visitor. When I spoke with Trevor Hunter and asked about any confrontations between Stringer and anyone else he could think of, he mentioned a writer who wanted to join their little mystery club. Supposedly, Stringer had harsh words with the man. Hunter said the fellow 'wouldn't have fitted in.' When I interviewed Anthony Young, he called the fellow 'a hack,' and Shaw said he was 'a Republican.'"

"What's his name?"

"A kid named John Steinbeck. You know him?"

"Johnny!" I sniggered. "It's true he wouldn't fit in, but he's no Republican, nor would I call him a hack—yet. Only time will tell if he writes anything worth reading, and yeah, I know him. He came to New York and worked construction for a time before he landed a job as a reporter. Heywood brought him to lunch a couple times. He's in California, now, I think."

I didn't understand why "harsh words" would be a motive for murder. "He's your only lead?"

"Well, he's in California, and Stringer's fellow writers all alibi out for the morning and afternoon hours."

"And what about Stringer's personal relationships? His girlfriend for one?"

"Cherish Winter was out grocery shopping at one o'clock, when Mrs. Vega heard the argument in the Stringer apartment. When she returned with the groceries, at around one-thirty, Stringer was not in the apartment. She fixed herself a sandwich and then went up to her studio in the attic and painted until seven in the evening. The artist she shares the studio with, Roberto Cellini, returned at around five o'clock after spending the day painting a mural in the lobby of the new Wentworth Building."

"The Wentworth—that's on 47th Street, right? Not far from the scene of the heist."

"That's right," replied Detective Sparrow. "Listen, I know what you're thinking."

"Oh, you do, do you?"

"Yes, that there might be something going on between this guy Cellini and Winter."

"Good guess, Detective."

"Since they share a studio together . . ."

"*Ah-ha*. I can imagine a romantic scenario, sure, with a drop or two of liquid murder. But, why go that far?"

"What do you mean?"

"Winter and Stringer weren't married. Why kill the man she could so easily have walked away from?"

"Yes. There would have to be a more pressing reason."

"A stronger motive," I considered aloud. "Stringer would have wanted to get rid of the interloper, Cellini."

"Yes, but it was Stringer's allergy spray that was doctored, so he was the intended victim. Yes, Miss Winter could have added the strychnine to the saline early in the day, before she left for work in her studio, whatever her motive. But wouldn't she have given herself a better alibi than being alone in her studio? I don't see her as the murderer."

"All right," I said, calculating a simple subtraction in my head. "The man arguing with Stringer at one o'clock was seen leaving the apartment at—?"

"One-ten, according to Mrs. Vega."

"And as the poison was inhaled, it is possible that the poisoned spray bottle was slipped into Stringer's pocket then, or anytime during the morning, or even between the time he left home at one-fifteen and his death at three-ten."

"That's right. So we interviewed the shoemaker who has the shop downstairs in the building. He doesn't remember seeing Stringer leave in the morning, only when he left the apartment at one-fifteen, and he said he was walking west. I have a man checking out a couple of other places Stringer frequented down in the Village. Somebody might have seen him early that day and between one-fifteen and three o'clock when he arrived uptown. Maybe his saline spray was placed in his pocket somewhere else, by someone other than his lunch-hour visitor. But, I need your help because there's much more to this than the murder of one man. It appears that someone is killing off the members of the Murder Club."

"What? How do you figure that? Only Stringer has been—you used the plural."

"That's because Mark Wendt was found dead this morning in an alley off Carmine Street in Greenwich Village."

That afternoon there were seven of us jammed into Chico's fancy new car. The Marx Brother was at the wheel, Soledad beside him, and I to her right with Woodrow on my lap. Behind us sat Mr. Benchley, FPA, and Aleck. It was three o'clock in the afternoon on a gloriously warm and balmy day as the car carried us through the Columbus Circle entrance into Central Park.

During lunch Chico posed the suggestion that we all head up to the Sheep Meadow for a game of croquet. This sport had become an obsession with Aleck, who, during the summer months at his retreat on Neshobe Island in Lake Bomoseen in Vermont, spent all of his waking hours putting the goddamn ball through the goddamn wickets with Harpo as his challenger. Harpo, whose solo harp performance was being filmed in Astoria this morning, was not with us at lunchtime, even though he was besotted with Soledad and anxious to see her. She had snuck out of the theater after the performance last night to avoid molestation by her most ardent admirer. Harpo, in love with both the mystery writer and croquet, not necessarily in that order, had spent thousands of dollars on the best hand-crafted equipment for the game. According to Chico, Harpo hoped to get done shooting so he could meet us up at the meadow for the game.

Last fall, after being faced with the curtailment of their tournaments due to the snows of winter, Harpo and Aleck had ventured to rent the roof of a building in Midtown. They had the deranged idea of laying down carpet to simulate grass, thereby giving them a wintertime field on which to continue their games. But, despite a tent, the carpet was drenched with rainwater and melted snow most of the time, which during the harshest months froze into an ice-rink. By January the plan was abandoned.

As we rode through the park with the top down, past the bright orange-and-yellow-and-red canopy of trees above vibrant emerald lawns, I told Soledad about my morning conversation with Detective Nate Sparrow.

"He wants me to be his 'inside man' on the case. What do you think?"

"I think it's exciting, Dory, and a bit dangerous, darling," she said, holding down the crown of her ecru-lace-brimmed hat.

"What's dangerous?" called out Mr. Benchley from the backseat.

"We are trying to have a private conversation here, if you don't mind, Mr. Benchley."

"Well, *I'm here*, so converse, ladies."

"After all, Dory, you'll be thrown into the thick of it."

"Who's throwing what—" piped in my nemesis.

"If someone is going around murdering the members of the Murder Club," said Soledad, "and *you* become a member, well, chances are—"

"I know, I know," I said, slicing my throat with a forefinger, sticking out my tongue and cocking my head to the side.

Soledad pointed a forefinger at me like a gun, said "*Pow!*" and then blew away imaginary smoke from the barrel.

"Or," said Mr. Benchley, wrapping his hands around my neck, "I strangle her now before she gets into any more trouble. And why, in heaven's name, are you wearing that hat?"

"I don't need your permission."

"Didn't say you did; just asking why you'd wear a thing like that."

"And do I go around asking why you refuse to wear the monogram-engraved sterling-silver stocking garters I gave you last Christmas? Your socks are always falling around your ankles."

"They pinch."

"I meant, I don't need your permission to wear this hat *or* to help Detective Sparrow."

"What? So you can go get yourself killed? When have I ever tried to stop you? Aleck? Have I ever tried to—"

"But," I protested, "Just last night—"

"Put last night behind you."

"Don't be oxymoronic."

"It's my nature. Where you, my dear, are often obtuse."

"I suppose I have your blessing, then."

"I'm not your priest, or your rabbi, so it really doesn't matter what I think, or so you say."

"Detective Sparrow *asked* for my help."

"Well, if he did, he's desperate, obviously—and before you get all athletic on me, remember that the last time you got us into the thick of things it resulted in a nervous constitution."

"I've never suffered from nerves."

"It was *I* who was so afflicted."

"And *that,* I suppose, is *my* fault?"

"Certainly."

"No one else turns his stomach the way you do, Dottie," said Chico.

"Mind your own business and watch where you're going, you stinker."

"She's no fun at all," said Chico, swerving off the shoulder and back onto the macadam, narrowly missing a lamppost.

"Anyway, if anyone should be seeking Murder Club membership it should be someone who writes mystery novels and that's certainly not you, Mrs. Parker."

"Why," said Soledad, "it should be *I*! I can play a real role in snagging the murderer!"

"Unless he snags you first," said Chico. "No, no, my brother wouldn't like it."

"Your crazy brother has nothing to say about it."

"Which one?"

"Take your pick."

"Harpo wants to know if you love him."

"*Uh*, no."

"He is throwing himself at your feet!"

"I wish him a safe landing."

"He would lay down his life to have you!"

"He will never lay down and have me."

"Have a heart, Sollie!"

"I have one and I'm keeping it to myself," she said curtly, before turning to me. "Anyway, I've never been a part of a real investigation before. You know, going all incognito, and everything?"

"You wouldn't be changing your identity, Soledad," said Aleck, "else they wouldn't let you join in."

"Yes, of course," she said, the floral-patterned sleeve of her dress fluttering in the breeze as she held onto the frisky hat. "Do they have any leads on who killed this fellow, Mark Wendt?"

"Detective Sparrow said that Wendt was poisoned, too," I said. "Looks like strychnine again. He was found dead in an alley a couple of blocks from Romany Marie's café, and the police on the case have been trying to check his whereabouts throughout the day leading up to the time he was found."

"Oh, to be part of solving a real crime!" said Soledad.

"Did you forget our foray in Paris?" asked Mr. Benchley. "The spies? The murderers?"

"Forget Paris!" she said, looking up at the sky as Chico pulled to the side of the road; Sheep Meadow was only a short walk beyond. "Look! Someone's flying a plane. Oh, how I love to fly! Dory, did I tell you about the Frenchman I met in Casablanca? The famous aviator, Louis Blériot? The first man to fly across the Channel? Oh, my, when he took me up in the clouds I thought I was in heaven! So he gave me flying lessons after the War, and I tell you, it's a marvelous pastime, as well as a practical way to get across the Channel to Paris when you've had your fill of fish-and-chips and bubble-and-squeak. I'll take you up some time."

"There's a banner off the tail," said Chico.

"Advertising," said Frank, giving us ladies a hand as we stepped out onto the grass. "Good thing it didn't rain overnight or our spats would be ruined."

"Good thing I left mine home," I replied.

After we all hopped out of the car, Woodrow dashed toward a patch of bushes. Aleck, who *rolled* out, began removing the game equipment that had been packed in the rumble-seat.

We began the short walk around the path toward the opening of the meadow. The park's shepherd and his dog were herding sheep toward the eastern edge of the meadow. Woodrow gave chase.

"Woodrow, Dory! He's running away!"

"Don't worry, Soledad," I said, touching her arm to stop her from running after him. "Woodrow is just visiting Eleanor."

"Eleanor?"

"The shepherd's dog."

"As in our Governor's wife, Eleanor Roosevelt? Why can't people name their dogs Nibbles, or Buster, or Bowser, or Bubbles?"

"Too many Ivy Leaguers claim those monikers these days," said Mr. Benchley. "Anyway, does that handsome Boston terrier of Mrs. Parker's look like a 'Bubbles'? Certainly not! He's got the stuff of senators, of statesmen, of presidents!"

"Yes, appropriate," said Soledad, "and from what I read in the newspapers these days, they are all tail-chasing bastards."

"Dogs have integrity, so you won't find any 'Herbert Hoovers,' though they've named a vacuum sweeper after him," I said.

A droning buzz, like a circling mosquito, grew louder, and when Chico started waving wildly we raised our faces to the sky.

"What fresh hell!" said Mr. Benchley.

"That's my line!" I said.

The aeroplane buzzed overhead from the east and circled above us; the banner floating from its tail spelled out "Harpo Loves Soledad." Soledad's jaw dropped, her expression first flummoxed, then infuriated.

As the biplane suddenly swooped down toward us, the sheep at the far-east border of the meadow became startled and began to *baa,* and the nice, compact band of animals formed by Eleanor's able wrangling suddenly dispersed in all directions, sending the bitch into an immediate tailspin in an effort to retrieve her stock and bring back order to the flock. Woodrow followed suit until Eleanor barked him away. He retreated under the shade of a maple, tongue hanging and duly rejected. The dogs' relationship oddly mirrored Soledad's and Harpo's.

Chico began jumping up and down, laughing and waving, egging-on the little biplane to circle again.

"Damned fool," *harrumph*ed Aleck, who then turned his back and set about the task of placing wickets on the lawn. When the aeroplane swooped down on its next pass, so low as to create a breeze, Frank asked him: "Where's the flyswatter?"

Aleck ignored Frank and everybody else who had come running from the surrounding paths and groves to watch and wave and encourage the yellow-cabined, stacked-winged phenomenon buzzing through the air. Aleck continued with his measurements before sticking in the next wicket.

Wings lifted toward the heavens and barely clearing the treetops, the aeroplane headed toward the east side of Manhattan. The *putt-putt-putt* of its little engine began to fade and the flying machine took on the appearance of glued-together matchsticks in the sky over the East River. Bystanders returned their hats to their heads and dropped their eyes from the sky, and the scattered spiral of sheep were coiling back into a neat little package again, when the droning sound of the motor grew louder and louder and, suddenly, there it was again, turning, dipping, and then coming straight toward us, wings tipping from side to side like a seesaw as it barely cleared the treetops.

"Holy *shit!*" I screeched, as it dropped lower and lower from the sky. "It's going to crash!"

"Naah," said Chico. "He's just showing off his aviation skills."

"You mean . . . ?"

"That's Harpo!" said Chico with a nod and smile of assurance. "I told Sollie he would throw himself at her feet, he'd lay down his life—"

"Oh, for God's sake!" yelled Soledad in a huff.

"But, if he doesn't pull that nose up—"

"Holy *crap!*" I yelled, and Mr. Benchley ran to where I stood frozen in the middle of the meadow. He grabbed my arm and pulled me out of the path of the oncoming plane. I turned to look for Soledad but all I found of my friend was her discarded high heels in the grass. I swiveled my head in search of her, and there she was, sprinting off toward Chico's car. I watched her get in, struggle with the choke, turn the key, and bang violently on the steering wheel. Then the car sprang to life and she drove off.

Harpo brought the plane down bumpily onto the meadow, taxied to a stop, and, motor idling *putt-putt-putt-putt,* leaped out into the cheering crowd that closed in around him. Pulling off his leather cap and goggles, he bowed to the applause, and yelled out to us, "Where's the love of my life? I've come to take her away!" just as police sirens whined their imminent arrival. "Sorry, got to fly," he announced, hopping back into the biplane, instructing a fellow to pull down on the propeller blade, and telling the crowd to move back.

"You've really got to tie down that fool," I scolded Chico.

"We've tried everything, Dottie, but the boy's double-jointed."

The biplane's tail lifted off into the air and the two police cars chasing after it came to an abrupt halt.

The flock of sheep uncoiled again.

Biplanes over the Hudson River

Stringer, Hunter, Wendt, and Cousins

Stephen Shaw

Anthony Young

Chapter Seven

"Sparrow wants you to help solve his case?" said Mr. Benchley. "Why, that's unnatural. The police always want you to butt-out!"

"And you want me to butt-out!"

"Of course I want you to butt-out! People are getting murdered. And I don't want you to stick your butt out and bring up the body count! Then where'd we be? Jane, can you imagine life without our Dorothy?" Forlornly, he looked down at his feet and shook his head: "No one to call me a fool; no one to shout profanities at me; no one to tell me to pull up my socks."

"He's just worried about you," said Jane, trying to make peace.

We were standing in the lobby of the Gonk, myself, Jane, and Mr. Benchley, waiting for the others to arrive for lunch. "I understand that," I said to Jane, when suddenly I looked up at the man brooding beside me and thought of all the times that his life was in danger during one of these investigations I had insisted embarking upon, and realized that Mr. Benchley has a wife and two sons he is accountable for. Who would be there for them if anything happened to him? He couldn't put his life in jeopardy merely for a lark. If anything happened to him—oh, I didn't want to think. . . .

There is so much more to him than the deliberately lighthearted, seemingly vacuous funny-man he shows to the world to mask a profound underlying melancholy. He is often self-effacing, self-deprecating, and always considerate of the feelings of others. Yet, I have in the past been able to read those deep concerns beneath his jovial banter. And now, circumstances are changing for Mr. Benchley, as my own life remains relatively stagnant.

A few weeks ago we celebrated his fortieth birthday. That milestone and the new opportunities that take him away from New York and our circle of friends—from me—for long periods of time have begun to complicate his life even as they offer him new opportunities, ones he never expected. I see his reluctance to move ahead, to leave New York. But Hollywood beckons, more loudly and persistently these days since he authored and starred in several short films for the Fox movie people. I must be honest about it: I want the world for him. But I feel left behind and a little bit abandoned as weeks go by when he is away from me. But most of all, I fear that as reluctant as he is to start a new life three thousand miles away, it is also a new and exciting time for him, and his future awaits him there, in Hollywood. And our friendship . . . how can it survive the distance? As the one truly great love of my life moves on, will I just fade away from him like a memory from the old days, only to be considered every so often when he's blue? Sometimes, when people who have shared great affection move away—neighbors, schoolmates—they pick fights so that the pain of separation is not felt so keenly. Was that what Mr. Benchley and I were up to?

I was about to say that I wouldn't get any further involved with the case, that I would telephone Detective Sparrow and tell him to find somebody else to help him, when Mr. Benchley asked: "Well, exactly what did he ask you to do? Don't tell me you were serious about what you were going on about in the park yesterday with Soledad—"

"He said nothing about joining the club, but he knows we have connections in the publishing world. He just wanted me to ask questions and find out why someone wants to kill members of this club. It was my idea about joining the club. He suspects the other members' lives are in jeopardy."

"Great! So you'll be his sitting duck."

"I told him that I wouldn't be the best person for the job, because I'm not a novelist."

"Yes? So you aren't going to do it?"

"No. But Soledad is."

"She was serious?" he said, his eyes widening. "I suppose it makes sense. But, she'll be—"

"A sitting duck?"

"—putting herself—"

"—in danger. I know."

"It's good to hear you finishing each other's sentences again," said Jane.

"Well, we can't let Sollie go out there all alone with nobody to protect her," said Mr. Benchley, his Victorian chivalry rising in his voice.

"No? I mean, *no*, we can't send her out there alone, Mr. Benchley."

"No, it wouldn't be right. But, what does Sparrow think she can find out, once she joins up?"

"Other than who wants them all dead? Well, I told him that the manuscript that Ersatz was writing and keeping so close to his vest might shed light on the reason for the murders. It might lead directly to the killer."

"The motive. . . . So they didn't find what Erzatz was writing when they found his body?"

"No, they didn't."

"Someone killed him for it?"

"I'm guessing so."

"So, first Ersatz is killed by Trevor Hunter, or someone *posing* as him, so that he can get his hands on what he's writing. Then Mark Wendt gets the bullet—well, the poison—but why? Had Wendt killed Ersatz for the manuscript and did someone poison Wendt to get his hands on it? It makes me think that something somebody doesn't want anybody to know about is revealed in the book."

"Assuming that it was a book he was writing."

"Or, this missing manuscript may have nothing at all to do with these killings," said Mr. Benchley.

Jane asked, "Has the detective asked the surviving members what they know about the manuscript?"

"Yes, but his interviews with Young, Cousins, Shaw, and Hunter have led nowhere. Sparrow says they look scared. He thinks that's why they've clammed up."

"The men are being blackmailed?" said Jane.

"Yes . . . perhaps the secret for the blackmail is in the manuscript. Yep, that's motive for murder, all right!" said Mr. Benchley.

"But, what if the manuscript never left Ersatz's apartment?" I said. "What if he hid it somewhere? What if he had put it into a locker at the train station—"

"Wait! What if he put it into a safety deposit box at the bank?" said Mr. Benchley.

"Yes!" I said.

"You think he had already put it into the bank before he died? But, he was walking toward the bank, not from it, when you saw him on the street."

"Still . . . it's a possibility. Maybe he was killed on his way to fetch it *from* the bank, and the murderer didn't know he didn't have it on his person."

"We can find that out easily enough. Detective Sparrow can get a warrant to open Ersatz's safety deposit box—if he had one there, or in any other bank around town."

"Sometimes, with a little cooperation from the police, one doesn't have to employ your Swiss army knife to break into a bank."

Detective Sparrow walked into the Algonquin's lobby. We asked him about a safety deposit box, and he said Ersatz didn't have one. And then he told us that the City Coroner had determined that the cause of Mark Wendt's death had been respiratory failure. "Analysis of Mr. Wendt's pipe tobacco pouch registered a high concentration of strychnine in the mix. He was poisoned."

"Well, that makes it difficult to point to any one particular suspect. The poison could have been added to the tobacco at any time," I said.

"Was it added to the pouch directly, or to the can his tobacco was purchased in?" asked Mr. Benchley.

"Why?" I asked.

"Because," explained Detective Sparrow, "if strychnine was added to the can—perhaps days ago, a week ago—and Wendt didn't refill his pouch from it until yesterday, it's difficult to narrow down just when and by whom the poison was placed there. But, yes, Mr. Benchley, there was strychnine in his humidor."

When the others arrived, we took our places at our Round Table, the detective next to me. He ordered a hamburger and gave me the floor.

"So, what do we know?" I asked the assemblage of my friends.

Ross, Jane, Heywood, and FPA had looked into any recently demised who may have had connections with our Murder Club members, as they had the resources of their publications at hand. I felt that before we could find the murderer of the members of the Murder Club, we needed to know more about their individual backgrounds and relationships, for there might lay the motive for the killings, and a motive might point directly to a suspect.

Heywood took out a small writing pad and read from it: "All right, now, let's see. Ernest Stringer was born in 'ninety-eight in Brooklyn to Jacob and Edith Stringer. He was an only child. His father was an engineer who emigrated from Germany in the early eighteen-nineties. Jacob worked for a company that designed bridges and he traveled quite a bit. His mother was murdered when Ernest was five years old. It is believed that Jacob killed her when he suspected she was having an affair with a wealthy amusement park owner. Jacob disappeared, leaving the child abandoned. Ernest was sent to an orphanage—Our Sisters of Mercy in the Bronx—where he remained until he was of age. He had a nearly fatal bout of scarlet fever when he was seven, and suffered all kinds of allergies and respiratory problems, so he didn't see any time in the service. He managed to put himself through a year at City College and was hired by the *Sun* as a copyboy, and then moved up to become their third-string critic—that's how Aleck knows him. Wrote a bestselling book published to good reviews in 'twenty-two. That's it."

"Now, about Anthony Young: He's forty-one, a moderate success with his history-professor-sleuth novels. Born eighteen-eighty-nine to Rose and Gerald Young in Minneapolis. Father, a stockbroker, moved the family—he had a brother two years younger, by the way—moved the family to New York City after the crash of 'ninety-three. Took a lowly job as an accountant with a Wall Street firm. Rebuilt his fortune. Anthony went off to prep school—Phillips Exeter Academy in New Hampshire—and on to Harvard, where he switched his major from business to Greco-Roman studies. There was some contention from his father, who had expected him to join the brokerage house he'd established in nineteen-hundred. . . . Went on to short-term professorships at several small New England colleges, teaching history; never attained tenure. When his parents died in a car crash while vacationing in Paris in 'twenty-four, Young inherited the firm and a small fortune."

"What about the younger brother?" asked Jane.

"Oh, Gerald, Jr.? The boy died at age four. Don't have details of his death. So, when Young suddenly became financially independent, he started writing his mystery novels. Now, there was a discrepancy. By my calculations, he should've graduated from Harvard in nineteen-eleven, but he didn't finish up until 'thirteen."

"Class of 'thirteen . . ." interrupted Mr. Benchley, who had graduated with the class of 'twelve. "I'll look into it. I remember there was an epidemic of measles sweeping the school when I was a sophomore. . . ."

"Anyway," continued Heywood, "after graduation Anthony did the European tour, spent a summer in Greece, came home before the war in Europe broke out. He never married, has no known children, but he fancies himself a ladies' man. Lectures at various women's clubs, civic organizations—you know the type: the expert on classical literature, Greek tragedies. Not many male friends outside the Murder Club men, and the people I spoke with at the paper who knew him years ago remember him as a prissy top. Belongs to a bridge club, Harvard Club, and that's all I've got so far."

Ross said, "Shaw, Stephen Shaw: The pompous ass was born in 'ninety-three to James Michael and Siobhan Shaw. The father was a Protestant minister in Northern Ireland who did not spare the rod on his five sons—or his wife, for that matter—this according to an obituary filed at the *Journal*, sent in by Shaw himself, for publication in the event of his death. If there is any truth to the story, who would know?

"His father was killed when his horse-cart overturned. Siobhan and her brother's family emigrated to the States at the turn of the century. Right off the boat the family, like many Irish immigrants at the time, was shuttled off to Albany. There's no mention of Shaw's schooling. Shaw left home at fourteen and came to New York. He subsisted by taking on menial jobs—newsie, dishwasher; was a voracious reader. One day decided to see the world, so, in nineteen-fifteen, Shaw set out as a hand on a ship that sank off the coast of Cobh. That ship was the *Lusitania*. Somehow, he survived. But the War was raging in France and Italy and he sailed home after a few months, signing on as crew on a freighter bound for Boston. On the ship he worked alongside a group of Italian anarchists. Once arrived in Beantown, where he got a job at a cording factory, Shaw became involved in a factory labor dispute. He was one of a dozen men fired for inciting the riot that got his arm broken from a policeman's swinging jack; forty-three other men were bashed, wounded, a couple were killed.

"From then on he knew his path in life—so he says: It was the labor movement that inflamed him, and after he followed the labor organizers to factories around the big cities of the Northeast, he began to write his exposés. He never married, has no kids, far as anyone knows, fancies himself an intellectual, an autodidact. Nearly put Niles Pickering's publishing house out of business, not because of any defamation suit—although Shaw and the publishers were sued by several city officials he had named as corrupt without any substantial evidence against them—but by the wrath of the mobsters he'd taken on."

"That'd be the Moffo Brothers," said the detective. "They have the Yonkers and Mount Vernon garbage contracts."

"About Mark Wendt," continued Ross, "according to a piece in the *Post*, he was born in 'ninety-seven here in Manhattan, Upper-Eastside neighborhood. Grew up on Ninety-third Street on the East Side—the Jewish neighborhood where the Marx Brothers grew up, by the way, according to Chico. Father killed—he was a sandhog—in a subway tunnel collapse; mother waitressed to support her only child. The kid was a pansy—Chico said that, not the *Post* article—a dreamer, who, when lost in his fantasies would wander across Lexington Avenue and get beaten up by the Irish kids, or by the German kids a few blocks south, which was—still is—the way of the streets around town. The kid always sported a shiner."

"Used to be the avenues were the only safe route for a kid navigating Manhattan; it was the cross-streets where you met trouble," said Heywood.

"Good to know," said Ross with a sardonic smirk.

"Growing up, Mark wasn't like all the neighborhood kids. He was small for his age and kids made fun of him and pushed him around. So he kept to himself and starting reading anything he could get his hands on. Things changed when he approached puberty, and he shot up like a weed. He didn't have many friends his own age, but the younger kids in his neighborhood gathered around him and he would tell them stories, mostly tales he'd made up himself, about knights and ladies and Arabian adventures. He hated school; all he wanted to do was read. It was discovered that had a nice singing voice, and when he was twelve he quit the sixth grade and joined a troupe of singers who performed for two-bits a night, a catfish dinner, and all the beer you could drink at an oyster joint on Forty-sixth Street. Somehow, that led to an audition for *Hello, Broadway*, the George M. Cohan show back in 'fourteen, around the time when Aleck, over there, was pretending to be a reporter—"

"And you were a thumb-sucking copyboy," said Aleck.

"Aw, shut-up, Fatty. As I was saying, Mark Wendt was a chorus boy in a string of shows. But what he liked best was to make up stories, which he began writing down. In 'twenty-two he got published. He's got five books under his belt, all about the Wild West. Never been west of New Jersey, but people eat that crap up."

"Has he any enemies, angry ex-wives?" asked Jane, flashing a knowing look at her husband.

"Who knows? He married a chorine, but she ran off with another guy years ago, before the books became popular. And if there are any enemies, they're smart enough to lurk in the shadows," said Ross. "Mark Wendt was an amiable guy, and not the type to look for trouble."

"What about Cousins?" I asked.

"I got that one," said Frank. Daniel 'Bigfoot' Cousins—he was tagged Bigfoot during his years at Columbia U. Bigfoot was born in nineteen-hundred, in Providence, Rhode Island, the second son of two born to Italian immigrant parents, Enrico and Carmella Cugini."

Aleck said, "Cugini translated into English is 'cousins.'"

"Your brain is in your ass," said Ross.

"Your mother wears army boots."

"Boys, go to your rooms!" laughed Frank. "Where was I? Oh, yeah, Daniel Cousins. Father was a fishmonger; the mother a seamstress. Father died of sepsis after he stuck his finger on a fishbone. Carmella then supported the family. Her sewing skills proved clever and she was industrious. She sold the jewelry that had belonged to her late mother, given to her by her father when she left the old country. She bought a few yards of fine silk and rented a room above a haberdashery. With the bolts of satin ribbon and the lace she'd brought in her trousseau to America, she began designing and selling lingerie to the Newport crowd, which led to a remarriage to a wealthy widower."

"Is she the Carmella of the Carmella Lingerie line?" asked Soledad. "Why, her chemises rival any I've seen in Paris. I wear them myself. It's the only thing that touches my skin."

Ross's eyes widened, he blinked, and then swallowed the lump in his throat before murmuring, "Touches your skin . . ."

Jane riled and said, "*Oh, yeah?* It's the *only thing* that touches her skin. Remember that, Ross."

A cornered fox at the hunt, sweat suddenly broke out on his upper lip. Could Ross save himself from his wife's wrath? "Well, what I meant was—there must be a catalogue—don't you deserve nice things, my love? Our anniversary is coming up—wait, that was last—birthday! But, what I meant to say—" continued Ross, digging himself deeper into the grave.

Frank said, "Nail the casket; you're dead already!"

"Yes, sorry, old man. . . . What did you just say?" asked Ross.

"Good thing we didn't engrave Jane's wedding band," whispered Aleck in aside to me. "I've been expecting this."

"Aren't we the harbinger of cheer?" I replied.

Chuckling, Frank flipped a page in his notebook, found his place and said, "As I was saying, from rags to riches for the Cugini clan. Bigfoot got his degree; one book, out of print, a halfway decent writer, but not at all prolific. Oh, yeah. There was rumor that a book he wrote had been plagiarized. I don't have any more about that, though. He's been writing ad copy—well, we knew that. . . . That's all I've got." Frank closed the cover of his notebook and leaned back in his chair.

"What about his military record?" asked Aleck.

"Wouldn't take him—his feet were too big," said Detective Sparrow. "And as none of them have arrest records, we have no leads that might trace back to criminal associates who'd want to kill them."

Aleck cleared his throat, removed a small notepad from his inside coat pocket, rebalanced his spectacles on his nose, flicked through the pad, and, with an officious clearing of the throat, took the floor. "Trevor Hunter. He is a very peculiar one. Supposedly has a half-dozen books in the works—or short stories, I don't know. He was born to a fortune. His maternal grandfather, a Canadian named Samuel Spencer, was a snake-oil salesman back before the

War Between the States, who later concocted a tonic for dyspepsia that actually worked. Made a fortune when a British pharmaceutical company bought the formula. You remember Cocana Cure? My father used to guzzle it down. Spencer's daughter, Margaret, married the company's son and heir, Simon Hunter, and in eighteen-eighty-five, after they had taken up residence in London, Margaret gave birth to a son, Trevor. Two other siblings followed, both dead now, Spanish influenza.

"After a fine public school education, young Trevor went on to Oxford. A 'friend' of Conan Doyle—so he claims. A flyer during the War—Royal Air Force, saw twenty missions. Leg shot up—that accounts for the limp. Trevor inherited his father's company and sold it in 'twenty-four. Moved to the States. Thinks he's a genius—delusions of grandeur. Never married, not much interest in long-term re-lationships with women, but he manages to seduce plenty, and is especially attracted to the married ones; few friends, male or female."

"A narcissist like you, Aleck," said Ross.

"You are too stupid to be an idiot."

I looked at the faces of my career-driven friends around the table. "Do we know anybody who *isn't* a narcissist?" I said.

"These two murdered men—Ersatz and Mark Wendt—were nice people. So, whom did they cross who would want to kill them?" said Mr. Benchley. "And the question arises: Ersatz was a one-shot novelist, and Wendt wrote Cowboy novels. Why were they involved with this Murder Club?"

Soledad spoke up: "I talked with Josh Latham some more about these men. He heard talk that Mark Wendt was writing a different sort of book—bored with the Western theme, you know how we writers get. Mysteries are the thing, these days, and Mark Wendt was planning to write one and told people of his intentions. Ernest Stringer was excited about a crime story he wanted to flesh out into a book. It wasn't like anything he'd written before, and he thought the others, especially Anthony Young, might help him through it. Josh also heard through the grapevine that Shaw was giving up his exposés—they'd gotten him into enough hot water—and was going to write what he called a 'thriller' about a federal agent chasing commies. Very cloak-and-dagger."

Edna spoke up for the first time after hearing the verbal biographies of the club members. "Yes, Soledad. In regard to what you said about Ernest: When I spoke with Ernest Stringer at a party last winter he sought my opinion on something. I have to say he appeared excited about his new project. Soledad, you know that when writing a mystery plot you try to depict the perfectly executed premeditated crime. This makes for a clever protagonist and gives your detective a real challenge. The detective must find the one overlooked detail that will bring the culprit down. There is always something."

"Yes," agreed Soledad. "To paraphrase Dostoyevsky's Raskolnikov in *Crime and Punishment*: 'A criminal is caught because at the time of his crime he loses the ability to reason.' One cannot predict the loss of a shirt button, the shedding of coat fibers, the passerby who sees your face when you leave the scene of the crime. It's the little unexpected things that may give one away, no matter how perfectly one plans the execution of a crime."

Edna nodded. "I believe that Ernest was writing a novel depicting the perfect murder, whose protagonist was *not* held accountable for his crime at story's end. I think this because when I asked if he was working on a new book, he said he was and asked me if I thought that his immoral approach was too extreme for a publisher to take on."

"Your advice to Mr. Stringer?" asked Detective Sparrow.

"Readers want vindication; they want a resolution; they want the criminal caught. And they want him properly punished. There are perfect murders committed every day that are mistaken as accidents, suicides, illnesses. But real life has to take a backseat in popular fiction."

"Edna is correct," said Soledad. "But I think that if, at story's end, the reader is privy to the identity of the criminal and the ending is open to the possibility that the villain will be caught and punished for his crime through some blemish in his nature—Greek tragedian's *fatal flaw*, a device that Shakespeare used over and over again—that innate flaw in his character that will lead to his eventual downfall, after the reader has finally closed the book he would find vindication and not be disappointed. With the right publisher, a book like that—one depicting the perfect crime—well, it could get itself banned in Boston and make a big splash."

"But, these men—Shaw, Ersatz, and Cousins— had paranoiac aspects to their natures. You'd think that the last thing any of them would do would be to share their book's plot lines with each other."

"Good point," agreed Aleck. "Writers are like some children: They do not play well with others."

"Oh!" said Soledad. "Whom did they upset, is the question."

Soledad's question led me to another. "Do you think it's possible that the men stumbled upon a real-life murder plot, one that had already been committed?" I posed. "A murder committed by someone who was willing to kill to keep his secret?"

"There isn't any crime if no one knows that a crime has been committed," said Jane. "Therefore, to cover one murder you have to commit others."

"So there had been a crime?" I said, "and these men, who stumbled upon it, were killed to keep the secret?"

"That might be so," said the detective. "It's a hard thing to prove because we have no suspicion of a past crime having been committed that our men may have known about."

"Hence, the perfect murder," said Soledad.

Detective Sparrow nodded. "And after interviewing Shaw and Hunter and Cousins and Young, I've come up with no suspects, no motive for their colleagues' murders. I have to say, they all appear to be cooperating, and yet, substantively, they have offered me nothing to go on."

"They are hiding something. Perhaps protecting someone?" said Jane.

"Their own sorry asses, no doubt," said Ross.

"If these fellows know anything, maybe they're too scared to tell," said the detective.

"Each must be terrified that they will be next," said Frank.

"If they won't help you find their colleagues' killer, what can you do?" asked Heywood.

"I agree that they must have stumbled onto something really big to be so afraid of revealing what they know," said Edna. "But, I fear there is more. Now that I hear about this missing manuscript, I feel in a way responsible for what's happened to Ernest. You see, not only did I say his premise could work in his favor, but I encouraged him to follow through with it, to write the book. I remember saying to him that he had nothing to lose by writing it. It never dawned on me that he could lose his life over such a thing, if the killer did the deed to get the manuscript Ernest was guarding."

Soledad comforted Edna: "You just wanted him to succeed, my dear. He hadn't a success in seven years, and you wished that for him."

"Yes, yes, I know," said Edna, flashing a quick smile and blowing her nose on the pristine handkerchief she'd pulled from her pocketbook.

"Have you interviewed all the people that these writers are associated with—" said Aleck. But Detective Sparrow cut him off.

"It's been done, Mr. Woollcott. These men kept whatever troubled them close to the vest. Young and Hunter said that they met weekly to discuss crime reports they gathered from the newspapers to craft into stories for their books. Young was teaching them how to construct their plots, how to reveal clues, and the psychological aspects of character. Hunter provided forensic information. They never shared their ideas outside of the club. And I have read the manuscript found in Ernest Stringer's apartment— *The Body in the Basement*—and it's not a murder mystery in the classic sense of the word. It's about the remains of a woman buried more than a century before the book's present-day venue. It's a ghost story. So there are no clues there."

"Isn't it possible that our Murder Clubbers became privy to a crime that struck close to home, a heinous crime kept secret until the men unwittingly uncovered it? That might be the motive for Stringer's and Wendt's murders. Have you looked into recent crimes—robberies, for instance, or deaths of anyone even vaguely associated with the men of the club, whether from seemingly natural causes or accidents or suicides?" asked Mr. Benchley.

"It's time-consuming labor. I don't have the men to put on checking out vague connections."

"Wait, Bob," said Heywood. "We can go through police blotters and newspaper coverage of the past, let's say, five years. Look through all the obits over at our respective newspapers. Something might jump out at us—related to one of the men, maybe? Aleck, put your assistant at the *Times* on it. I can get my friends at the *World* on this, too. Frank—how about you?"

"I've got it!"

"Ross?"

Ross nodded and so did Jane. "Jane and I will do the publishing houses and the agencies. We'll get the skinny on who kicked the bucket or was caught with their hand in the till or up some guy's 'skirt.'"

Mr. Benchley said, "I'll check out my contacts in high and low places—"

"Mostly low," I said.

"Polly Adler may have heard something from one of her girls."

Polly was a high-class madam who ran a high-class cathouse on 58th Street east of Fifth Avenue. Detective Sparrow winced at the unwanted knowledge, which was better left to the vice squad. "Polly Adler, *hmmm?*"

Mr. Benchley squirmed for a second, and then said, "Yes, Miss Adler; she's a business contact."

"I'll bet she's had contact with your *business*," I said.

"Let me remind you, Mrs. Parker, that my business is private."

"And should remain so," giggled Soledad. "We don't want you to start a riot!"

Mr. Benchley blushed a Victorian rose and ineffectually began to explain the reasons for his visits to Polly's to Detective Sparrow. "I conduct my business at her house."

Sniggering.

"I mean, I often go there when I need to relax—"

Sniggering and snorts.

"—to sleep, to work, away from the relentless enticements of my friends' activities—"

Sniggering, snorts, and sneers.

"—in order to meet my deadlines!"

Hearty laughter all around.

"These people won't let me work, I tell you!"

Even though what Mr. Benchley said was true, Sparrow shot him a look of disbelief. After all, who frequented a bordello for the purposes of getting a good night's sleep and one's writing assignments done? "Nice work if you can get it," said the detective with a chuckle.

Heywood came to Mr. Benchley's rescue by summing up: "So, when we have these lists of the recently deceased, or victims of extortion and scandal, we can cross-reference and come up with a short list of people who were possibly victims, and the suspected instigators, wherever it may lead. Then we can determine how closely they stand to our Murder Club members. Perhaps then we might find the person targeting these men."

"When can I meet this madam, Polly Adler?" asked Soledad, excited at the prospect.

———◆———

We climbed the stoop to the brownstone on 58th Street and after ringing Polly's doorbell were admitted into the foyer by her maid, Lion.

"Good afternoon, Mr. Bob," said the spritely little Negro woman whom everybody addressed as "Lion" because of the fierceness with which she protected her mistress, Polly. She ushered us into the sitting room.

"How's my little darling?" responded my friend.

"Fine, just fine, Mr. Bob."

"Is Miss Polly seeing callers today?"

"Miss Polly is always available for Mr. Bob," Lion replied, flashing a radiant smile.

"I'll bet," I whispered to Soledad.

The truth is that Mr. Benchley is a regular at Polly's, as are dozens of our friends, myself included. Polly may run a bordello and speakeasy, but she also entertains, in her front rooms, the crème-de-la-crème of New York society and the business world. It is the place to go for a relaxing evening where you could enjoy the "real deal" right off the boat from the rum-runners off the Great South Bay of Long Island, along with conversation as stimulating as the proffered hooch. I have spent many a delightful evening on her plush sofas, imbibing and happily chatting with my friends.

But this place is also a haven for Mr. Benchley—not because of the nature of its purpose, but because when my friend finds the distractions of his everyday routine interfering with his writing assignments, this is the place to which he retreats.

"Mr. Bob" always has a room available to him, a room with a desk where he can set up his typewriter and get down to the business of completing his writing assignments without interruption. This is where he can take a break to enjoy a sandwich or a steak dinner delivered to his room by his favorite maid, Lion, who will not allow any of the other maids to serve him. After a good night's sleep, his suit would be presented pressed, his shirt, underwear, and socks laundered, and she'd bring his breakfast on a tray. Lion's smile lights up a dark room, Mr. Benchley always says.

Of course, as a home away from his Scarsdale home where his wife, Gertrude, and his two young sons reside, Mr. Benchley also has his apartment in town at the Hotel Royalton, directly across the street from the Algonquin. He had given up his rooms at the Gonk a few years ago because he couldn't get any work done just knowing that his friends were in the bar downstairs, or in my rooms, or playing cards in the room Aleck kept there for that purpose. He had moved just across the street to the Royalton in the misguided belief that the move would cure his nervous tendency of quitting work to see who was downstairs in the lobby. But, he never gave a thought to the fact that it was all too easy to just cross the street from his new place to his old—and so his distractions continued. My friend is a brilliant man, but brilliant men are often quite stupid about the obvious.

Polly Adler is a savvy businesswoman who prides herself in providing the best of everything to her customers and the best care, protection, and motherly concern for her girls. She encourages the women to read, to keep up with current events, to continue their education, to take care of their bodies, and to save their hard-earned money for the day when they would be leaving her for marriage or other careers.

Sure, she'd been closed down many times, but she is always released quickly, thanks to her contacts in City Hall and on the Bench. She has strict house rules: No one enters her establishment without credentials. There is an expectation of gentlemanly conduct of the men who frequent her house—whether movie star, stock broker, Arab prince, or bookmaker. Guns are left at the door. And yet, no matter how careful she is, there is always the occasional guy who's drunk too much of her good booze, and who starts throwing his weight around, or sometimes the furniture. Polly calls in her protection if she can't get rid of the problem-boy herself. Her pistol might do the trick, but sometimes you just had to call in the infantry. Polly sees herself as a procurer, an entrepreneur who provides a much-needed service to the community, and she does what she does with grace and style.

Now down the stairs floated the tiny madam with the big brown eyes. The Russian Jew, born in a village near the Polish border, is barely thirty years old, dressed in a trim blue suit and a string of pearls. A dozen or more years ago she found herself on the streets of New York City, penniless, alone, and hungry for the opportunity to make something of herself and the chance to earn a decent living.

"How's business, Paulie?" asked my friend, his Worchester, Massachusetts, upbringing enhancing his vowels. He gave her a hug and a smooch on her cheek.

"Well, you know how it is, Bobby," she laughed, and then batted her eyelashes, as she knelt down to pet and coo at Woodrow Wilson, who relished every moment of her attention and flipped over on his back to enjoy a belly-rub. In her thick Russian accent she pressed on. "The only sin is to be poor. These past few years, anything that is economically right has been morally right. So business has been quite good."

"I want to introduce my friend, the mystery writer, Soledad Soleil—Mrs. Parker you know."

"Yes, Dorothy, how are you? It's a pleasure to meet you, Miss Soleil—I have many of your books in my library. I hope you'll do me the honor of signing them for me?"

"My pleasure, and call me Soledad, please."

"Call me Polly," she said as she gestured for us to sit. Woodrow leaped up like a young pup to sit next to Polly on the divan. After accepting the offer of cocktails and answering Polly's polite queries, Mr. Benchley got down to business.

"Polly, have you heard about the recent murders of Ernest Stringer and Mark Wendt? They were writers—"

"Yes, Stringer wrote the sex stories, no? Lion recognized the name when she saw the story in the paper. I have not read them, but I am told they are quite entertaining. They, too, are in the library—right next to your books, Miss Soleil."

"Erotica?" Mr. Benchley raised an eyebrow.

"One does have to earn a living, Bobby," said Soledad. "Poor Ernest hadn't had a novel published in seven years. Lots of writers have relied on the income during their salad days."

"I don't disapprove. I just didn't know—I haven't seen them. He wrote them under his own name?"

"Lion will fetch them for you, Bob. Read them at your leisure."

"I'd like to see them, if only to see who published them," he said.

"That I can tell you," said Polly. "Harvey Price brought them here one night."

"Price!" said Soledad. "Price Publishing? Since when do they publish—"

"Lion, fetch the books—and while you are there, bring down Miss Soleil's as well."

Lion put down the drinks tray and rushed out of the room on her mission.

While we awaited the maid's return and we sipped our cocktails, Mr. Benchley told Polly what we knew about the murders. "Why would Harvey Price publish pornography?" mused Mr. Benchley, more to himself than to us.

"Sure cash," said Soledad. "There's a healthy market, as you know, for that sort of thing."

"But, to admit that he is the publisher," I said, "would hurt his reputation."

"It was Marianne he told, well, you know, at a time when. . . . Price was always very drunk when he'd arrive here asking for Marianne. Marianne left my house last month. They were her books that she left behind."

"Oh? Why did she leave?" I asked. "Where'd she go?"

"It was time," said Polly, and I could tell that it wasn't a topic she wished to expound on. Knowing Polly, if the young woman wanted to leave for marriage or a career, she would do everything to encourage her; but if she had asked Marianne to leave, it had to do with untoward behavior on the girl's part.

"Mark Wendt. . . ." said Polly. He I did not personally know, either, but I know his books about the cowboys. They help me fall asleep."

"You'll have to take a tonic from now on, Polly: Wendt went."

Soledad let out a giggle at my remark and Polly, too, and then, realizing that the man was dead, turned serious faces back to Mr. Benchley.

Mr. Benchley righteously cleared his throat in a gesture of disapproval. "It appears that somebody is killing off the men who belong to what they call

'The Murder Club.' Have you heard any talk about it among your clientele?"

Polly didn't respond right away. She nodded and I could see the wheels turning in her head. "The newspaper, a few nights ago. Who was it, now?" she asked herself, searching the ceiling for the answer. "Oh, yes, it was that fellow . . . do you know Mr. Stone?"

"Stone?"

"Wait," she said, rising to walk over to her guestbook. All of her clients' names were marked down in code. She flipped the page, ran her finger down the ledger, looked up and smiled. "It was Stonewall."

"Stonewall?" said Mr. Benchley.

"That is the man. Martin Stonewall. He came here with one of the regulars." She mentioned the name of the regular patron, but neither Mr. Benchley nor I recognized the name. But Soledad did. Stonewall was at one time an editor at Scribner's, and had recently started a press of his own. They published racy books.

"Mr. Stonewall had too much to drink. So, at around two in the morning Lion and I helped him outside, and while Lion flagged a taxicab to take him home, a newsie came up to us to sell a paper. The headline said, *Writer Found Shot at Bank Heist.*"

"That would be Ersatz—I mean Ernest Stringer." I said.

"Yes. Stonewall grabbed the paper from the newsboy and said, 'They killed the wrong son-of-a-bitch!'"

"They killed the wrong . . . like the victim should have been somebody else?"

"I don't know, Bob, but that's what he said. That's all he said."

Lion returned with an armful of books that she placed on the table beside Polly's chair. Polly picked out the four mysteries by Soledad and handed the three volumes of erotica to Mr. Benchley. Soledad and I leaned in over our friend as he riffled through the pages of Stringer's books. They had racy, double-entendre titles and were authored by Anonymous. The dustcovers were lurid depictions of scantily clad women in compromising positions, expressions of fear widening their eyes, the shadowy figure of a man leering over them. They lent a rather dark aspect to the books. They were published by Pulse.

So, I thought, *Harvey Price published the books under a different mantle, Pulse.*

"Polly, how did you know that Ernest Stringer wrote these books? It says they are authored by Anonymous."

"Miss Polly," interrupted Lion, "I told you. That's 'cause Mr. Harvey told Marianne who was the writer of those books. You see, she was reading them out loud upstairs to some gentlemen when she was entertaining Mr. Harvey and his friends. I was there, fetchin' drinks that night. Marianne said she wanted to meet this Mr. Anonymous of the nasty books, and she would not read out loud no more unless she was told who he was and where she could find him. The men was getting wild, wanting her to read them more of the sex stories, and they pressed on Mr. Harvey to tell Marianne once and for all the real live name of Anonymous—"

"Yes, thank you, Lion," said Polly, making me wonder if that was one of the issues that had led to Marianne's departure.

"—and they all laughed when he said they was by Ernest Stringer, the famous writer. And Marianne, she put the real name of the man down there on that cover, see? So I filed them in the shelves under *S* 'stead of *A* for *Anonymous*."

"Thank you, Lion," said Polly.

"Too bad about Mr. Harvey, *tsk-tsk-tsk*. . . ."

"What do you mean, Lion?" I asked.

"Did something bad befall Harvey Price?" asked Polly.

"Sure did. His wife got wind he'd been coming here, and she put a stop to it."

What did Martin Stonewall mean by *They killed the wrong son-of-a-bitch*?

I called Sgt. Joc Woollcott and asked him to let Detective Sparrow know we had information on the murders, and could he meet us next-door from the precinct house at Gino's Italian Restaurant. And could the detective check if the names of Martin Stonewall, onetime editor at Scribner's, and Harvey Price, publisher of Price Publications, were ever mentioned or questioned as associates in any crimes over the past couple of years. But then Joe said that there had been reported another murder, and that we'd best wait at Gino's after five in the afternoon.

"A murder, you say?"

"Another one of the Murder Club men. Daniel Cousins."

Polly Adler

Chapter Eight

Stunned by the news of Daniel Cousins' murder, Mr. Benchley, Soledad, and I began walking downtown, zombie-like, and it was only natural that we should gravitate toward the closest comfort station, which was Tony's Speakeasy, for a round of drinks.

From a telephone booth at a Western Union office I called Jane and Ross at the *New Yorker* offices, and then I reached Aleck at home with the news about Daniel Cousins. They agreed to meet us at Tony's and then we'd go to Gino's at five o'clock to meet with the detective. Aleck said he would telephone Heywood and Frank to pass on the news and ask them to join us at Gino's.

The days were getting shorter, and although the mornings and evenings were crisp, by afternoon the sun warmed the city. It was the best season to walk around town, to relish the balmy air, to linger for a time, to window-shop. No need to rush down into the subway, or hop a streetcar, or seek the warmth of steam heat in an office or apartment. These were walking days, exploring days, and there was always something new to see.

Despite the best of weather, though, we were all a little out of step with the pedestrian march. I was unconscious of the flow of human traffic along the sidewalk until suddenly we were at the door of Tony's Speakeasy. It was between-time, before the rush of patrons who stopped in after work for a drink and a chat with friends.

Aleck, Jane, and Ross had arrived, and my spirits were lifted at the sight of Chico and Harpo enjoying a late lunch of Spaghetti à la Tony. Groucho and Zeppo had afternoon calls at the movie studio in Astoria, Harpo explained, falling all over himself when he saw that Soledad was with us.

He leaped to his feet and the napkin tucked in his collar fell to the floor. He stooped to retrieve it and hit his head on the table on the way up, causing his gin cup to spill over. In an attempt to wipe up the mess, he used the napkin, but when that wasn't enough, he tugged at Chico's dinner napkin. As it was securely tucked into his collar, the recoil unbalanced Chico, whose elbow hit down hard on the little table, sending him, the table, the dinner plates, the basket of bread, and the condiments crashing to the floor.

These kinds of mishaps would put Harpo into "entertainment mode" to save face. With exaggerated flair, Harpo gathered all the items — the plates, the cups, the utensils, even the strands of spaghetti in red sauce—examined them thoroughly, wiped the plates with his dinner napkin, and then wrapped everything up in the checkered tablecloth, tying the ends into a neat, if soggy, bundle.

"All he needs is a stick," said Chico, rising from the slimy mixture of spaghetti and wine. After Mr. Benchley gave him a helping hand, Chico grabbed Aleck's walking stick and handed it to his brother, who slipped it through the bundle, hobo style, loaded it over his shoulder, and walked out through the door to the kitchen.

"With a suitcase like that he can finally leave home," said Chico, to the laughter and applause of the customers.

"Wish you would do the same," said Jane, disgusted with the way the men fell all over themselves around Soledad.

"Pack me a tablecloth," said Ross, "and don't forget the meatballs."

Harpo pushed through the swinging kitchen door, the cook's apron tied around his waist, and took a deep stage bow.

Woodrow was not averse to eating from off the floor, and he did a good job cleaning up the meatballs and the parmesan cheese that had missed Harpo's attention. A waiter mopped up the rest, and Harpo tucked a five-dollar bill into the fellow's shirt pocket. He was always generous to service people.

A table for four opened up, so we pulled it over to where the boys were sitting.

"Don't you love me, Soledad?" said Harpo all cow-eyed.

"No," she replied matter-of-factly.

"A *teensy-weensy* bit?"

"Forget that teensy-weensy bit, Harpo," she said. "That's getting far too personal."

"Oh! You thought—well, whatever you think about my . . ."

"Attributes."

"Thank you, Aleck—*attributes*—I hope that means what I hope it means—seriously, Sollie my love, my *zaftig latke*, my little *shiksa tchatchke*, if you won't say you love me, I will *plotz* right here!"

"Dear God!" said Aleck, "get that knife away from him!"

"Calm down, Aleck," said Heywood. "*Plotz* means he could *explode*, is all."

"This is no *schmaltzy spiel* from a *meshuggener schlemiel*; I *kibitz* you not! You must marry me!"

"Chico, tell this *schmuck* to get his *schmutzy* hand off my *tukhus*, or I'll *potch* him in the *schnozz!*"

"Actually, Sollie, that's my hand on your—"

A loud slap cut him off.

Jane scoffed and said, "Oh, brother!"

"Yes?" said Chico and Harpo simultaneously.

"If you won't let me woo you—"

"I won't let you woo me."

"Can we fool around?"

Soledad burst out laughing. "You're incorrigible!"

"I am? Wow! Did you hear that, Chico, I'm . . ."

"*Incorrigible.*"

"Thank you, Aleck. Gee, I hope that means what I hope it means!"

"It doesn't," said Jane.

"It means you've got *chutzpah*," said Ross.

"Why do you encourage him?" said Jane.

"All right, if that's your final word," relented Harpo.

"It is."

"But—"

"No *buts*."

"We can be friends, no?"

"Yes, dear man, no."

"Well, that's all right, then."

"Thank God that's over with," I sighed.

Harpo turned toward me and winked conspiratorially.

Ten minutes later, after I had told the boys the news about Daniel Cousins' murder, a pall had fallen over the table.

"Another writer bites the dust," said Chico. "I'm still trying to get over Mark Wendt's death. We knew that kid all his life, you know?"

Harpo sat motionless now, speechless, and that was alarming because it was so out of character for the cyclonic and loquacious—when he was offstage, that is—Marx Brother. And Soledad, who truly liked and admired Harpo, even though she'd been hounded by his amorous attentions, was unusually solicitous toward him, for she, too, was taken aback by his stillness.

Harpo often says, "The only reason you egg-heads want me around is because you think I'm the only one of the gang who pays attention to you when all of you talk at the same time. I'm not listening, I'm just confused."

But now he wasn't confused, he was just sad. When it was time for him and Chico to go off to the theatre, Harpo spoke: "Three down, three to go. If I were Young, Shaw, and Hunter, I'd leave town. It's only a matter of time."

Ross, Frank, and Heywood were already there when we arrived two hours later at Gino's. They had taken a table near the rear of the speakeasy. They were ready with the newspaper reports extracted from their papers' files. And as Aleck put off his order of cannoli for an order of eggplant parmesan with a side-order of spaghetti Bolognese, the rest of us shuffled papers and cross-checked dates to compile a master list to consider.

"What I really want to know is what Martin Stonewall meant by his comment at Polly's: 'They killed the wrong son-of-a-bitch,'" I said, while riffling through the pages we'd exchanged.

"What I really want to know," said Soledad, pouring a martini from the coffeepot Gino had placed at the center of our table, "is where does Gino store his hooch?"

"Why, in the fish tank, of course," I said.

"But there are fish in it."

"Yes, but the fish swim in water," I said. "There's a glass partition halfway through the tank. Water up front, gin at the back. You can't see where the gin starts and the water ends. One of those tubes is the fish-tank aerator; the other is the gin line."

Gino overheard my reply to Soledad's question, and his dark face turned very pale. "Dorothy! How can you know that?"

"It's just my genius in deductive reasoning."

Mr. Benchley blew a raspberry.

"Working from the premise that some people miss the forest for the trees."

"How does that apply?" said Mr. Benchley.

"I haven't the slightest idea. I just thought it sounded good."

"Well, then, I see," nodded my friend. "You make perfect sense!"

"In your twisted little mind, I suppose I do, Mr. Benchley."

The alarmed expression on Gino Di Cenzo's classically Roman face made me want to reassure him: "Don't worry, Gino. The Feds are too stupid to figure it out, and people who do will credit you with your brilliance."

Detective Sparrow arrived twenty minutes later, and his timing was good, because my friends and I had narrowed down our list to several events that might link, by association, the members of the Murder Club.

As the detective entered the speakeasy, he was greeted by Gino with a slap on the back and an exchange in Italian. The two men shook hands, passed a few more pleasantries, and then Sparrow joined us at our table. He pulled up a chair between me and Aleck.

"You speak Italian," I said like an idiot.

"Yes."

"You are fluent!"

"Yes. You seem surprised."

"What other languages do you speak?"

"Other than the language of love?" he said, a wicked smile crossing his lips as he tilted his head near mine.

I blushed.

"Just Italian."

"Picked it up in the neighborhood or overseas during the War?"

"At home," he said and smiled. "I'm Italian. First generation. I was born Natali Speranza. Kids used to call me Nate at school, and Speranza became Sparrow."

"Natali. . . . A Christmas baby?" asked Aleck.

"December twenty-fifth, yes."

"Natali Speranza!" said Soledad, rolling off the vowels, savoring the sound. "Christmas Hope," said Soledad. "How delightful!"

"Delightful doesn't cut it in the Force. The guys call me Sparrow for short."

I understood a lot more than what Natali Speranza was willing to tell. There was awful prejudice against the Italians. During the War, it was the German-Americans who suffered. The Italians, as the newest immigrants, often were grouped with anarchist factions who wished to bring down the government, or associated with the few mob racketeers, criminals running neighborhoods and wreaking murderous havoc around our country's big cities in order to control the production and transport of spirits. The New York City Police Department was packed with Irishmen. And the Irish, who were once looked on with disdain, enjoyed the seniority of looking down on the more recently arrived Italians. But, I supposed, Sparrow's toffee coloring and blue eyes helped him fit right in.

I left these thoughts when Sparrow asked, "What have you got for me?"

"There have been many deaths in the publishing business over the past year or so," said Heywood, "some people only remotely associated with the Murder Club members."

"Give it to me."

"These stand out: The death of Niles Pickering—he was the publisher of all of the members of the Murder Club at one time or another. He died from natural causes, slumped over his typewriter in his office."

"Yes, he had a heart condition," said Ross.

Heywood continued: "And then there was the sudden suicide last fall of an editor at Mycroft Publishing, a fellow named Jim Morrow. He left a typewritten confession of the murder of one of his authors, Frederick Feldman. This came as a surprise, because Feldman's death had been deemed a suicide. Jim Morrow's confession of murder was never made public. But, a friend at my paper has a friend who has a friend who worked as a maid for Morrow's wife, and she—the maid—found the confession in the trash."

Detective Sparrow asked, "What's the connection to the club?"

"My friend at the paper heard that Cousins claimed an unpublished book he wrote was plagiarized by Mycroft Publishing. The publisher had Cousins' manuscript more than a year before Frederick Feldman's version of the book came out under the Mycroft mantle. Cousins had the rejection letter from the publisher at Mycroft, Jim Morrow, in which he applauded Cousins' book but said there wasn't room for it on their list. Hard for Cousins to bring the case to court and prove plagiarism even if Feldman's novel shared the same story, the characters uncannily similar. The publisher was smart enough not to steal word-for-word from Cousins' book."

"They conspired to steal Cousins' book, then?" said Sparrow. "You said Cousins was paranoid, though."

"Well, with good reason, I'd say. How would you feel if the premise and characters of a book you wrote became a bestseller, and it had someone else's name on it?"

"Cousins was probably right about his novel being stolen," said Aleck. "It's not uncommon for editors to toss one author's original premise or plot, sometimes an entire book, to another writer they like, to someone who hasn't produced anything in a long time. It's not right, of course, but they usually get away with their larceny."

"I wonder," said Frank, "if the clubbers found out about the Morrow-Feldman affair and helped Daniel Cousins to use the scandalous information?"

"You mean to expose them? Blackmail?" said Detective Sparrow.

"Morrow's society wife wouldn't like to hear about it," said Ross.

"Yes, and the clubbers might have tried to blackmail the two men," said Soledad.

"First, the writer, Feldman, is believed to have committed suicide by hanging. A month later, Morrow followed by hanging himself after confessing he murdered the writer," said Mr. Benchley.

"All right, there's something you should know," prefaced Detective Sparrow. "I was on the case when Morrow killed himself. I can't tell you anything about Mrs. Morrow's maid finding the note in the trash, but yes, he left a confession to the murder of his lover, Feldman. It was suppressed. No mention of it at the inquest, so the press knew nothing about it."

"A coverup?" I asked.

"To protect Morrow's wife and children," said Frank. "Let's say, June Morrow had connections, so it makes sense that the affair and the admission that her husband was a murderer were suppressed. It's not the first time suicide notes have disappeared or been bought."

"But, you people knew about the affair?"

"Sure, Detective Sparrow, sure there were whispers," said Frank. "Not the murder angle, of course. There was nothing that would have sold papers from the Morrow-Feldman affair. Two suicides? *Nah*. But a murder-suicide, that's different. Had the press got a whiff of that—well, June Morrow has friends in high places. Anyway, there are Morrow's children to consider, and the absence of a confession, well, where's the story?"

"Was Morrow ever a suspect in Feldman's death?" asked Soledad.

"No. There were no suspects because murder was never considered. The inquest determined Feldman's death was unquestionably a suicide."

"So Jim Morrow committed the perfect murder," said Soledad. "There is no crime if no one knows there's been a crime committed."

"Must have been guilt, terrible remorse, then, that drove Morrow to confess and then to kill himself," said Aleck.

"Yes, but it's odd, don't you think?" I said. "I mean, Jim Morrow tried to protect his wife and kids from knowledge of his homosexual affair, but in the end he confesses to a greater sin, the heinous crime of murder. That's some lasting legacy, all right!"

"June Morrow's life has been ruined by an adulterous scandal. And to boot, her husband reveals he is also a murderer!" said Aleck. "Why did he murder Feldman?"

"Who knows? Lover's quarrel, blackmail, jealousy?"

"In order to hang someone, it takes premeditation," I said, pondering why Morrow would turn on his lover. "These men were desperate. I wonder what—who—drove them to their tragedies?"

"You think Cousins may have pulled the chairs out from under them, figuratively speaking?" said Detective Sparrow.

"I can only guess. I really hate to accuse anyone to suit my fantasy scenarios," I replied.

"I thought you all agreed that despite his big feet, Daniel Cousins was a nice man," said Aleck.

"A nice man who was double-crossed and unable to do anything about it, so we have to entertain the possibility that he struck out where he could," said Ross.

"What else you got?" asked Sparrow.

"Stephen Shaw—lots of enemies acquired through his exposés. Corporate enemies who'd like to see him dead, I'd say," said Ross. "But Shaw is still walking and talking. That's all I've got."

"Mark Wendt," said Heywood. "Mark Wendt pursued the killer of a woman who lived in his apartment building, and with whom he was emotionally involved."

"Romantically?" I asked.

"I can't say. You see, her husband had been insti-tutionalized and Mark was the couple's friend. He got the woman a job at his publisher's, as a secretary. Last winter, as she was crossing a street in Little Italy, she was run over by a speeding car. Witnesses described the car and the driver, and the police investigated, but the car's owner had an alibi. He and his car were supposedly out on the Island at the time, on his estate on the North Shore. Three people confirmed his story. Mark didn't let it go. He hounded the man, a bootlegger. Ties to the Morello gang."

"You think Morello—?" asked Ross.

"Doubtful. He doesn't get involved in other people's business—not this kind of personal business, which is not *business*, if you know what I mean," said Heywood, and Sparrow nodded agreement. I didn't know what the hell he was talking about.

"The bootlegger who owned the motor was John Davis Welles," announced Heywood.

"But, wait! He just died," said Aleck. "Had a heart attack while dining at the Waldorf," said Aleck. "It was in all the papers this morning."

"That's what I was about to tell you," said Heywood.

"Another heart attack . . ." I said.

"But, if Welles had a close connection with the Morellos, who's to say Wendt's murder wasn't a mob hit," said Mr. Benchley.

"The mob executes people with a bullet to the head; they don't poison your tobacco," I said.

"You are correct, Mrs. Parker," agreed Detective Sparrow.

"Anybody got anything on Trevor Hunter?" I asked. Before Sparrow could say it, I continued: "He's been cleared, I know, Detective. He's got an alibi—he was with Anthony Young."

Heywood referred to his notebook, and, shaking his head, closed the cover and then spoke. "Trevor Hunter is a singular specimen: He's a loner, a scholar, an intellectual who spends most of his time, when not writing, pursuing a variety of interests most people would view as decidedly Victorian: botany, mycology, phytopathology—"

"What?" I said.

"Plant diseases."

"How do you spell that?"

"It would take all day."

"Carry on, then," I said officiously with a wave of my hand.

"Forensic anthropology, osteology—"

"Bones, Dory, bones," said Soledad.

"He also has a keen interest in fluid, hydro-, and aerodynamics. He was a pilot during the War. And then there are the pseudo-sciences—phrenology, alienism, and parapsychology; he dabbles in the occult."

"He sounds like a fun date," I said, and Soledad snorted.

"Exactly, Dottie," said Heywood. "Hunter relates best to the scientific and esoteric discussions. Ergo, he has few friends."

"Lots of brainy people are admired, though," said Ross. "Varied interests doesn't mean you're boring."

"Yes, that's true," replied Heywood. "But the man is brusque, impatient, has poor social skills, and as leader of his club—"

"You're describing Aleck, you realize?" said Ross.

"There are people who dislike him, certainly, but I found no one who hates him enough to want to see him dead," said Heywood. "And I couldn't find a connection between him and any recent deaths." Ross nodded agreement.

"As far as the other murdered writer, Ersatz—I mean Ernest—Stringer was writing pornographic novels," I said. "I doubt he'd want that bit of information thrown around the business."

We told our friends about our little chat with Polly Adler.

"So, that's why you wanted me to look into the backgrounds of Harvey Price and Martin Stonewall," said Detective Sparrow. "Well, neither of the men has ever been arrested, so we don't have criminal files on them."

Frank spoke up: "*Aha!* I have that one! I can tell you about Ernest Stringer's connection to Price, besides the pornography thing: It has to do with Price's partner in his publishing company.

"It's been a wild ride for Price Publications the past year. The company was floundering and it appeared they'd have to close up shop. Then, last spring, John Mitchell, Price's partner, had a massive stroke and died. The company's life insurance policy on him paid a hundred thousand to the company. Suddenly, they're solvent! I wouldn't be surprised if Ernest got wind of something that wasn't quite Kosher about Mitchell's death."

"Blackmail?" asked Sparrow.

"Been done before," said Frank.

"And Ernest was desperate for cash. . . . *Hey*," I said, "blackmail explains the five thousand bucks he had in the bank!"

"So we should entertain the possibility that Price murdered Mitchell for the insurance money and then killed Ernest, his blackmailer?" posed Detective Sparrow.

"I suspect our Murder Club friends have been up to no good," said Ross. "Two possible blackmail schemes."

Detective Sparrow said he would check to see if there had been any unusually large withdrawals — say, five thousand dollars — from Harvey Price's bank account around the time of the deposit made into Ersatz's account. That was all Sparrow had to go on in the Ernest Stringer case. And he would interview Price.

"So, what've we got?" said Sparrow. "We've got a bunch of wild speculations and no single suspect for a string of publishing industry deaths that most likely have nothing to do with these murders. Not to be rude, but I don't suppose you'd *entertain* the possibility that your imaginations are working overtime?"

"You have to admit, Detective," said Soledad, "that there is credence in the Price-Stringer connection. The pornography, the five thousand dollars in the bank. And the man Wendt was after for running over his girl is suddenly dead. And don't forget Cousins and his plagiarized book and the deaths of the two men who stole his work."

"Maybe there is, Miss Soleil, but there is still no single suspect that links the murders of Stringer, Wendt, and now Cousins."

"Well, then," said Soledad. "We'll have to find that missing link, whoever he is."

"I think we need to follow the trail of Ernest Stringer's stolen manuscript," I said.

"What trail?" said Detective Sparrow. "The trail's been cold since he fell dead."

"Ernest must have been writing about *someone* who didn't want to be exposed for whatever that someone did," agreed Aleck.

"That's all speculation," said Sparrow.

"Speculation is the first step in solving a murder mystery," said Soledad. "One has to use one's imagination: Speculate and speculate, come up with theory after theory and hypothesis after hypothesis, and then dismiss any theory, any scenario you've imagined in which the evidence you've gathered doesn't fit. You can't just get stuck on one theory, which is what many detectives do. Evidence, motive, opportunity—each are like the pieces of a jigsaw puzzle. Any hypothesis you conceive is the picture you imagine will take form when all the pieces are fit together. If you are so doggedly certain that the resulting picture—your hypothesis—will show a cow grazing in a pasture, but suddenly you're seeing a cow flying in the sky, you've got to turn that board around or discard any preconceptions you've had, don't you?"

"You mean, the picture may not turn out to be the pastoral vision you had hoped to see, but a nursery rhyme instead—'the cow jumped over the moon'?" said Ross.

"Exactly. Both pictures make sense only in context. In only one, however, do the pieces at hand fit easily, *sensibly*. It takes an engaged, creative, and, most important, an *open* mind to piece together the evidence, the motive, and the opportunity, *not to see what you want to see, but what's really there.*"

"When it don't fit, quit!" agreed Frank.

I said, "At the moment we have no evidence, no motive, no suspects, and everybody close to the men had opportunity, so we have no pieces of any puzzle to form a picture with! All we do know is that three of the six Murder Club members are dead and the others very possibly in imminent danger. Unless there is a serial killer out there targeting these men, all we do know is that our boys have had a few serious disputes with people over the years. It doesn't necessarily mean that anybody they've had trouble with wants to murder them."

"You're right, of course, Mrs. Parker," said Mr. Benchley. "Aleck, for instance, Detective, has had numerous serious confrontations in court with the Shubert Brothers, who don't want him reviewing their shows because he says they all stink, and he's still walking this earth."

"That's my point, exactly. Let's entertain the possibility that there's a serial killer on the loose, not three disgruntled and angry enemies," I said. "Let's make *that* our hypothesis for now."

Aleck said, "Detective, don't you agree that the other men may be in danger?"

Detective Sparrow's lips set in a hard line; he studied our expectant faces, and then he replied, "Yes, I think they may be. I can suggest protective custody, if my captain agrees, and if these men are willing."

With that, Detective Sparrow rose from the table and said he would interview Harvey Price about the death of his partner. He then bid us a good afternoon.

I turned to my friends crammed around the table. "Let's look at what we've got."

"We've got nothing," said Frank.

"That's about it, Honey Lamb," agreed Ross.

"Well, tonight I'll be at Romany Marie's Café and I'll be reciting several of my poems. Let's see what I can find out there."

"You didn't tell me about this!" said Mr. Benchley.

"I called this morning to arrange it. After all, Marie did invite me to perform an evening of recitation. And she did say that tonight is when the men of the Murder Club meet for coffee before they go off for their discussions."

"You weren't thinking of going on your own, were you? There's a murderer out there."

"Of course not; don't get your shorts in a twist. Sollie's coming, too."

"My shorts don't get twisted; I wear—it's your *neck* getting twisted that's at issue!"

"Woodrow Wilson will protect us."

"Very funny!"

"As funny as she'll ever be," butted in Ross.

"Oh, shut up, you!"

"Why does everybody tell me to shut up all the time?"

"Ask you wife."

I turned to Mr. Benchley. I had always intended to take him along with me, but I didn't need a parental reprimand. "Want to tag along?"

"I think that's a good idea," said Soledad.

"I suppose. His teeth are sharper than Woodrow's."

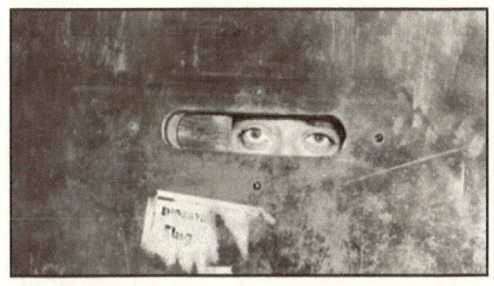

Give the man the password.

Gino's

Tony's

Playing games at Chumley's

Chapter Nine

The plan was for Soledad to seek entry into the Murder Club, rather than I, she being the mystery novelist and a great source for all sorts of nasty ways to accomplish murder. She dressed the part, wearing a tweed suit—a good cut, but slightly out of date— borrowed from Edna Ferber. She accessorized with a pair of wire spectacles, and hid her gloriously shiny finger-waves under a plain felt hat from off the floor of my closet. Sensible shoes, rented for the evening for five dollars from a Plaza Hotel maid, and the only indication of her success, a string of pearls, finished off the costume. With only a touch of face powder to dull her creamy complexion, she almost managed to transform herself into a horsey-set, to-the-manner-born aristocrat. All she needed were a brace of pheasants tossed over her shoulder, a half-dozen beagles swarming around her feet, and a shotgun broken over her elbow for full effect. She could not disguise that sleek figure and those patrician cheekbones.

I chuckled as we watched her enter the café, and made a two-dollar bet with Mr. Benchley that she was wearing her pricey Carmela Lingerie silk underthings, along with her Cartier diamond necklace under that high-buttoned silk blouse. I realized that Mr. Benchley's eager acceptance of the bet was not because he believed to the contrary, but rather an excuse to "inspect" the truth of my suspicions. The dog!

When Soledad walked into the café alone and took a table-for-two on the aisle just a few feet from the front door, we watched with amusement as she ordered Marie's specialty dish, *ciorbă*, a soup made with vegetables, meatballs, eggs, and sour cream and served with crusty bread. Awaiting the arrival of the meal, she watched the door, her hand resting on her carpetbag. Half an hour later, when the door swung open, she pulled from the bag the appropriate book—one of three she'd brought, each authored by the club members—opened it, and held it up so that the title might be seen by anyone who glanced in her direction. And of course she chose a novel by mystery writer Anthony Young.

Young searched the room with frowning intensity. The foppish professor's usually perfectly aligned bowtie was askew, his paunchy stature slightly shrunken in his suit. His florid demeanor had turned ashen, and when he removed his hat, his scalp peeked through the thin veil of his comb-over. As he ran a hand through what remained of it, the lamplight caught wispy strands floating into the air.

"There's Young," I said to Mr. Benchley. "He looks seriously nervous."

"Well, I should say so. I'm surprised he'd dare to leave his house, considering that three of his friends are now seriously dead."

We watched as with perfect timing Soledad hitched up her skirt as she crossed her shapely legs, which was enough to stop Young dead in his tracks. She lowered the book, removed her eyeglasses, and caught Young's eye. A light glowed in his frumpy countenance—he was snagged.

"Why, hello there," she said as he remained rooted in place. She rested the open book on her breast, like a coquette coyly flirting behind her fan. It was a calculated move; Young could not fail to see the title.

"Hello!" His face brightened to full wattage before dimming suddenly.

She resumed her eyeglasses and took up the book to read.

Young hesitated; when his attention was called by people at another table near the window, he smiled and waved slightly at them, but I could see his curiosity as his attention was drawn back to the attractive woman reading his very own novel.

He took a decisive step toward her. We were not able to hear the conversation because the guitarist began to play, but the language of their introductions was universal:

Are you enjoying that book?

Oh, very much!

Soledad's graceful fingers stroked the book's spine with a vertical motion. Up and down, up and down. . . .

Young, bobbing from one foot to the other, smoothing his little moustaches and pulling at his shirt cuffs, finally revealed that he was the author of the amazing book she was reading and extended his hand. Soledad put her hand to her mouth in a gesture of surprise before telling him who she was. They shook hands.

Won't you sit down?

Delighted!

A glance toward the rear of the restaurant before pulling out a chair and then flagging a waiter. Lots of smiling, lots of chatter. . . .

I'm grand; you're grand; blah-blah-blah. . . .

Suddenly, I was being introduced by Marie. She called me *the preeminent woman writer of our times, a great poetess.* I wondered, in my neurotic way, whether she had said the same of Vincent Millay, who frequents her place—could she be mistaking me for her?

I turned desperate eyes on Mr. Benchley, but he wouldn't save me from the horror of reciting my own words, so I walked up to the little stage in the front corner of the room, smiled and nodded uncertainly, and began to recite from my book of poetry, *Enough Rope.*

As I droned on, in came Shaw, the tough longshoreman, the smell of the sea at low tide about him. He unbuttoned his peacoat, hooked his thumbs under his belt, and, standing spread-legged, searched the room with his icy-blue eyes like a squinty-eyed albatross searching the ocean for an unsuspecting fish. He spotted Young right away, in an unexpected posture, I suppose, because he frowned, removed his cap, and tossed his curly head to indicate that Young should follow him to a table near the kitchen. Young was obviously torn between duty and the dame. He hesitated, and began to resume his seat. But duty won out, and over Soledad's objections he kissed her hand and then scurried off to the back table to join Shaw.

The two men conferred for a few moments, their gestures wild, before exiting through the kitchen.

Soledad turned to see them gone, turned back to catch my eye, quickly tossed a couple of bucks on the table, and exited the front door.

Things were not going as we'd planned!

Mr. Benchley casually rose from his seat and, carrying my purse, indicated that I should wrap up my recitation. I hurried through the last couplet, and nodded to the audience's applause as I backed up toward the door, waving to the much-confused Marie, who signaled the guitarist to strike up a ballad.

At the corner we spotted Soledad a block north, and the two men walking ahead of her. A third man joined them and there was a brief exchange. Was that Trevor Hunter? It was difficult to discern under the low-voltage streetlamps. The figure was tall and reedy, and who else was it likely to be? And then the three men split up in different directions. Shaw began walking toward me and Mr. Benchley, Young was walking west, and the third man, Hunter, crossed the street moving east. Soledad slipped into the shadow of a doorway and emerged when the danger of being seen by the men had passed. She moved into the light of a streetlamp so that we could see her once again. Through telepathy we knew that she was going to follow Hunter, and Mr. Benchley and I were to follow the others. As Young and Shaw were heading toward opposite sides of town, Mr. Benchley and I quickly split up. I followed Young; he was on Shaw's tail.

Onward through the crazy-quilt patchwork of irregular streets, I stayed a safe distance behind Young, ducking into doorways and alleys as he zigzagged from Waverley Place and then across Sixth Avenue. Turning west, he continued along West Washington Place to the junction where Grove Street ended in a T. From there he turned left, heading south a block onto West 4th Street, and in less than a minute, took another right onto Barrow Street.

It was after eleven o'clock, and although the evening was temperate, it was a weekday and only a few cafés were still open for the neighborhood clientele.

The storefront businesses were mostly closed and shuttered for the night, so there were few people out on the streets and I had to keep my distance because Young kept looking over his shoulder, suspecting he was being followed.

When he turned onto Bleeker Street, I nearly lost him when into my path two men came out of a building carrying a stretcher on which lay a dark, shrouded corpse. Another black-suited man opened the back hatch of a hearse and I had to scurry around them and into the street to regain sight of my quarry.

I caught a glimpse of Young turning right onto Morton Street, and when I arrived near the corner, I watched as Stephen Shaw turned onto the street from the south. Safe from being spotted by either man, I turned onto Morton only to meet up with Mr. Benchley. We stared at each other for a long moment like long-lost friends who had forgotten each other's names, wondering why the men had taken such circuitous routes to arrive at the same address. We moved into the shadow of a stoop and peeked over it to see Young and Shaw entering a building three doors down.

Quickly, though cautiously, we followed after the men. The two writers had led this wild goose chase to the same location, which suggested that the third man, Trevor Hunter, had the same idea in mind. It was obvious to me that the men were afraid of being followed.

I realized that if they were all afraid of being followed, then there must be some veracity to their fears. I was about to voice this thought to Mr. Benchley, but he pulled me into the small foyer, which was lit by one bare, hanging light bulb. Beyond the tiled walls lined with mailboxes was another door leading into the lobby, and peering through the glass partition I could see nothing but the dark void, its boundaries barely discernible for our reflections in the glass. Mr. Benchley looked at the names on the six mailboxes. "Shaw lives here," he said, reaching into his pocket for his Swiss army knife to attend to the door lock. I took a chance and turned the knob. He sighed with disappointment at the ease of our entry.

We were halfway up the stairway that led up from the left side of the lobby, a weak illumination from the floor above guiding our way, when we heard the swoosh-and-thump of the outside door opening and closing. We stopped in our tracks to see who might be coming in and were surprised by the arrival of Cherish Winter.

Aware that she wouldn't see us right away, we scurried back downstairs and around into the deep shadow of the stairwell and waited for her to enter the dark lobby, which she did. We listened to her footfalls on the stone steps. One flight up and we heard the echo of her advance across the ceiling above us.

A knock at a door. The sharp *click!* of locks disengaging. The swoosh-and-thump of a door opening and closing above us.

Mr. Benchley and I made our way gingerly, silently up the stairs, and then along the hallway. A popular melody streamed out from one of the apartments and echoed along the corridor. Someone had been frying onions. Mr. Benchley looked at the numbers on the doors and pointed to one on the left.

I wondered whether Soledad had arrived before us, and whether she was already inside the apartment with the others. I whispered to Mr. Benchley, "Soledad?"

He shook his head. "Don't know."

I thought we should stop all the intrigue by simply knocking on the door. I was about to rap on it when Mr. Benchley caught my hand, just as a crash and a woman's sharp cry sounded from within.

Mr. Benchley gave me a worried look and was about to pound on the door when we heard a horrific screech, "*What the fuck! What the fuck!*" followed by a voice that was undoubtedly Cherish's.

"Oh, I am sorry, Stephen—"

"Forget it. Don't bother trying to clean it up. We've got other things to discuss."

"I don't know what else to tell you," said Cherish. "You should all go to the police and—"

"No police."

"But someone is picking you off, one at a time," said Cherish. "And where's Hunter? I thought he was—"

"He should have been here by now," said Anthony Young, his voice agitated.

"Unless he was—oh, he'll be here," said Shaw.

"I don't know why we let him get us into this mess," said Young.

"What do you mean? What are you talking about?" said Cherish.

"Shut up, Tony. You're just a yellow-bellied coward," said Shaw.

"*Yellow bellied cocksucker! Yellow bellied cocksucker!*"

"Shut up!" growled Shaw.

"*Shut up! Shut up!*"

"Cover him up, for God's sake, Shaw!" said Young, with a desperate edge to his voice.

"Don't mind anything he says, honey. He's just scared he'll be next."

"And that's why you must go to the police. They can protect you," said Cherish.

"It's too late."

"What do you mean, Shaw? We'll decide what we need to do when Trevor gets here," said Young. "It's not up to you!"

Young's last words were like a stage cue, because as soon as they were uttered, there was the heavy tread of footsteps echoing from the stairs coming up from the lobby.

Mr. Benchley eyes widened with alarm. He looked around for a way out of the hallway, for a place to hide so we wouldn't be seen, but there was nowhere to go except in through another apartment door. He grabbed my hand, about to pull me away from the door, but it was too late. Trevor Hunter had arrived on the landing and saw us.

Mr. Benchley knocked on the door.

Stephen Shaw opened it with a force that should have taken it off its hinges. His glower said he had expected someone else. "Mr. Shaw, hello!" said Mr. Benchley, pulling me into the apartment before the man could object.

The place reeked of flophouse staleness, of fried onions, dirty socks, and old cigars. Sometime in the recent past a cat had lived here.

An ungodly, inhuman shriek sounded from within the dreary room, and that's when I saw the parrot, its head bobbing, white-and-black droppings coating the floor around its stand. "*Who the hell? Who the hell?*" it screeched with the eerie intonations of its owner.

"Shut up, Friday!"

Shut up, Friday! Shut up, Friday!

Yes, at one time a cat had lived here; the bird must have verbally abused it to death.

Anthony Young walked over to stare at us as if we were poisonous insects encased in glass at the Museum of Natural History.

"You know Mrs. Parker, of course?" said my friend.

"Mrs. . . . ?" said Shaw. "Yeah, I know of her."

Young pointed at me and said accusatorially, "You were at Marie's tonight."

"How-do-you-do," I said, offering my hand. "Call me Dorothy."

He eyed my proffered hand suspiciously, as if I had one of Harpo's joy-buzzers concealed in my palm. His handshake was like holding a dead fish.

"I'm Anthony Young, the author—"

"We're all authors here," interjected Shaw, gruffly.

"—and this is Cherish Winter, *the artist*," said Young, rolling his eyes at Shaw.

These two men were at the opposite ends of the male spectrum: Shaw was a big man, craggy-faced, brusque-toned, barrel-chested, bristly-bearded, muscle melting into middle-aged flab. Pelts of dark hair peeked out from his shirt cuffs and crawled over the backs of his hands, an exemplary specimen of the term *hirsute*. A regular werewolf but for the teeth, which I glimpsed when he snarled: They were small, like yellow corn kernels tightly fitted along the cob row.

In contrast, Anthony Young was a bouquet of spring flowers. Cologne aside, he had a spongy, flushed faced, and was the prime example of male vanity—a monkey grooming himself on a sunny rock. He kept running a hand over his rapidly thinning hair and brushing strands off his impeccably tailored shoulders. He was a regular creampuff of an aging dandy who looked as if he were sutured into his plaid lavender vest, which peeked over a buttoned-up dove-gray suit jacket. He had short legs and stood in Italian leather shoes. I suspected he was girdled, by the rigid posture he presented. Since I last saw him at Marie's he had straightened his bowtie.

"Yes, Miss Winter we know. How are you, Cherish?" I said.

Trevor Hunter lurked silently behind us in the doorway. My back was to him but I could practically feel his impatient breath at my neck. From him there arose a peculiar smell that I couldn't quite place. It reminded me of frankincense—no!—something heavier, sweeter—of course! Opium!

"Why are you here?" said Shaw, all sandpaper and scowling, and displaying his corn row of teeth.

"*What the hell! What the hell!*"

"We were on our way to visit Cherish, you know? To see how she was faring, you know? She lives on Jones Street, you know, and we saw her walking along and tried to get her attention, you know, but she didn't hear us call out to her, and we followed her here," I said.

"Well," said Mr. Benchley, "you know."

"You followed her?" repeated Hunter, moving around us to get into the apartment. I looked into his rheumy eyes, followed the sharp hook of his nose, and noted the triangular hollows beneath his high-boned cheeks, which lent an unattractive skeletal aspect to his features. With his heavy protruding brows—those peculiar sable pelts—he had a face that a Cubist might render on canvas by applying a jumble of paint in geometric shapes. Oddly, he reminded me of one of the oils hanging in Ernest's apartment, a portrait in the Cubist style, and I realized that he was the subject of one of Cherish Winter's paintings!

Although I had never formally met the man—I'd seen him enter a restaurant last year sometime and also saw him at one of Edna's book-launch parties—I felt an instant dislike. I sensed something slightly . . . foul.

Why would these men ever have had anything to do with one another? I wondered. I saw no camaraderie, no affection, only tolerance at best. Why this motley assemblage?

"Well, yes, you see, she dropped this," I said, reaching into my pocketbook and riffling through the mess in search of something, anything, to prove my claim. I retrieved my little address book and offered it over to the woman. "We must talk, Cherish," I said, pressing it into her hand.

"Yes, yes, of course," she said, clutching the small black book. "Thank you for finding this. I was in a hurry and—"

"I'm sorry to hear about all the troubles you fellows have had recently," said Mr. Benchley. "Stringer, then Wendt, and now Cousins, *tsk-tsk*."

"Cousins!" yelped Young. "What do you mean? Daniel? *No!* Oh, my God!"

"*What the fuck! What the fuck!*"

"*How? When?*" demanded Shaw.

"We don't know all the details, only that Cousins was very seriously murdered," said Mr. Benchley.

"When one is murdered it is always serious," growled Shaw.

"Yes, of course," corrected my friend, "I only meant—well, you know. . . ."

"That's why we went to see Cherish, to tell her, but she wasn't home. She was walking down the street and didn't hear us call," I said. "The truth is, someone is targeting you. You aren't safe until the culprit is caught. You need police protection."

"We can take care of ourselves," said Shaw.

"He's a clever killer, that's for sure," I said.

"What?" cried out Young, and then, more soberly, "We will stay together."

Suddenly, Young wasn't so sure because the other men didn't readily agree. When Shaw turned away from his appeal, Young frantically insisted: "Won't we, Stephen? Trevor? There's safety in numbers, you know."

"And your numbers are dwindling," I said, and instantly regretted my careless remark, because Anthony Young looked like he was about to suffer a coronary thrombosis right there in front of us. He yanked at his bowtie and the veins in his red forehead bulged purple.

"Blast! Pull yourself together, Tony," instructed Shaw, pushing the man down onto the ratty sofa and then pouring him a glass of rum.

"*Blast! Blast!*"

As I had already rocked this rapidly sinking boat filled with the survivors of the Murder Club, I decided to press on. "Who the hell did you fellows piss off?" I said. "Who the hell is picking you off one at a time like this?" I said.

"*Who the hell! Who the hell!*"

"For God's sake," I said. "We can do without the Greek chorus!"

"*Ohhhh, Jesus!*" cried Young, his hand shaking as he accepted the drink from Shaw.

"Stop whimpering, you idiot!" scolded Shaw. "We don't need you cracking up on us like—"

"Like? Like who?" I asked.

"Like a hysterical old woman," said Trevor Hunter.

I wanted to punch Hunter in the gut—or other, more sensitive regions of his body—for that remark, but he was bigger than I am, and wrangling was not going to get me anywhere. I flashed him a withering look. Behind his back.

"You have to admit," said Mr. Benchley, "these murders read like something contrived for one of your mystery books."

"That's absurd," said Hunter.

"Well it ain't coincidence that somebody's wacked off half of your little members these past three days!" I said.

Young gasped at my euphemism, "wacked off."

Hunter cringed at "ain't."

Shaw took offense at "little members."

Everyone was appalled at the image I had un-intentionally expressed. Mr. Benchley giggled and said, "An unfortunate choice of words, my dear, given to misinterpretation."

"That didn't come out right. Let me rephrase—"

"Please," said Mr. Benchley, discouragingly. "We all know what you meant."

"I was trying to say, three of your friends are dead. Three down, three to go."

"Better, but no cigar," said my friend, shaking his head.

I thought that the threesome was poised to throttle me. But, however appalled they were at my choice of words, upon looking closer I saw more fear than violence in their faces: Young had blanched an oatmeal gray; Shaw's eyes narrowed and his corn row peeked out between tight lips; Trevor Hunter squinted, his sables twitching frantically.

"Mrs. Parker does make a point, you know? And only you boys can help lead the police to the killer."

"It's *not* too late," I added, remembering Shaw's response to Cherish's suggestion of going to the police.

"What do you know about it?" demanded Shaw.

"I can only assume that you have some idea of why all this is happening."

"We *don't know* who's trying to, uh, kill us," said Young, frustrated, near tears, unraveling.

"You must have some idea of who has something to gain by these murders," said Mr. Benchley.

I asked, "Who doesn't like you? I mean, sure, lots of people don't; I don't have enough fingers to list—"

I caught Mr. Benchley's critical, raised eyebrow and edited the rest of what I was about to say: "Who hates the lot of you and wants to see you dead?"

"No cigar . . ."

"Mrs. Parker is right," said Shaw. "Sure, we have our detractors, but if the corporate mob wanted to kill me for my exposés, for revealing the truth of their injustices, I would've been killed a long time ago. And Tony, over here, is an insipid little prick, when he's not crying like a girl, so who'd bother to take him out?"

"That's not nice, Stephen. Just because I don't go around steamrolling—"

"Shut up!" yelled Shaw, and the chorus came in on cue.

"*Shut up! Shut up!*"

"Well, you don't have to—"

"I said, *shut the hell up!*"

"Mr. Hunter," I said, turning to the lanky bones hovering over me, "who'd want you dead?"

"I can think of a few," said Young. "The sewer rats he runs with. . . ."

"It's true," said Trevor Hunter, fixed firmly at his assumed post near the door. The image of a carved stone gargoyle lurking overhead, peering down from its perch, ever-ready to spring to life, flashed in my mind.

"I know all sorts of people," he said.

"Criminals!" said Young.

"Yes, some are thieves, some miscreants, mostly harmless scoundrels who assist me in my work, my research. I can't say any one of them wants me dead. I keep them in their habits, if you know what I mean."

A regular *mensch*, I thought.

"But who's your Moriarty?" I said.

He stared, and it was intimidating to have those heavy lidded, pale-green eyes boring into me. But then he laughed. It was easy, self-deprecating, devoid of scorn and totally disarming. The release brought levity to the drama of the last few days and melted away his fierce-looking exterior to reveal a hidden humanity. I still didn't like him.

I wondered about these men. Hunter was condescending; Shaw was blustering; Young was supercilious; all displayed aspects of conceit, but each man had to be more than what I saw on the surface.

Most of my friends were blatantly arrogant. Look at Alexander Woollcott! Still, there was so much more *good* in Aleck than his sometimes haughty and offensive behavior might suggest.

Because of the disagreeable faces these men projected, I imagined that each could draw the attention, and ultimately, the wrath of an unstable mind—someone they had insulted, dismissed, someone possessing a homicidal arrogance.

Shaking his head, Hunter said, "I'm not really Sherlock Holmes, you know."

"You didn't seem surprised when we told you that this afternoon Daniel Cousins had been murdered," I said. "Why is that?"

"I was expecting to hear it."

"Oh?"

"It was in all the late editions, Mrs. Parker."

"A shame, poor Daniel," said Young. "Deep down he really was a nice fellow."

"Wait," I said, "Deep down? What did you mean by that? Deep down below the layers of not-so-nice, you might find nice? Or that Daniel Cousins was nice deep down to the bone?"

"I don't know, Mrs. Parker; I really don't know what you mean," whined Young with a pout, massaging his eyes and running his hands over and over his head as if to rid himself of something caught and tangled in his hair. "I don't feel very well."

"Pour him another drink, Shaw," said Hunter.

"Was there someone, some other author who wanted to join your club? Someone you may have turned away?" I asked.

"What club?" asked Shaw.

"Why, Mr. Shaw," I replied. "Everybody knows about your Murder Club!"

"What do you mean, *everybody knows!*" cried Young, leaping to his feet and spilling his drink.

"It's not a secret that you writers get together to discuss your work," I said. "I just wondered if there was someone harboring bad feelings."

"*What the hell! What the hell!*"

"Oh, for God's sake, Shaw, shoot that bastard, or I will!" ordered Hunter.

Mr. Benchley stated, "I think it would be wise for you gentlemen to stay close together, after all."

"We can take care of ourselves!" bellowed Shaw.

"I hope for your sakes—" I began to say, but Mr. Benchley interrupted.

"We must leave you, now. Goodnight, gentlemen." He put a protective hand on Cherish's elbow to escort her out of the apartment.

We hurried her down the hall and when we arrived at the stairs I turned to see Trevor Hunter, his old glower returned, watching us from the threshold of the apartment.

When we arrived on the sidewalk I looked up and down the street for Soledad. She must have gone back to her hotel, I thought, as we walked in the direction of Cherish's apartment.

Cherish volunteered answers to our questions before we even had a chance to pose them. "Trevor called me a couple of hours ago," she began, "to say that the men wanted to talk with me tonight at Stephen's apartment. When I got there, only Tony Young had arrived. Trevor was late, right on your heels."

"But you expected Daniel Cousins?"

"Yes, of course," she said, stopping to grab my arm. "Trevor said he spoke with him earlier in the day. But, now Daniel's gone, dead, too. Three men poisoned, and when will it stop? Where will it end?

Poor Daniel. Ernest liked him best of the lot, you know."

"You are saying that Ernest didn't like the others too much in the first place," said Mr. Benchley.

"I suppose not; he hardly talked about them to me."

"Why did they want to see you? What did they want?" I asked.

"To talk about, you mean?"

I nodded.

"Trevor went on and on about a missing manuscript, whether there were carbon copies."

"That pesky manuscript, again . . . the one Ernest was working on?"

"I know nothing much about it. I told them I had nothing in the apartment that they hadn't already searched through."

"They've gone through Ernest's things?" said Mr. Benchley.

"Yes, of course. I let them, after they explained that the manuscript was a work they had each contributed to."

"Are you saying they were all collaborating on one book?"

"Yes. When you were at the apartment the other day I had no idea what Ernest was keeping so close to himself. After all, he never mentioned there'd been collaboration among the men."

"Cherish," I said, "there is the possibility that even though you cannot find the manuscript, the person—or persons—who are killing people associated with it in some way or another might assume it is still at your place."

"Mrs. Parker is trying to tell you that you are not safe there until the killer is caught."

"I see," she replied, slowing her pace once again as she considered. "Maybe I should stay in my attic studio."

"Why not stay with Mrs. Vega?" I suggested.

"Yes, you are right, of course."

We left Cherish at the door to her apartment building and took a taxi uptown.

Chapter Ten

OCTOBER 15, 1929

I went to bed at three in the morning and woke with a start at six, Woodrow's stretched-out paws pushing up against my back. He already took up most of the bed, and he snored, chomped, and made little mewing sounds when he dreamed. No different from any two-legged bedmates I'd known. But, when I'd wake up with a disagreeable attitude, he never snapped back at me. And better yet, he actually liked to cuddle.

I turned on the bedside lamp and saw that I had three hours before a deadline on a poem that would bring me a much-needed two hundred dollars cash. But Woodrow whined and pawed the bedcovers, and I knew exactly what his little dance meant.

When I called the front desk to ask the clerk to send Jimmy, the bellboy, up to take Woodrow for his morning walk, I was told that it would be at least an hour before he was free of his duties. There was a convention of pickle salesmen going on at the Hippodrome down the street, and a busload of attendees had arrived to check into their rooms moments before my call.

Knowing that I would have no peace if I didn't take care of Woodrow's business before I got down to mine, I opened a can of dog food and filled his water bowl. While he ate I got dressed in an old sweater and skirt and threw on my raincape.

When the elevator reached the lobby we found ourselves amid the raucous rabble of Hoosier hucksters, a hundred carnations tucked in a hundred lapels. The place smelled like a funeral parlor. They had come to the Big City to drink, vandalize, cheat on their wives, and exercise their bragging rights over the size and crispness of their pickles.

Woodrow and I pushed through to the front door of the Gonk. As we stepped aside for the luggage cart to be wheeled in from the sidewalk, Mr. Benchley appeared at my side. "What's going on? Is the circus in town?"

"Pickle convention at the Hippo," I replied.

"Goodness! How many *are* there to need a hall that huge?" he said as he ushered me out onto the sunny street. "Gorgeous day!" he said, as we walked toward Fifth Avenue.

"Don't know about that, yet," I replied. "What are you so cheery about?"

"Who says I'm cheery?" he said, bobbing his walking stick as we passed the Harvard Club and the Yacht Club on the north side of 44th. While waiting for the traffic sign to flip to "Go," he said, "I just had breakfast with a friend at the Harvard Club and I asked him about the Anthony Young question."

I looked at him blankly. The traffic bell rang and the sign flipped over, allowing us to cross for our walk down Fifth Avenue toward 42nd Street.

"The discrepancy about his Harvard graduation year, remember? He should've graduated class of 'nineteen-eleven? Young didn't graduate until 'thirteen?"

"Oh, yes, I remember you were going to look into it."

"There was a scandal of course, my friend reminded me of it, only I never connected Anthony Young as one of the five boys involved."

"Involved?" I said, momentarily preoccupied as Woodrow pulled me across the tide of pedestrians toward a fireplug.

As we stood at the crossing at 42nd Street, the New York Public Library all white and sprawling along the two-way thoroughfare, I looked to my left at the astoundingly beautiful Art Deco–style structure rising up from Turtle Bay a few blocks to the east on Lexington Avenue. The scaffolded crown of the Chrysler Building appeared near completion, its steel-clad arched terraces blinding in the sunlight, and I recalled hearing the news that the building at 40 Wall

Street had just been finished and towered just a couple of feet taller than the Chrysler Building, making it the tallest in the world. Walter Chrysler had been bested, after all, by *a couple of feet!*

"Instead of going to Bryant Park, let's walk this way," I said to Mr. Benchley, and when the signal changed we crossed east on Fifth Avenue, which delineated the East Side from the West Side.

"You were saying," I shouted over the clang of the streetcar bell and the incessant honking of automobiles and delivery trucks bounding along the Avenue. The sidewalk was thick with people walking to and from Grand Central Terminal and from the subways and streetcars on their way to work in the office buildings that lined the streets. The metallic buzz of riveting echoed along the corridor of brick and steel, the leitmotif of our evolving city.

"For gosh sake, Dottie, what are you feeding that pup?"

"Looks like Gino's meatballs," I replied, pulling Woodrow from the edge of the curb and back into the flow. Mr. Benchley only called me "Dottie" at moments of surprise and shock, so this was perfectly appropriate. "You were saying?"

"Yes, Anthony Young. He was . . . how can I say this delicately?"

"What the hell did he do?"

"It's not what *he* did; it's what the other four boys did to him."

"No!"

"*Ya-voll!*" he said, stopping short and causing a pileup of pedestrians in his wake. An obscenity thrown by a disgruntled passerby prompted us to move along and we skirted the jammed-up main entrance of Grand Central Terminal at a quickened pace.

"How bad was this frat initiation?"

"Oh, it had nothing to do with any initiation. It was beyond the usual harmless schoolboy club humiliation. He was stripped and assaulted . . . sexually."

"*Shit.*"

"Young was sodomized by all four of them, allegedly."

"Allegedly? Was it alleged or proven?"

"The four boys were expelled."

"And Young?"

"Innocence lost, semesters lost. His father insisted he return to Harvard the next fall. The incident was covered up—Young Senior had connections. The university hushed it up—bad for their reputation, even though the assault occurred off university grounds."

"That explains a lot about him. I thought Anthony Young was just a supercilious little prick. But I can see how Dr. Freud might agree that we are the sum of our experiences."

"Is that what Freud said?"

"I have no idea. His psycho-jargon is ambiguous."

"Look at that over there," he said, pointing to the Chrysler Building. "I suppose Freud would say that Walter Chrysler suffers from penis envy, and that's why he's building the biggest shaft the world has ever seen."

"Lots of little men rising to dizzying heights," I said. "But the building is not the tallest, after all."

"The bank won?"

"Yep!" I said. "Well, maybe he can bring up the height—stick a weathervane on top or something."

"Well, the good news is that nobody died building that monster."

We watched as the workers strode in and out of the fencing around the building site. The clanging of tools and hum of equipment rose up and echoed before being swallowed up by the clamor of the city.

I turned to my friend. "Hearing about Anthony Young's history—well, it reminds me of the Longfellow quote: 'If we could read the secret history of our enemies we should find in each man's life sorrow and suffering enough to disarm all hostility.'"

"Miss Dana's School?"

"Yes, but time and time again I forget that lesson."

"Well, Anthony Young has had his revenge."

"What do you mean?"

"He's outlived his tormentors. Two of the four died in the War, the other two last year."

"*What?*"

"I said, two of the—"

"I heard what you said," I replied. I moved toward the curb and watched the construction crew's progress atop the building while Mr. Benchley bought a copy of the *World* from a newsie hawking the latest editions.

A biplane was flying over the top of the great building, the *putt-putt-putt* of its motor obscured by the roar of machines on the construction site. I thought of Harpo and his newfangled hobby. Aleck's nose was out of joint since Harpo's attention was no longer focused on the game of croquet, but instead on this new obsession.

Mr. Benchley returned to my side. "Yes, well, both of Young's attackers who survived the War died suspicious deaths. Poisonings. One fellow's wife is on trial for murder in Cincinnati," said Mr. Benchley, rustling through the paper. "*Ah*, here it is."

"Is it about her trial?"

"What? Oh, no, I was looking for something else. News of Daniel Cousins' death. Something's been nagging at me."

"Your wife?"

He ignored my nasty comment and said, "Ah-*ha!*"

"For heaven's sake! What are you looking so smug about?"

"No mention as to the cause of death. Just that Cousins was found dead in an alleyway—*blah-blah-blah-blah*—here it is: 'Homicide squad is investigating the possibility of foul play.'"

"I fail to get your point, Mr. Benchley. Stop being oblique!"

"Why is it that when you fail to understand what I clearly state it is because *I* am oblique? Have you ever considered that it may be *you* who are obtuse?"

"I am not slow to understand! You are oblique!"

The drilling from the construction site across the street reached a crescendo, making it difficult for us to argue without screaming. "C'mon, you old crank," I said, leading Woodrow around the corner of Lexington toward 44th Street and home.

Mr. Benchley followed dutifully, clucking disapproval but wearing that cocky expression of superiority.

"What's the big deal?" I said as the noise of construction receded. "What is it that you know that I don't know, but that I'm supposed to know? And will you wipe that smug expression off your—*Oooooh! Oooooh! I see!*"

"'And there was light!'" laughed my friend.

Chapter Eleven

"Damn! I forgot to buy a typewriter ribbon! How the hell am I going to get this to the magazine in time?"

"Hand me the pencil copy, my dear."

He squinted over the numerous erasures, and the insertions, both in ink and pencil. "*Hmmm*, a regular palimpsest! An abstrusely rendered canvas, yes, but I should be able to. . . . *Hmmm*, it's no longer than *The Iliad*," mused Mr. Benchley. And then with a smile: "I will take this across the street and type it up for you at my place while you get properly dressed. Are there any *more* changes you want to make?"

"No. It'll do."

"What about this? Perhaps you might want to—"

"*Exactly* as it is; I like 'lagging feet.' *Do not change a word!*"

"All right. Get going. I'll be back in a jiffy," he said as he made for the door. "By the way, did you hear from Soledad last night?"

"There was a message at the desk. I called her back and she said that she lost Trevor Hunter. Seems he gave her the slip after dodging into a speak. She's certain he spotted her. She'll join us later for drinks at Gino's."

While waiting for the bath to fill, I finished the coffee and sweet roll sent up by room service and then went over to my typewriter. Yes, the ribbon was at its end. I removed it from its little cage and was about to throw it into the trash when sunlight from the window shone through several of the keystroked letters against the dark field of the inked ribbon.

That's when it came to me, my *eureka!* moment, the proverbial light bulb in my head, and all the other clichés about epiphanies and lightning strikes that illuminate the creative mind with instant revelations.

The tub was filling fast, and my friend would soon return, so I did my thinking while selecting a pale-blue-wool dress and matching bolero jacket I had bought last month and had been waiting for cooler weather to wear. I pulled a navy-colored cloche from a hatbox and laid out silk stockings and underthings on the bed. After an exhausting search through the jumble on the floor of my closet I finally found first one and then the other of the navy high-heeled pumps I'd bought on sale at the end of last winter's season.

While Woodrow snoozed on my pillow, I hurriedly bathed, fixed my errant curls, powdered and rouged my face, sprayed myself with Coty's *Chypre*, and slipped into my clothing. Mr. Benchley soon returned with a neatly typed poem in triplicate carbons. He had even slipped the original into an envelope and addressed it to the editor of *The Saturday Evening Post*.

"We'll get Jimmy to deliver it for you."

"But, they have to cut a check!"

"Call and tell them the copy is coming and to return the check with the messenger."

"Oh, you are so clever, you clever man!"

"From oblique to clever in just an hour's time."

A telephone call to Detective Sparrow confirmed our suspicions. He would meet us there, at Ernest Stringer's and Cherish Winter's apartment, he said. As Mr. Benchley and I taxied down to Greenwich Village I told him of my typewriter ribbon discovery. Our mission to drop in on Cherish now had two purposes.

Detective Sparrow was waiting for us in his squad car when our cab pulled up at the storefront apartment building. We entered the walkup and knocked on the door. There was no answer. Repeated raps produced Mrs. Vega peeking out from her door down the hall. "Hello!" she said, coming out into the hall. "If you're looking for Cherish, she's gone out, I think."

"Do you have any idea where?" asked Sparrow.

"Well, she isn't in her studio because the young fellow she shares the space with came by a while ago looking for her, too. She probably went out with the other fellow."

"What other fellow?"

"Oh! Yes, how could you know? It's been a busy morning. A man came by this morning. I opened my windows to air the house; it's a lovely day. I could hear them talking."

Mrs. Vega had many kind, neighborly instincts; the eavesdropping was probably unintentional.

As if she read my thoughts she said, "They were speaking very loudly. After a few minutes I was afraid to close my window, because then poor Cherish would hear it close and think I was snooping; you know how people are."

"What was it about?"

She hesitated, and then, decision reached, she said, "I almost knocked on the door. It sounded like Cherish was crying, and then the man said he would take care of everything and it would be over soon."

"What would he take care of and what would be over, do you have any idea?"

"No, really, I don't know," said Mrs. Vega, her eyes filled with concern.

"Did you see this man?" asked Detective Sparrow.

"No, I'm afraid not. The telephone rang—it's in the living room. My sister in Brooklyn. Well, by the time I got off the telephone and went back to the kitchen, I didn't hear anything coming from next door. I waited a little while and then knocked on the door, but Cherish did not answer."

"Do you have the key to this apartment?"

"No, I don't have a key. Wait! Lift out that ball on top of the newel post. I think that's where Ernest and Cherish kept a spare one."

Mr. Benchley lifted the wooden ball and in the shallow space within was a key. "*Darn*," he said under his breath, and then mumbled something about his Swiss army knife.

Key in hand, Detective Sparrow unlocked the apartment door. He looked over at Mrs. Vega and thanked her in a tone that said, "That will be all." She meekly backed in through her own door.

Once in the apartment I immediately walked over to the desk and the big Royal typewriter, lifted the ribbon cage, and was stopped by a thundering "*Don't touch that!*"

With rubber-gloved fingers, Detective Sparrow removed the ribbon and placed it into a paper bag he withdrew from his pocket. "This goes to the lab," he said, "and the typewriter, too, and everything else on that desk."

"You'll never fit all that in your paper bag," I said lamely, as he picked up the telephone receiver and dialed his precinct house.

After he hung up, he turned to us and said, "Mrs. Parker, Mr. Benchley, thank you for your help. Your insights just might give us what we need to solve this case."

"You want us to leave?" asked Mr. Benchley.

"Wait a minute! What exactly do you mean, Detective?" I said. "How does what we've told you solve anything? We don't know that there's any evidence on that ribbon. It may be a multiple-strike ribbon, a mess of overlapping letters. It's easier to read tickertape than what you'll find on there. And if Stringer had written a book with the other men of his club, what makes you think it was typewritten at all? It may have been in longhand. And the comment Cherish Winter made last night to us, about *three* men poisoned, may have been only an assumption, even though Daniel Cousins' cause of death was withheld from the press, as Mr. Benchley confirmed this morning from the newspaper reports. Of course, she may have thought he was poisoned because the first two men were murdered that way. It could be as simple as that. But maybe there is a more sinister explanation for her comment."

"You are absolutely correct, Mrs. Parker."

"I am?" I replied, perplexed. "I don't understand."

"Are you under the impression that I now think Cherish Winter had something to do with these murders?"

"Well, don't you?"

"I have no reason to suspect her. I just think that she knows more than she's saying. The answer may be on that typewriter ribbon, as you've cleverly suggested, Mrs. Parker. As for the remaining members of this Murder Club, I put in a request to the captain to collect them down to the station. As soon as I have his okay, we will get them to a safe place where they'll be under protective custody until the murderer is apprehended. That goes for Miss Winter, too."

"All right, Detective, we're going," I said.

"Oh," I said turning from the door, "how was the poison that killed Cousins administered?"

"Whiskey flask laced with strychnine. He was found in the alley behind the Black Cat Café. A waitress said that he came in alone and ordered coffee, and she saw him spike it with the liquor from the flask. He looked ill after a few minutes, and he left the café a few minutes later. A cook found him sprawled near the trashcans."

"So, again, there is no way of knowing just when the poison was added to his flask."

"That's right."

Mr. Benchley asked, "This fellow, Stonewall? He's the man who, upon leaving Polly's, remarked at the news headline announcing Stringer's murder, 'They killed the wrong son-of-a-bitch'—what does that amount to?"

"Yes, Martin Stonewall," replied Sparrow. "I spoke with him. He admits that he was very drunk at Miss Adler's that night. When I pressed him he said he was surprised that Stringer was dead, and that he *knew* that Stringer had written the porn for Price. Stonewall fiercely disliked Price. Stonewall had always been great friends with Price's partner, John Mitchell. He said it distressed Mitchell that Price had decided to set down stakes in pornography, no matter how desperate they were to save their failing company. Seeing the news of Stringer's death made him think of his friend, Mitchell, he said, and he wished that it was Price who had died instead. He was very drunk, after all."

"Yes, but from the mouths of babes *and* drunks, as they say, comes truth," said Mr. Benchley.

"The remaining men know something, I'm sure they do. They don't just look scared, they look guilty. They're hiding the truth," I said.

"If they don't tell us what they're hiding," agreed Detective Sparrow, "what they're hiding might get them killed."

We lunched with our friends at the Gonk, where the topic of conversation was Hollywood and the mass exodus of many of our friends to the land of Orange orchards and year-round sunshine. Tallulah, Helen Hayes, and the Barrymores had already been recruited for the movies by lucrative contracts. Most New York playwrights were already scripting for the "talkies," Mr. Benchley and Donald Ogden Stewart as well. I sensed that it was only a matter of time before the central core of our luncheon club would splinter and scatter toward new horizons. Where would I be a year, five, ten years from now?

Aleck, Mr. Benchley, Woodrow, and I walked up to Gino's after lunch for dessert. I would skip the cannoli for one of Gino's "corpse revivers." Soledad was already there, sitting at the "soda-counter" when we arrived. She was sipping a "Maiden's Prayer" and was bubbling to tell us her news. She carried her drink over to a table near the window—the table from where, less than a week ago, we had watched the bank robbery.

"I'm having dinner with Trevor Hunter tonight," she said. "Close your mouth, Dory darling."

"But . . . how did . . . ?"

"I telephoned him this morning, and if you are surprised now, you should have heard *him*! I decided on a frontal attack, to come right out and tell him I was following him last night."

"But . . . but . . . ."

"You're repeating yourself, darling," she said, patting my hand. "I told him that when I saw him on the street, I had recognized him and tried catching up with him and failed. Then I told him why."

"Mind telling us why?"

"I told him that I was a friend of Conan Doyle's—you know, his mentor, so Hunter claims—and I decided to use that connection as introduction. A dozen years ago, when I was in London after the War, I met Conan Doyle, and he was gracious toward me when I was writing my first book. I got to know his second wife, Jean, quite well, you know. I met Houdini in 'twenty, when he came over to see Conan Doyle. But that's neither here nor there. So, I told Hunter that I had read his books and admired his work, and employed all the usual flattery necessary to disarm the fellow. He seemed properly contrite and we chatted briefly about the Doyles and I told him this and that and then he asked me to have dinner with him."

"I don't think he'll be able to, Soledad." I said.

"Why? Was he knocked off since I spoke with him this morning?"

"Not that I'm aware of, but Detective Sparrow told me he's placing Hunter and the other two survivors of the club under protective custody."

"Well, if he shows, he shows."

"If he shows up for dinner, I doubt you'll find out much about who's killing his friends. He's been tight-lipped with the cops. They've all been."

"You didn't mention us or the case or—" asked Mr. Benchley.

"Certainly not. Not after Dory, here, told me about your encounter at Shaw's place last night. Any connection with you would surely make him clam up. But, I failed last evening to gain access to the Murder Club, and I lost Hunter while I was tailing him later on. Detective Sparrow has asked for our help, and perhaps I might glean something to bring the killer to justice. These old boys are protecting someone, or some secret they share. I wouldn't be surprised if they are privy to a scandal in the Hoover administration! My first guess was that they knew who engineered the—oh, but that's a secret, I can't talk about that—and then I thought maybe the men of the club were all part of a soviet spy cell and—"

"That was the *last* book, Sollie," said Mr. Benchley.

"Yes, well, there's intrigue and scandal around every corner these days, Bob," said Soledad, and I could hear the little trill of excitement rising from her throat. "I have heard some dicey rumors about that *other* Hoover—J. Edgar?" she said, looking left and right, and then cupping her hands she whispered, "The man is a cross-dresser!"

I glanced at the two men we were with—Aleck, who was involved with giving the waiter his order, and then Mr. Benchley, who preferred wearing boxers to union suits.

"So are half the men at this table," I said.

"Oh! Why, yes, of course! Aleck did make a formidable appearance as Catherine the Great during the Festival of Fools in Paris, when he wasn't getting his panniers stuck in the gate, that is."

"What's this?" asked Aleck.

"Nothing, old sport," said Mr. Benchley. "Sollie was just saying she won't forget Paris."

We were saved when the waiter asked for my order. Mr. Benchley shook his head when I started to ask for a meatball for Woodrow. I ordered my pup a plain beef patty instead.

"I'm off," said Soledad. "I've got scads to do before this evening. I'm making it an early night. Harpo is taking me flying at dawn."

"What? You and Harpo?" I squealed.

"What the hell, he's mad about me and I can't unstick him."

"Dear God!" cried Mr. Benchley. "You're putting your life in his hands!"

"Certainly not! His hands will never touch an inch of me, Bobby. Don't worry; Louis Blériot was my flying instructor. I can loop-de-loop with the best of them," she laughed, and gathering her purse and scarf said, "I'll call you tonight with the details of the dinner!"

When she had gone, Aleck asked, "So, what's been going on with this murder case? You didn't mention any progress during lunch."

We brought him up to date. "This is maddening. Too many dead people. It's a puzzlement," said Aleck, removing his fountain pen from his coat. He unscrewed the cap and on the back of a menu began to write. When he was done, he showed us the chart.

Ernest Stringer: Poisoned
   Price Publishing 's John Mitchell dies, insurance pays Harvey Price, whereabouts unknown. Stringer has $5,000 in bank. Blackmail?

Mark Wendt: Poisoned
   Woman friend dies in hit-and-run. Wendt investigates. Long Island racketeer who is suddenly killed.

Daniel Cousins: Poisoned
   Might have tried to expose plagiarists Mycroft publisher Jim Morrow, and his lover, writer Frederick Feldman. Murder/suicide?

Anthony Young: Poison-deaths of two of his four Harvard classmates 18 years after the rape.

Stephen Shaw: Corporate/mob enemies?

Trevor Hunter: No known enemies

"The question is," said Aleck, "what do all these men have in common other than membership in this Murder Club?"

"They all own typewriters," I said.

"They all live in Greenwich Village," said Mr. Benchley.

"They were all authors published by Pickering before Niles Pickering died and the company closed shop," said Mr. Benchley.

"Niles Pickering," I said. "He's the only common thread!"

"Do you suppose his death has spawned this Avenger? If so, why?"

"Perhaps we need to find out more about Niles Pickering."

"What's to find out?" asked Aleck. "He was a good man with a fine reputation who worked hard for his clients, too hard probably, and he died of a massive heart attack at his desk. No one ever had a bad word to say about him. And believe me, if *I* didn't have a bad word to say, *nobody* did."

"I think Detective Sparrow should look into his death more closely," I said. "Niles Pickering has always been the only person linked to all of these men."

"Before you go off half-cocked, Dorothy, and open old wounds for his family by having the police start an investigation, let me talk with his wife, June."

"I didn't know you even knew Pickering that well," said Mr. Benchley.

"Well, sure. Niles and June spent a week in Antibes at my rented villa two years ago, the summer Harpo and I met you in Paris. They play a very challenging game of croquet. June still does, anyway. I'll give her a call."

"Will you do it right away, Aleck?" I asked.

"'Wittle Acky' will do it right now, if Gino will let me use his telephone." Aleck stuffed the rest of his cannoli into his mouth, dabbed with a napkin, and pushed his great girth back from the table.

I was feeling restless. I belted down the dregs of my drink, and when Mr. Benchley asked if I wanted another, I said, "I'll get it." Indicating his coffee cup, I asked, "Same as before?" He nodded and I walked over to the bar and asked the bartender to repeat the orders.

While I waited for the young man to work his magic, my eyes followed the circuitous routes of the fish swimming in the tank, which was fitted into the wall behind the bar. It was an unusual feature for a speakeasy—unusual in that it was so prominent in the room. The fish swam about with a mesmerizing effect. The light shone on their colorful, iridescent scales.

Gino stood behind the bar, his curly dark head and Roman profile reflected in the glass of the tank. The two-headed Roman God Janus came to mind—the guardian of Heaven's Gate. And what were those placid little fishies doing but guarding my gin, my personal gate to Heaven? Or oblivion . . . or Hell. Other menacing classical images flashed in reckless succession: Cerberus, the three-headed dog, and the Centaurs guarding Dante's Circles of Hell. Appropriate, I thought, from the Temperance League's point of view. The River Styx flowed gin. . . .

"Clever of Gino," said Mr. Benchley, breaking my reverie. "The fish tank is the perfect cover for his gin tank."

"It is human nature, isn't it, to accept what we are offered at face value?"

"You are waxing philosophic, my dear. It's too early in the day for that."

"We see only the surface. What's easy to see. What people *want* you to see."

"*Uh-oh*, here we go; a blue funk."

"We've been stuck," I said. "Stuck with a theory that there is a killer out there, an avenging angel of sorts, taking out the members of the Murder Club because they may have, perhaps unwittingly, effected tragedy in the lives of a few people they had been associated with. What if there was no one seeking retribution? What if . . . ?"

Aleck reappeared with a perplexed expression on his face, cutting me off. "June told me that a month before he passed away, Niles decided not to publish the books of a dozen authors, rather than to close his doors completely. Niles's doctor wanted him to retire. He had a weak heart, and the pressure of his work . . . well, June said that, among the dozen authors, all of the Murder Club members were included."

"He died at his desk, a heart attack . . ." I said to myself.

"That's what they said," said Aleck.

"Was there an inquest?"

"No. He was not alone when he suffered the attack. You're thinking foul play, aren't you, Dottie dear?"

"I don't know what I'm thinking; I'm grasping at straws."

The bartender slid our drinks onto the bar.

"But I am now convinced we've been on the wrong track. Looking out when we should be looking in. Things are not how they seem. We have to turn the puzzle around. It's all very clever, really, but hard to prove."

"Want to elaborate, my dear?" said Mr. Benchley. "I have no idea what you mean by that *oblique* observation."

"You will," I said, knocking back the corpse reviver. "Is your Swiss army knife ready for action, Mr. Benchley?"

"I should say! I was about to retire it," whined Mr. Benchley.

"You haven't heard a thing I've said."

"Mrs. Parker!" he replied, outraged. "Once a Boy Scout learns to depend on his little blade, he does so for the rest of his life. Now, what were you saying?"

"It might come in handy when we break into the apartments of our Murder Club boys."

"Why not just ring the bell?" said Aleck.

"That wouldn't be any fun," I said. "Anyway, Hunter and Shaw and Young may already have been rounded up by the police for their own protection. Which is a good thing, because I suspect one of them—or all of them—may be murderers."

"*What!*" bellowed Aleck, sending a breeze through my hair. "Young is too much of a wimp to murder anyone; he's scared of his own shadow. Shaw is all show, all hot air, and Hunter is so self-involved with his own delusions of grandeur that he wouldn't bother with anything as petty as murder."

"I beg to differ, Aleck, although I've never heard anyone say that murder was petty! Well, think about it: Six authors meet regularly to devise murder plots for the novels they are writing. Every damned mystery writer worth his salt strives to devise a plot featuring a perfect murder, a murder so cunningly executed that only the brilliant skills of a Sherlock Holmes type of detective can unravel the mystery. When we were talking with Edna yesterday, she mentioned that Ersatz spoke with her about writing a novel in which his murderer gets away with his crime—"

"Yes," said Mr. Benchley, "and I said something to the effect that if no one knows a crime has been committed, there is no crime."

"That's right," I said. "And there have been many deaths surrounding our Murder Club member-ship that appeared to be of natural causes or suicide."

"You believe these deaths were in fact murders?"

"Well, yes," I said. "I think so. And wouldn't they be considered perfect crimes? I think our boys were playing the avenger against others who had done them wrong."

"It makes sense," said Aleck, "except, who is murdering the boys in the club?"

"Someone who knows what they've been up to, I should think."

Mr. Benchley considered my last statement. "You know, whenever you hear about a gang of two or more thieves, one often squeals on the others rather than standing firmly beside them. There's always one weak link who tries to save his own neck."

"That's it," I said, nodding. "There's always one guy who gets scared, or whose conscience kicks in, the weakest link who caves in and gives away not only himself but his cohorts as well."

Aleck said, "Let me get this straight: You think Ersatz and the others killed a bunch of people they held grudges against, making their deaths appear to be from natural causes or the result of suicide? And then some clever person figured out what they were doing—"

"No. I think there's nobody outside of their group targeting them. I think the killer is on the inside. As it is only a theory," I said, "we need to prove it. Now, Ersatz was the first of them to fall. Cherish talked about something he was writing. Maybe it was or maybe it wasn't a manuscript. He was nervous, paranoid, she said. He may have been the first link to break—and therefore the first of the boys to be killed. And since we have to wait for the police lab to decipher what he typed using that ribbon, and the men are safely in police custody by now, I think we can feel free to check out their living quarters for clues or the proof that they've been up to something naughty."

Mr. Benchley said: "Trevor Hunter is the likely ringleader. We'll break into his place first."

"Why do you suppose Hunter is the mastermind?" asked Aleck.

"Because he fancies himself a modern Sherlock Holmes. And besides the fact that Conan Doyle's Holmes possessed a pharmacopeia of diabolical poisons, if you remember Heywood reporting that Trevor Hunter's wealth came from his father's remedy for dyspepsia, after which he built a huge pharmaceutical company, it's pretty likely that the poisons used to kill his fellow members, as well as their outside enemies, came from him."

"Why not just tell Detective Sparrow and wait for him to get a search warrant?"

"We'd get nowhere fast doing that," I laughed. "And Mr. Benchley needs the practice. Where does Hunter live, I wonder?"

"In the Village, I know that. The address should be listed in the telephone directory," said Mr. Benchley.

Skimming through three pages under the surname "Hunter" we found no listing for a Trevor. A thought popped into my head, so I looked further, found the surname I was looking for, and ran my finger down the page. There must have been ten pages of listings under this other surname, but I finally found an address under "Sherlock Holmes" on Barrow Street.

———◆———

As we approached the door to Trevor Hunter's/ Sherlock Holmes's Greenwich Village apartment, there was a bounce in Mr. Benchley's step as he affectionately fondled the Swiss army knife in his coat pocket, a smile of eager anticipation on his face.

"All right, then," I said, "take out your tool, and work your magic."

"That's all you women want," he replied with a cocky wink, "a handyman!" Mr. Benchley knocked on the scarred door.

When there was no reply, he eagerly set to work. The lock sprung open and we opened the door and entered into what could only be described as a "hovel." A breeze poured in through a half-open window in the single room that served as living room, bedroom, and kitchen area, the latter defined by a hot-plate on a rickety old table. The bathroom must have been down the hall, because there wasn't one inside the flat.

"What a dump."

Mr. Benchley's eyes took in the room. "Some might say, 'homey.'"

I nodded, thinking of Shaw's and Stringer's sorry rooms. "Looks like these guys all hired the same decorator."

Something dark moved past my peripheral vision.

I screeched: "*Yikes!* Was that a rat? Did you see that? Was that—"

"Might have been," said Mr. Benchley. "But I think the roaches carried him off thattaway!"

"Shit! I can't take rats! Oh, my God! Over there!"

My companion, seeking safety, hid behind me.

"Scaredy-cat!" I screamed, bumping into him as I turned to flee.

"It is!" laughed Mr. Benchley, as a very young black kitten came out from under a pile of clothes in the corner, stretched its little legs, and shook off the sleep from his head. The ball of fluff sat and stared at us with blue eyes so big they filled half his head, and then after a few seconds began to *meow* from hunger.

"So sweet," I said, scooping up the kitten, whose tiny claws dug their way up toward my shoulder, catching in the weave of my suit. "Since you're not a rat, I may just take you home with me."

"Oh, no you don't," cried a scraggly little girl of about six years as she bounded through the door. "He's not a rat! He's mine," she said with a proprietary pout as she aimed a scuffed Buster Brown at my shin. I moved aside before impact. But seeing that she meant business, I quickly handed over the cat.

"We got no rats around here, lady," she scolded. "Bad kitty. Naughty Esmeralda!"

"Esmeralda is a girl's name."

"So what?" said the kid, hugging the cat against her faded pink sundress. The sweater she wore over it suffered from much wear and had gaps in the knit the size of bullet holes. "I like da name."

"Well, I'm glad you're reunited with—uh—Esmeralda!"

"Ha!" she said scornfully, "I *cawt* ya, ya mean, tryin' ta steal 'im."

"My, you are a *precocious* little thing, aren't you?" I hissed through a thin smile.

"Id ain't nice ta say bad woids."

"That's what I tell her all the time," said Mr. Benchley.

"What I meant was that you are a . . . clever child. A smart—"

"Ma says I'm a smart-ass, if dat's whattcha mean."

"I'm sure," I said, exasperated.

"So, we know your kitten's name, but not yours," said Mr. Benchley.

"Dat's right."

"Well, what do people call you?"

"Besides 'smart-ass,'" I said.

"Yes. What's your name, dear child? I'm Robert Benchley—Bobby to my friends—and this is Mrs. Parker."

"Don'she got no friends?" she said, pointing at me.

"Certainly I have friends, you little—"

"Mrs. Parker!"

I turned to my *sometimes* friend: "*Aaah*, stick it!"

Why am I letting this kid get to me? She's just a fresh-mouthed kid. I'm the adult here, I said to myself.

Instead of slapping her face, I slapped a smile on mine and said: "Call me Dorothy."

"Dere's a goil in school cawled Dorothy."

"Oh, really?"

"She cusses an' she's aw-ways stawtin' fights. I ain't s'posta play wid huh. Ma says she's a badfloons."

"A bad influence?"

"Dat's it."

"Comes with the name, I suppose," said Mr. Benchley, and I pulled a face at him.

"So, kid, what do you know about the man who lives here?" I asked.

"Crayzy."

"Well, all right," I said. "But did you notice anything else strange about him?"

"I told ya, lady, he's nuts."

At times like these, when dealing with children, I'd forget that I often regret not having any of my own.

"Ma says don't tawk ta him."

"Why's that? Isn't he a nice man?"

"Aw, heck, I told ya! He's crayzy! Gotta go; I ain't s'posta tawk ta strangers."

"You live next door?" asked Mr. Benchley, leaning down face-to-face with the child. "Your mom home?"

"*Maaaaaaaaaaa!*" screamed the kid, scaring the kitten to fly from her arms and into Mr. Benchley's hair before it leaped off and scurried down the hallway. Mr. Benchley staggered back as if Rudy Vallee's megaphone had been placed over his head. The kid gave chase; Mr. Benchley held the sides of his head, the model for Edvard Munch's *The Scream*.

A door flew open in the hall.

"*What the—*" sounded a gravelly voice. And there appeared a larger version of the kid, a cigarette bobbing between her lips as she threatened: "Getcha ass in heeyah! Oh, da stoopid cat. Din't I tell ya don't hang 'round da hawl bodderin' folks?"

She swatted at the tangle-haired kid and pushed her into the apartment.

Charming.

The woman glared at us as she stepped back into her apartment. "Whaddaya starin' at?"

Charming.

"I'm Bob and this is Dorothy—"

"Yeah?"

"We want to ask you about Mr. Hunter."

"You ain't cops. I don't gotta tawk ta ya."

"Well, no, but—"

"Ya from da papers or sumpthin'?"

"Well, no, but—"

"I got nuttin' ta say." The hag slammed her door on us.

We reentered Trevor Hunter's room and stood side-by-side on the only square foot of uncluttered space. "Why would someone from money live like this?"

"I don't know. Dope."

"Who're you calling a dope?" I said. "Haven't I been abused enough by—"

"No. I mean, *dope*. Opium, cannabis, cocaine."

"Ah-*ha!* That's what he was smoking in his 'oily briar pipe'!"

"Yes, I'm afraid he's adopted many of the habits of Holmes."

"He plays the violin?"

"Tucks it right under his chin . . ."

We began a slow visual search of the room. It was necessary to brush aside the debris collected on the floor—papers, wrappers, soiled clothing—

"*Yikes!* A dead rat!"

"The little girl said there were no rats! Can't believe a thing that kid said!"

"Now, now, Mrs. Parker. The little monster didn't want us defaming her neighborhood."

"This place looks like a crime-room photograph," I said, focusing on the macabre papers tacked on the wall, many columns cut from newspapers about murder investigations and trials. There were autopsy photos, mug-shots, and reports.

"So our Mr. Hunter is an addict. Just found what appears to be his stash of cocaine."

"I get no kick from cocaine."

"You know, Mrs. Parker, I think this dump has been trashed."

"By someone other than the man who lives here?" I replied, thinking it over.

"A jumble of trash on the floor. . . . And yet from what I can see after a cursory inspection, there appears to be a strange sense of order in what is hanging on the walls."

"And if whoever ransacked this joint was out to steal valuables, he would have taken the dope. So he was looking for something else. A manuscript?"

"You seem to be stuck on the idea that Stringer had a manuscript."

"I suppose I am," I said. "It's just that when Cherish Winter mentioned that Ersatz was furiously writing and guarding his work, along with his sudden paranoia, it made me think that it must contain something worth killing for."

"An original *Divine Comedy* is worth killing for; a *Gutenberg Bible* is worth killing for; a *Hypnerotomachia Poliphili* is worth killing for; the Holy Grail—whatever it may turn out to be—was, and still is, worth killing for. A slice of Lindy's cheesecake is worth killing for. But an original manuscript by Ernest Stringer? Not so much."

"Look!" I said, my eye catching a newspaper headline from the *Detroit Register*: *The Trial of Mary Connelly Begins Today.* I read aloud the beginning of the news story dated three weeks ago: *"On trial for the poisoning death of her husband, Richard Connelly—"*

"*Hey!*" said Mr. Benchley, "Richard Connelly! He was one of the boys who raped Anthony Young while he was attending Harvard! I told you about that."

"Here're obits on Jim Morrow and Frederick Feldman. And the notice of the results of the inquest on the Feldman death deeming it a suicide," I pointed out.

"There weren't any news stories linking the men or suggesting their relationship."

"No, we knew there wouldn't be. . . . *'Millionaire Businessman Dies While Dining.'*" I read aloud. "*'John Davies Welles suffered a fatal heart attack while dining with friends at the Waldorf-Astoria Hotel last evening. . .'* That's the man who Mark Wendt believed ran over his girl!"

"Look at this!" said Mr. Benchley, removing a thumbtack from a column of newsprint. "*'John Robert Mitchell, Publisher of Price Publications, Dead.'* Listen to this: *'The fifty-four-year-old John Robert Mitchell died suddenly last night after dining at the Harvard Club with his partner, Harvey Price.'*"

"He's got it all here! He murdered them all, I'll bet!" I said.

"So it appears. Who in his right mind would collect the proof of his handiwork other than its perpetrator? And yet, this is really not proof. It's a scrapbook!" said Mr. Benchley, looking around the room.

"Stuff!" I said, walking around the cramped space, inspecting a briar pipe hanging on a pipe stand. I began to riffle through a wall of bookshelves that reached all the way up to the ceiling. The shelves were bowed with the weight of books, and everything appeared precariously balanced, causing me to step back with the possibility that the shelves and their contents might just topple down on me.

The collection was a mad exercise in confusion. Some books were placed vertically, some jammed into any available horizontal space, everything askew and cross-hatched like a crazy quilt. Many of the titles were forensic or physiological in nature, and having to do with the commission or investigation of crimes. There were books on plants and pharmaceuticals, their uses and abuses, and many sinister-looking publications, the spines of which denoted that the contents dealt with diabolical practices in far-off places around the world—Africa, Asia, the Caribbean Islands, Ancient Egypt. Here were the Pharaohs' crimes of matricide, fratricide, patricide—a family affair of poisons and murder; a history of the Borgias, and of several scheming popes and Vatican scandals; and books on torture, dismemberment, disembowelment, self-mutilation, cannibalism, and violent sexual practices. There was an extensive collection of religious dogma and hedonistic practices. There were books on Judeo-Christian executions, the Inquisition, and Roman blood sport; on voodoo, zombies, vampire lore, and premature burial; on American Indian practices and Mayan brain surgeries. We found articles about Satanism—many on the Black Arts—and exorcism and the Roman Catholic Church, as well as speculative journals about secret organizations ranging from the Masons, Opus Dei, and the Knights Templar to Yale University's Skulls. The "how-to's" included mummification, the distilling of toxic plants, embalming techniques in the ancient world, animal dissection, and taxidermy. Whatever filing system Hunter employed to find any one particular edition lay beyond my comprehension. None were shelved alphabetically, nor were they sorted by any particular topic.

A great place to hide something.

"He's got an arsenal over here," said Mr. Benchley, opening the door of a cabinet. "Mostly antique revolvers. More stuff," muttered Mr. Benchley, eyeing a collection of sabers mounted on the wall next to the gun case. He spun a huge globe beside the cluttered desk.

I glanced over at my friend and saw the big Royal typewriter on the desk. My mind shifted away from my perusal of the shelves to a mental note: *Stop at the stationers on the way home and buy a typewriter ribbon.*

"And still more stuff!" he mumbled, his eye huge as he peered at me through the magnifying glass. "Unless you are a Holmes aficionado, or you want to know how to shrink a head, there isn't much of value around here. No paper in the carriage with cryptic words typed out for clues," he said, flicking the carriage lever to the left and making the bell go *ding*. "Perfect A-flat! *Mi-mi-mi-mi-miiiii!*" he gargled out.

It's a Royal, I realized, my eyes back on Hunter's typewriter. *Same model as mine. Wonder if there's a spare ribbon box in his desk drawer?*

Mr. Benchley was now examining the items on the desk. A string of worry-beads clicked through his fingers. Then, he tossed a Ping-Pong ball in the air. When I refused to play a game of catch, he frowned and began searching the desk drawers. "There's got to be a bottle of whiskey somewhere around here."

"I would think so. Imagine coming home to a dive like this. I couldn't live in it sober," I said. "But then, I don't live anywhere sober."

I remembered my mental note. "Hey, it wouldn't exactly be considered stealing if there happened to be a new, spare typewriter ribbon in one of those drawers, do you think?"

"Yes," was his reply, as he lowered his head to peer into the eyepiece of the microscope.

Thwarted, I asked, "Any clues?"

"Ah-*ha*." He picked up binoculars from off a hook near the door. "Ah-*ha!*" he said again, staring at a wall through the field glasses.

I stopped perusing the bookshelves to await announcement of his discovery, but without another word he dashed through the apartment door and out into the hallway. I picked my way toward him through the clutter.

"Ah-*ha!*" he exclaimed again, and then reentered the apartment, closed the door, and continued on toward the lone window. He yanked at the dirty, torn shade blocking the sun. The roller engaged and dust motes danced wildly. Then he threw up the sash of the partially opened window and leaned his head out.

"Ah-*ha!*" he said, ducking back in to face my bewilderment with a broad, knowing smile. Whatever he discovered, he was not about to share it with me too readily.

"All right, *Mr. Ah-Ha*, wipe that cocky grin off your face and "

"As I suspected, Mrs. Parker! Now, let me show you: There's a window to the right of this room, if you'll take a look out the window, Madame!"

"Well, that's from the apartment next—"

"—door? *Ah-ha!* But you see there is no door to that windowed space leading in from the hallway."

"There's more to this place—another room?"

"Over there!" he said, pointing at a wall clear of any press clippings.

He handed me the binoculars and told me to look through them. All I saw was a narrow bed pushed up against the wall, and a tapestry that was hung on the wall behind the bed depicting a family or club crest. A coat of arms. It was the only uncluttered wall in a room overpowered by possessions. And if I had stopped to really look around me, I would have seen that the tapestry was the most important clue in the room, for the very reason that it hung alone and apart from the chaos surrounding it.

"Look at the molding surrounding that tapestry. Notice that it's the only wall in the room that has molding. There's a gap. It doesn't quite lie flush against the wall, so at first it appears that the wood is buckled, but it's not."

I put down the binoculars and saw the lineal shadow cast on the wall from the sun coming through the opened window. My friend was correct.

I helped Mr. Benchley shift the bed aside, and lifted an edge of the hanging, which I suspected obscured a doorway, but there was none, only the bare wall. It was pockmarked and beaten like the rest of the walls in the place. Because of a strong breeze from the open window, the clippings that covered the other walls—newspaper articles with headlines screaming "Murder," notes and photographs and innumerable charts depicting I knew not what—began fluttering wildly like moth wings beating a window screen.

Mr. Benchley pushed aside the tapestry and I held it out of his way while he began tapping on the wall. "It's not plaster and lath; it's hollow behind here."

After much inspection by my friend, the tapestry began to weigh on me so I leaned against the wall for support.

I cried out and Mr. Benchley managed to break my fall when the wall gave way to my touch. "Open Sesame!" he said, and then whistled.

I rubbed my butt, which had made contact with a bedpost, and after a string of foul exclamations I watched as Mr. Benchley disappeared into a dark space behind the tapestry.

I jumped at the sound of a metallic *click!* Was it the turn of a key locking us in?

It was only Mr. Benchley flicking open the cover of his cigarette lighter.

"*Oooff!* You gave me a scare!"

"I didn't touch you!"

"Never mind," I said, looking around the room, its boundaries obscured by the shadows cast by Mr. Benchley's light. I felt as if we had stepped into a dark corner of existential proportions. I was struck with a sharp sense of dread, a strange, albeit unreasonable, foreboding, as I peered into the darkness—a setting foreshadowing some Victorian tale of horror. My skin crawled.

I grabbed at the tails of Mr. Benchley's waist-coat as we progressed further into the room, my eyes trying to make out what lay ahead. Light caught the forward-moving undulation of a serpent-like figure, opaque and ghostly, causing Mr. Benchley and I to collide, and I gave out a little shriek. The inanimate objects in the room shifted in the light of the flickering flame.

"It's only that swan's-neck glass retort apparatus over there, Mrs. Parker," my friend assured me, as he reached up and pulled a lamp chain, flooding the room with light. The hooded lamp swung back and forth, throwing shadows in all directions. He steadied the shade and my momentary flight of fancy was chased away. I gazed at the convoluted glass object I had previously believed was alive and about to attack us.

"It's a little still, Fred! Do you suppose Hunter was distilling gin?" I laughed lightly, and then shivered from the proverbial footsteps over my grave. Even with the lamplight, I was still uncomfortable in my skin. There was something sinister about this hidden room.

"I knew the fellow had a laboratory!" announced Mr. Benchley. "With all those volumes out there, and the microscope, I knew there had to be more!"

There were Petri dishes, test tubes, bulbous retorts, small and gigantic, glass pipettes, Bunsen burners, funnels, condensers, beakers, funnels, and a maze of pipes. "Paging Dr. Jekyll," I said, my voice wobbling nervously.

I was suddenly cold, chilled to my bones. "Bugs!" I screeched when my eyes landed on a small aquarium.

"Beetles, by the looks of them."

"This place is crawling with vermin."

"Don't be afraid, Little Dorothy, they won't bite you. Just don't touch them. I think those are Blister Beetles. Give you an awful, oozing rash."

"I have no intention of touching them. And how do you know about Blister Beetles?"

"Fraternity pranks, of course. You can't believe the ruckus they—well that's a story for another day. It's the primary ingredient in making Cantharidin, commonly known as Spanish Fly."

"Is that what you studied at Harvard?"

"Certainly not!"

"Well, then, how do you know these things?"

"From a book I picked up entitled—"

"*How to Make Spanish Fly*," we said in unison.

"What I want to know is where he keeps the gin," I said, looking over the assortment of brown bottles and green bottles, some tiny, others gallon-sized, that were labeled and lined up alphabetically on a row of shelves. Some displayed skull-and-crossbones, indicating poison.

"Ah, Calalar beans," said Mr. Benchley, inspecting the labels. "Used by African witch doctors. And *Tinctura gelsemii*, made from the root of yellow jasmine."

"What's it used for? Burning off warts or something?"

"It's a poison."

"How do you know that?"

"From a book entitled—"

"Don't tell me: *How to Make Tinctura jellysalame?*"

"*Gelsemii.* Besides, it says so on the label."

"Why, this place is a pharmacopeia of lethal concoctions."

"So it appears," agreed my friend, continuing his inspection. "And everything is in alphabetical order. Ah, the Borgias' everyday arsenic, odorless and colorless when mixed into your cocktails, and basically does the job. *Bacillus anthracis*—a smidgeon of that will definitely put a stop to your party plans. Belladonna—you might know it as Deadly Nightshade—"

"Doesn't everybody?"

"—or Devil's Berries or Death Cherries. Black walnut, Bulgarian umbrella—naughty stuff that! Catuwoba, and coline—made from hemlock. Curare! *My, my* . . . datura! *Tsk-tsk-tsk!*"

"*Tsk-tsk-tsk!*" I parroted.

"Mandragora! Mescaline! Monkshood! How better to kill werewolves than by administering monkshood! Tricky though; need a full moon and it's hard to make a werewolf take his medicine, you know?"

"So I've heard."

"*Hmmm*. Morphine . . . kills pain—maybe forever. Nitro benzene, phosphorus—yes, phosphorus can put an end to all your problems. Stropanthus, yes, one would need stropanthus for one's arrow quivers. . . . Strychnine! Tansy! Thallium—first you lose your hair and then you lose your life. Quite unpleasant."

"Got any cyanide? I could use a shot right now."

"Yes, here's some, but that's not how it's best dispensed."

"Lend me that book you picked up: *How to Dispense Cyanide.*"

"Can't. Lent it to a friend who hasn't returned my calls."

"Well, we can assume this is where all the poison came from."

"You know what they say about when you 'assume' anything?"

"Not that old joke, please."

"It makes an 'ass' of 'u' and 'me.'"

"You had to say it, you just *had* to say it!" I chided. "But, it's all here at Trevor Hunter's fingertips! Anyway, I don't like the man."

"You don't like the man," taunted Mr. Benchley, "so he's got to be the killer!"

"Well, we are standing in a room filled with diabolical poisons!"

"So we are, my dear, but tell me, have you ever heard of poisons that were not diabolical?"

"Gin," I replied. "Drinking gin leads to a slow death."

"That's all right," said Mr. Benchley, "I'm not in a hurry."

"I rest my case."

"We need to telephone Detective Sparrow with our discovery," said my friend. "Whether Hunter actually dispensed these poisons is up to Sparrow to determine. Our work is done."

"Is it?"

"Well, so far we've avoided getting kidnapped, shot at, bludgeoned, or stabbed in the back, so I'd say I've helped you get out of this relatively unscathed. You want to press your luck?"

"*You've* helped *me?* What do you mean, *you've helped me get out of this relatively unscathed?*"

"Well, I was against this whole thing in the first place. You knew how I felt about playing cops and robbers! I only tagged along to protect you."

"You! You! *You!*"

"*You* repeat yourself."

"You—"

"See? Now, watch your temper. Apoplexy can kill!"

"Yes! I'm apoplectic, all right, and I am going to kill—you!"

"*This* is the thanks I get."

A thought struck me and I froze in place. I was so stricken that Mr. Benchley thought I'd had a stroke.

"Dottie! Dottie, dear! What's wrong?" he cried at my blank, wide-eyed stare. He shook me. I blinked and then focused on his face.

"What if Detective Sparrow *doesn't* have the men in protective custody yet? That means that Soledad—Oh, my God! Soledad!"

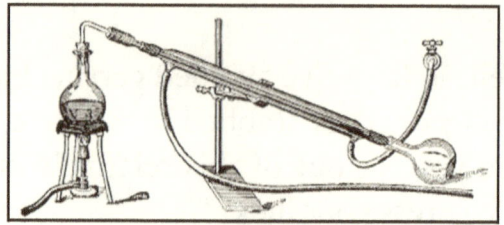

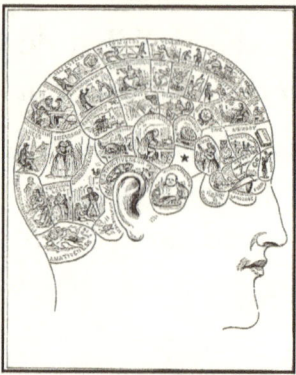

Phrenology

Mr. Benchley as a mad scientist

Chapter Twelve

"Where is Soledad?"

That was the question I asked the front desk clerk when I telephoned the Plaza Hotel and received no answer from her room. It was the question I asked when I telephoned Aleck and Ross and a dozen mutual friends and her hairdresser on Madison Avenue, before I posed the question to Detective Nate Sparrow of the New York City Police Department.

"We can't find her, Detective!" I yelled frantically into the receiver. "We've looked everywhere, Mr. Benchley and I. We've called all of her usual haunts and she's nowhere to be found!"

"She'll turn up," said Sparrow, and I called him out for his cavalier attitude.

"She'll turn up, did you dare say?" Turn up *where?* Dead in an alley, floating in the East River? What the hell do you mean by that?"

"Has she missed an appointment with you?"

"Why, no."

"Does she usually keep you informed about her comings and goings around town?"

"Why, no," I said, growing more and more frustrated. "We just can't find her!"

"Can I ask what is so pressing that you must—"

"Trevor Hunter."

"What about him?" I could hear a crunching sound and then a *smack*. He was eating a sandwich, he said, when I asked "What the hell was that?"

"Do you have him in protective custody? If you have him guarded, then she's safe."

"We haven't had a decision about that from my captain yet."

"Sure. Wait for the others to drop dead before—"

"I personally telephoned Shaw and Young that they had to take precautions."

"Well, what do you know? Think they're not already thinking along those lines?"

"No need for sarcasm, Mrs. Parker."

"I'm the ruling queen of sarcasm!" I hissed. "What about Hunter?"

"What about him? He's not answering his telephone. And why did you say a moment ago that if Hunter is under police protection, Miss Soleil is safe?"

"Soledad was going to have dinner with him," I said, "dinner with a murderer!"

"What makes you think—"

"We've been looking at this whole fiasco from the wrong angle. Nobody from *outside* the group is seeking revenge against the members of the Murder Club. One of the members is doing the killing!"

"How did you arrive at that conclusion?"

"It makes sense. First, we'd discarded the idea of multiple killers and adopted the theory of one lone *avenger*. But that is reaching rather far, don't you see? The shortest distance between two points is a straight line, and everything we've come across and considered is zigzagged all over the map!"

"What?"

"Take Gino's fish tank. You can't see the gin tank behind it, can you? One sees what is presented, what one is tricked into seeing. Now apply the principle of Occam's Razor."

"That the explanation requiring the fewest assumptions is usually the correct one?"

"Bingo!"

"A fish tank, Occam's razor, a straight line?"

"If we look at the members of the Murder Club who are still standing, only one, Trevor Hunter, has the means—the pharmaceuticals, that is—and he was the last person to see Ernest Stringer alive. Remember, I watched him follow Ernest on the street just before the bank heist. If you saw the array of poisons we found sitting around his hidden laboratory, you'd see that he is the only logical person who fits the bill—"

"Don't tell me you broke into his house!"

"Mr. Benchley and I are not the police, so we don't need warrants. A little bit of lock picking won't jeopardize your case against Hunter."

"Right, but a breaking-and-entering charge against you and Mr. Benchley—"

"We're not worried about that, assuming you won't blab it around. We're worried about our friend Soledad!"

"But, why would Hunter kill his friends?"

"I think Ernest discovered something quite nasty about the man, and he died because of it."

"We'll know what he was last writing about as soon as what's on the typewriter ribbon is revealed."

"You've had it for hours! How long does it—"

"As soon as the processing is complete, I'll call you."

"'I'll call you,' *hmmm?* That's what they all say."

We finished up our talk with Detective Sparrow's assurances that he would send a man to the Plaza Hotel to await Soledad's return and the arrival of Trevor Hunter, who was to escort her to dinner.

The key to finding Soledad was to track down Trevor Hunter. Hunter had no reason to bring harm to Soledad, insisted Sparrow, if he were, indeed, the killer. But he asked that Mr. Benchley and I meet him at Hunter's home on Washington Square so that we might show him this secret, hidden den of poisons.

"What? Washington Square? It's a hovel on Barrow Street."

"Mrs. Parker," Mr. Hunter's home on Washington Square is a grand mansion that his father bought before the turn of the century."

"Are we talking about the same place? We were at his rooms on Barrow Street, listed under the name of 'Sherlock Holmes.'" I explained our little excursion through the telephone directory.

"This is interesting," he said. "All right, I'll get a warrant to search the place. A *warrant*, Mrs. Parker. I don't want to jeopardize a case against Mr. Hunter, if he is indeed the killer."

"You are no fun at all."

He laughed and said, "Oh, I don't know about that. You need to give me a chance."

———————◆———————

"Where in fresh hell have you been, woman?" I scolded into the telephone.

"What's wrong? Is somebody dead?" replied Soledad, her voice low and husky. "It's not Aleck, I hope? He was holding his chest after he ate that entire stuffed leg of lamb last night. I fear that one day he may explode—like President Harding."

"Nobody's dead, I'm glad to say, now that I hear your voice."

"Ask her where she is," said Mr. Benchley, leaning his head on mine and listening through the earpiece.

It was after eleven o'clock, and Mr. Benchley and I had been closeted in my rooms together for hours playing gin-rummy at a nickel a game and eating Chinese food from containers while awaiting telephone calls from Detective Sparrow about his search warrant and Soledad in response to the numerous messages I'd left for her at the Plaza. There was barely an inch of rye whiskey left in the bottle, and Woodrow was making whining overtures about his late walk. After losing my shirt—a dollar-ten—to Mr. Benchley, I was ready to go for a late-night trot around town.

"Is that Bob chattering in the background?"

"Where are you, Sollie?" he said into the mouthpiece.

"What in heaven's name—" I said, wrestling the receiver back to my ear. "Where have you been, Sollie?" I repeated.

Mr. Benchley made a face: "It's more important to know where she is *now* rather than earlier!"

"Shut up!"

"Yes, that's Bob. The only people you ever tell to shut up are Bob and Ross, and Ross is undoubtedly at home under the watchful eye of the caustic Jane. Well, I heard Bob's question, and you should have remembered, Dory, because I told you I was having dinner with Trevor Hunter. You really need to write things down, darling."

"Yes, I know, I didn't forget, but, all right—*where are you now?*"

Mr. Benchley gave me an I-told-you-so smirk.

"With Trevor, of course. I'm with him right now, at his beautiful townhouse on Washington Square, and we want you to join us for drinks in a little while, if you're free. Bring Bob along. Bring the whole darn gang along."

"You're with him right now? Did you say *townhouse?*"

"Yes, dear," she said, "we're at his townhouse. He cooked me the most marvelous dinner—"

"Oh, my God," said Mr. Benchley. "She needs to get to a hospital!"

"You didn't eat any of it, I hope?"

"Why, of course, darling, why wouldn't I? Trevor prepared the most delectable cervelle de veau."

"What's that?"

"Calves' brains," she said, and I wanted to scream.

"You see, the trick is, first you need to sauté the—"

"Never mind that; I don't have a pencil."

"You sound very upset," she added, but gave me no chance to reply. "We're going to Chumley's, Dory—"

"Chumley's."

"Eighty-six Bedford Street—"

"Yes, I know where it is."

"The garden entrance."

"We need to talk, Sollie, we need to talk. And act natural, as if nothing has happened."

"Well, nothing has happened, darling, except a fabulous dinner. Have you ever had steamed sea urchins?"

"No, thank God, I haven't."

"Well, then you are missing a most scrumptious treat."

"One can't have everything."

"Got to go. See you at Chumley's!"

Before Mr. Benchley and I taxied down to the Village, I dialed the police station and asked for Detective Sparrow. He was not at his desk, so I asked to speak to Sgt. Joe Woollcott, who was on duty this evening. The officer who answered the call told me that Joe was taking a late dinner break but should return momentarily, as he was just across the street picking up Chinese food from the Golden Pagoda.

"They deliver now, you know," I informed the officer.

"I didn't know that! When did that start?"

I remembered seeing the boy on the delivery tricycle the day of the bank heist. "I don't know, but they do now."

"Well, Joe can use the exercise crossing the street. Oh, here he is; he just walked in. Chop Suey and fried rice and—"

What followed was the clanking of the receiver on the desk, the voices of half-a-dozen starving policemen rushing around, and what sounded like the crumpling of paper bags. Finally, Joe's voice.

"It's Dottie. Dottie Parker, Joe."

"Is everything all right? Is Aleck okay?"

"He's fine, Joe. I'm—"

"That's a relief. The other day I saw him stuffing his face with that cake Gino makes—a cassata? He sure loves that Italian cheesecake—but you'd think he was a condemned man eating his last meal. I thought you were calling to tell me he'd dropped dead or something."

"Not yet, Joe, but you'll be the first I call. I need to find Detective Sparrow."

"Sparrow's downtown, Dottie."

"He got the search warrant?"

"Looking for a judge. It's the last Thursday of the month, so that means the police chief's poker game down at headquarters. Couple judges there. Hey, Mel, hand me over that soy sauce. . . . Okay, what do you want I should tell him?"

"If he telephones in or comes back, whichever comes first, tell him that he needs to get down to Chumley's—the speakeasy on Bedford Street. That's where he can arrest the Murder Club Killer."

"What! Did you say you have the killer?"

"Tell him what I said. Oh, and Joe? There was a typewriter ribbon that was being—"

"Hold the line a sec . . ."

After what sounded like a mad scramble of shuffling feet and vocal protestations, and knocks and thumps assaulting the telephone receiver, Joe came back on the line to say he had to hang up to book an arrest. The line went dead.

Chumley's opened a couple of years ago. Its proprietor is an Englishman with definite socialist leanings. I'd heard talk about its intellectual patronage, of course. It is a regular hotbed of sedition, and, according to our friends, Bunny Wilson and John Dos Passos, who hold Marxist views, The Pen and Frog Society has regular meetings on the second floor, accessed through the one-person dumbwaiter behind the toiletry shelves in the ladies' room. And it is upstairs where the plot to overthrow the U.S. government is always on the agenda.

Of course the front for sedition is another illegal venture, and although the police know nothing of the treasonous activities being conducted on the second floor, they are well aware of the variety of "tea" being served downstairs. Why, all a cop with a thirst for gin needs to do is stop in and ask for an "English tea." If he prefers Seagram's 7, he just asks for "Canadian tea." The "Tennessee tea" will get you a Jack Daniels in a porcelain teacup. It's the real stuff, too, and the cops show their appreciation by placing a timely telephone call to the management when they know the Feds are on their way for a visit.

So when Mr. Benchley, Woodrow, and I, who had never been inside the place, arrived by taxi on the corner of Bedford Street we had to look around a bit. There was no number 86 scrawled on any of the building façades, but after a while, with a little bit of deductive reasoning, we spotted the gated alleyway.

We walked through a tall, wrought-iron gate in the archway, through a narrow alley between two buildings that opened into a small courtyard. Just ahead was an arched wooden door. We knocked and a square wooden panel slid to the side and an eye stared out at us. We didn't know the password, but Mr. Benchley said we were meeting Trevor Hunter. There was the grating of metal on metal as the bolt was drawn and the door was opened to us.

The long, shiny mahogany bar faced the entry and was packed three people deep. Beyond were booths lined up like little stable pens in the main room. These were filled with patrons, some loudly animated, laughing, celebrating, some in the dumps, depressed, but all literally "in their cups." A narrow shelf just wide enough for cups and ashtrays lined the right and left walls of the dimly lit smoke-hazed room, and people were standing along the circumference chatting and drinking and indulging in a variety of inhalants.

Woodrow looked up at me and let out an anxiety-ridden yawn. Mr. Benchley followed his example. "These late hours, you know," he said in lieu of apology.

Through the diffused, orangey glow of the room we searched for Soledad and Trevor Hunter to no avail. But then I spotted Stephen Shaw exiting the ladies' room. *Of course,* I thought, *the ladies' room.* He was a perfect fit for Pen and Frog membership. I wondered if he really believed in all the radical propaganda and condoned the violence that the fellows upstairs proposed. It was one thing to believe in and fight for social justice, to help advance great social causes such as the Labor Movement, but was he in it because he held these principles to heart, or solely because his battling nature led him anywhere he'd have the pleasure of a fight?

He made eye contact and ambled over to us. We said hello and asked if he had seen Trevor Hunter.

"He was here, but now he's gone," he stated matter-of-factly, and then he signaled the waiter and insisted on buying us a round. Before we had a chance to pursue the whereabouts of Hunter and Soledad, he said, almost accusatorily: "You two are friends with that pussy, Dos Passos."

"Well," I said, "he has a descriptor for you, too."

"I guess he does, I guess he does!" he sputtered out, and bellowed with laughter, which choked in his throat. He coughed and hacked and the noisy sputum rattled in his throat. From his searching eyes I figured he was looking for a spittoon. Finding none, he spit into a filthy handkerchief pulled from his pocket, and behaved generally unhygienically.

"Looking for Hunter, are you?" he said. "I wouldn't bother. He was hanging onto a fine piece of ass when he left."

"That was our friend, Soledad Soleil, the famous mystery writer," said Mr. Benchley with outraged haughtiness. "I'll ask you to refrain—"

"And *she* has a descriptor for *you*, too," I said, "and it ain't good."

"You are a little firecracker, aren't you?"

Just as I was about to level him with something devastating that would have had him running to a dictionary or the *Funk & Wagnalls*, Mr. Benchley put space between me and Shaw and came nose-to-nose with him.

"All right, enough!"

Woodrow growled.

I liked Mr. Benchley's authority, and Woodrow's daring, but I was afraid that Shaw's steady, amused glare was just the precursor of a messy cleanup on aisle six.

"Where'd they go?" said Mr. Benchley, not backing away.

"He said he wanted to show her something," he leered and raised an eyebrow, "and I figured he meant—"

"Yes?" challenged my friend.

Shaw thought better, or found us too tedious to bother with.

"I have no idea."

"That's grand."

"He said it was just around the corner on Barrow Street."

Of course, it dawned on me, *Chumley's is in close proximity to Hunter's lair.*

Without a word spoken, Mr. Benchley settled our bill with the waiter. I turned to Shaw—I couldn't resist: "Your life is in danger, Shaw. You need to get into protective custody right away. Then again, perhaps for the sake of all that is good, forget it."

Woodrow Wilson sprang eagerly out through the door and into the courtyard. He sneezed and shook his wiry body in a gesture of "good-riddance," and led the way through the narrow alley and up the street to Barrow.

The door of the apartment was opened wide to reveal Trevor Hunter sprawled in the middle of the room, the secret panel to the laboratory a gaping dark square in the wall. Woodrow stood warily at the door. I dropped his leash, and while Mr. Benchley checked for signs of life in Hunter I called out to Soledad, making my way into the lab, groping around before finally finding the light chain. She was not there. Sirens whined in the distance, and soon there was the heavy tread of multiple feet on the stair. Policemen entered and took in the bloody scene.

"He's alive," Mr. Benchley told them as they assessed Hunter's condition.

"You two," ordered a burly cop, "stand outside. MacArthur, keep an eye on these two."

Realizing that the cop in charge thought we must be responsible for the man lying prone on the floor, Mr. Benchley said, "We just found him like that."

"Right. MacArthur, take them downstairs and lock them in the squad car. *And* their little dog, too."

"But, you don't understand—" I objected, before being roughly led out into the hallway.

"Dey din't do it," said a smoke-graveled voice. It belonged to the mother of the fresh kid we had encountered here earlier.

"*Oh, yeah?* What do you know about this?"

'Oy made da cawl, whaddaya tink? Oy hoid da woman yellin' and den da gunshot."

"This woman?"

"*Nah*, not huh. Da *tawl* one, da movie stawr type."

"Soledad!"

"Oy cawled da cops. Oy noo dat guy's crayzy, but she'n da udda guy ran outta heah. *Dey* shot 'im."

"Did you get a look at their faces?"

"Wat, ya tink Oy'm crayzy, too? Dey wudd'a shot me! *Nah.* But Oy saw dem from da window. Oy seen 'im—da man—befowuh comin' 'ere ta see dis guy. Yeah, Oy saw 'im. He wuz pushin' huh down da shtreet. He hadda gun. Oy saw da gun."

"All right, said the burly cop in charge, and then ordered another policeman to take the woman's statement, just as Detective Nate Sparrow appeared on the landing, followed by three officers from the Eighteenth.

After conferring with the cop on the scene, he told the officers to let us go. "Mrs. Parker and Mr. Benchley are taking part in the investigation of the Murder Club Killings."

Mr. Benchley looked at me with astonishment. "This is the first time we've ever gotten off so easily, Mrs. Parker."

"It's the first time we've ever been *official*, Mr. Benchley."

"I suppose our rebellion against authority finally had to come to an end, my dear."

"You mean we're part of the *system*, now? Part of the grand social *problem?*" Oh, dear, oh, dear."

"Alas, it was bound to happen. After all, how old are we now?"

Another siren shrieked through the quiet neighborhood and abruptly ended its shrill blast outside the window. White coats of the ambulance corps barged into the apartment.

"Cancel the coroner," said the burly cop as Trevor Hunter was gingerly shifted onto a stretcher.

Hunter moaned, reviving consciousness, and he looked at us and the others in the room. When it dawned on him what had happened, his eyes widened beneath the heavy brows and he tried to lift his head, but fell back in pain from the gunshot to his shoulder and the crack on his head when he had fallen back and hit the edge of the desk. It was the impact that had knocked him out.

"Soledad!" he spoke out haltingly, and he pressed his eyelids closed and grimaced. "Anthony . . ."

"Was it Young who shot you?"

"He was here when . . . when we got here . . . show her my lab. He was . . . in my . . . there —" he indicated the laboratory. "He was . . ."

Another, more pressing concern interrupted his flow of information. "He took her? Soledad?"

"It appears so," said Detective Sparrow, and the burly cop nodded agreement.

"She's in danger . . . Anthony Young, he killed—" he said before passing out.

It was after four o'clock in the morning. Mr. Benchley and I were sitting on a small sofa in a waiting room at Bellevue Hospital waiting for the doctors to allow us to see Trevor Hunter. Woodrow was gently snoring at my feet and the rhythm of his breathing had the hypnotizing effect of sending me into unconsciousness. I awoke with a jolt when Mr. Benchley's head landed with a thud on my lap. We looked angrily at one another, and then, aware that there were others in the room, our responses fell silent.

"A heartwarming Skid Row scene," said Detective Sparrow as Mr. Benchley and I moved apart. I wiped the dribble from my chin and quickly rearranged the disarray of my apparel. I bent down to straighten my seams and to put on my shoes and noticed that Mr. Benchley's socks had fallen down around his ankles. When I poked him and pointed to his feet, he took it as a complaint, but bent down to pull them up. Nearly strangling himself, it took Mr. Benchley a long moment to understand the cause of the resistance. He unhooked his elbow from the loosened noose of his tie.

"Can we see him?" I asked the detective, who had stooped to his knees to pet my snoozing pup.

"How did you manage to get Woodrow in here?"

"I have ways. I've taught him how *not* to click his nails on polished floors. So, can we speak with Hunter? He may have some idea where Young might have taken Soledad."

"I already have, briefly."

"Why didn't you wake us, detective?"

"He doesn't know where they could have gone. I spoke with him when he regained consciousness and before he was given the anesthetic so they could dig out the bullet from his shoulder. He told me that he and Miss Soleil had surprised Anthony Young, who had broken into the place and was helping himself to the poisonous substances on the shelves of Hunter's laboratory. When Hunter objected to the violation, Young began to push and shove, and tried to strangle Hunter. Miss Soleil slammed a badminton racket over Young's head, which went through the net. And she had the presence of mind to yank the handle hard. This sent Young crashing into the gun cabinet, where he pulled out a loaded Winchester. When Hunter lunged for him, Young shot him, grabbed Miss Soleil, and used her as a shield to get out of the apartment. I've sent men around to Anthony Young's Ninth Street townhouse. He never returned there."

"He's on the run with Soledad as his hostage, if he hasn't killed her already!"

"Let's hope he left her tied up somewhere."

"Yes, let's," I said with sarcasm dripping from my words. "For *God's* sake!" I added angrily.

"Listen," said Detective Sparrow, "we have alerts all over the city—the bridges, the train stations, the bus terminal—"

"He's smarter than that. He'll hole up somewhere in the city."

"I don't think so. He's a frightened man, and that sort gets reckless. He'll find a way out of town. We just have to figure out how, when he plans to do it, and where he's going to go."

"Got a crystal ball?" I said impatiently.

"Miss Soleil appears to be a smart lady. Smart enough to get away from this man. In the meantime, I think you might want to read this."

Mr. Benchley took the typewritten report from the detective and said, "This is what was on the type-writer ribbon?"

"Good thing it's an old machine and he used a single-stroke ribbon. Now we know what Ernest Stringer was so carefully guarding. It's an indictment of sorts—far from a complete one, however. It doesn't exactly say—well, read it, and you'll see what I mean."

Chapter Thirteen

Fall 1927

Two years ago. . . .

Six authors we were, and of the others, I had only slightly known Mark Wendt of the cowboy books, whom I had met briefly at a book party, and Daniel Cousins, who signed on with Niles Pickering around the time I did.

I'd see Cousins at the cafe I liked to go to down on Bleeker Street to write and chat with other writers and artists. Aside from an occasional short story, he had had nothing published three years after his first book came out. Neither had I. When I'd see him at the cafe, I'd invite him to join me. He was a pleasant fellow, but there was something about him. Cousins played things close to the vest.

Mark Wendt was a quiet man who was enjoying a string of successes with his adventures out West, but I had heard through a friend that he wanted to be taken seriously as an author, and one day, while I was at Romany Marie's during the fall of '27, I looked up from my notebook to see him approaching my table. He smiled and asked if I remembered him, which, of course I did, so I pulled out a chair.

After the usual pleasantries, we talked about Niles Pickering's death, and he mentioned that Niles had not renewed his contract with him. I admitted I had been dealt the same hand, but I said I was surprised that Pickering would let go of such a prolific -as well as profitable- author such as he. Creative differences, he said; he refused to write any more cowboy books. Because of his candor, I suppose, I confessed to Wendt that I was at a standstill in my career. I hadn't produced anything anybody wanted for several years, other than a few short stories for small magazines, since my first and only novel of five years ago. I was reticent about talking about my situation. I, like Cousins, kept things close to the vest, and when he asked how I managed without a steady income, I didn't tell him about the other, less salubrious fare I had been hacking out for Jim Morrow that kept food in my mouth and a roof over my head. Mark said that he greatly admired the book Pickering had published years ago, and that it was better than most of what he'd seen published lately, and he wished he could write as well as I.

I was shocked. Here was a man entertaining thousands of readers with book after book, while I was just a one-shot deal, a flash in the pan with one bestseller because I just couldn't pull myself together to write anything else worth publishing. Mark Wendt said he "wanted to be more"; he wanted to be an artist like me. I found his admission flattering but disconcerting. He'd found a niche and was a success; I was struggling and had no real vision. I felt ashamed for not telling him how low I'd come but I kept mum.

Anthony Young used to stop in at Marie's sometimes in the evening and one time he was holding forth like the avuncular professor he was to several young aspiring writers about a murder case he had read about in the newspapers that intrigued him, a conversation that I happened to overhear from the next table. Somehow I was drawn in and several hours later, after the young people had gone, we continued our discussion over whiskey at Chumley's.

I found Anthony Young to be a charming raconteur, very learned and far more astute than his mystery series suggested. The rather prissy effeteness Anthony presented to the world seemed to melt away in the light of his kindness and intelligence.

We were so very different from one another. The faces we presented to the world were in sharp contrast. I was scruffy and serious; he was meticulous and lighthearted. I was the pessimist; he, the optimist. I liked the man tremendously, and it was mutual, I believe, because I wished in many ways to be more like him, to emulate his self-confidence, and to embrace the good fellowship he naturally projected, and he seemed to admire my dedication to the literary arts and my ambition to write the Great American Novel. I imagined that when he looked at me, he had confidence in me, that I would one day achieve my goal. This is a rare thing to be had from another author, in a business that is cutthroat and money focused, and a great gift from an

author as successful as he. It raised a
newborn confidence within me, which was
heady and inspiring and renewed my hope
for the future.

It was very late and while we drank in
a darkish corner of the near-empty speak,
in walked Stephen Shaw accompanied by
Trevor Hunter. Shaw saw us, and wanting
nothing to do with us, threw a savage look
our way - I could see his obvious contempt
for Anthony - and so he sidled up to the
bar.

Hunter, I knew casually. I'd see him at
Marie's having dinner with Bucky Fuller,
who I always thought was a pretentious prick
who took advantage of the cafe proprietress
with his costly and ridiculous decorations
of her place, which had to go finally because
of their lack of functionality. I didn't
think Fuller, who projected the image of
the great _artiste_, deserved the free meals
he was fed there. So, because of my dislike
for Bucky Fuller, I had nothing much to do
with his friend, Trevor Hunter.

But, when Hunter caught sight of us he
came over to say hello. I suspected that
as Anthony Young and I were in deep
philosophical discussion, what Hunter
really wanted was to find out what we

were talking about. Any amusement would have trumped Shaw's blathering political observations, I'm sure. For they were an odd couple, Shaw and Hunter: the rabble-rouser and the sophisticated intellectual.

I had no real opinion of Trevor Hunter; he always struck me as a dark soul, the impression fostered by the thick black brows that dominated his face and the high white forehead that suggested a superior intelligence. I was to learn that his face didn't quite depict the man accurately.

It turned out that Young knew Hunter quite well. His affiliation as a student of Conan Doyle prompted Niles Pickering, who had been publisher to all of us, to suggest that Young consult Hunter on occasion when researching his mystery novels. I learned sometime later from Anthony that Hunter was quite generous with his knowledge of drugs and forensics. And this association eventually became a friendship. It was Hunter who taught Young how to fly an aeroplane, a hobby that was to become a great passion for him, and it was Young who oversaw the magnificent renovation of the dreary townhouse on Washington Square that Hunter took over after his father died.

Shaw left at the bar and having imbibed too much over the course of the evening – he was quite drunk – bounded over to our table, his nose out of joint. I suppose he felt slighted at Hunter's abandonment of him, and he carried his effrontery over to our table. Hunter bought a round of drinks and managed to placate Shaw with outrageous comments alluding to Shaw's genius. I knew what he was doing, even though I wondered why Hunter had even bothered to seek out the companionship of such a brutish character. I later found out they had met earlier in the evening downtown in a Chinatown opium den.

Hunter was well aware of Shaw's paranoid and confrontational nature: Shaw once accused a bartender fifty feet across a room of talking derisively about him to a girl sitting at the bar with her fiance. The bartender had never seen Shaw before in his life, and was surprised when the brawny bear suddenly bolted at him full speed from across the room to leap the bar and pummel him mercilessly, before a dozen men pulled him off.

I can't say exactly at which moment our discussion suddenly shifted from Shaw's recitation of his numerous complaints

- those on the grand scale of American politics on down to his own petty, personal gripes, real or imagined - but suddenly the four of us were engaged in a discourse on revenge.

Hunter cited references in the Hebrew Bible to "an eye for an eye" as not meant to be taken literally, according to rabbinic teachings, rather that such injury demands monetary compensation equal to the value of the loss. "Do not seek revenge." "Love your neighbor as yourself." Forgiveness of indiscretions, of injuries inflicted is the goal of man, as "Vengeance is mine," saith the Lord.

Young spoke of seeking vengeance as the great theme in literature, from the affinity for revenge in Greek Tragedy, and the extremes of Medea's madness, to Hamlet's retribution of his father's murder and Othello's betrayal and his jealous rage, to the horror of Poe's stories.

"There are those I could kill," said Shaw, nodding slowly, teeth bared, and I saw the glint of his steely eyes in the dimly lit room and imagined he was choosing his victims right at that moment, and that Anthony Young was on his list. The zeal with which he spoke held a vile intent, and sent a prescient shiver through me. I remember thinking, if ever there was a man who would kill for the thrill of it, it was Shaw.

Making light of his remark, I said, "How would you do the deed? A poisoned coronet as Medea might have done, or a stab in the back?"

Anthony Young gave out a hollow laugh before stating, "The first is more efficient; the second far too bloody."

Shaw leaned his big chest across the table and brought his dark face close to Anthony's and hissed through a grimace of delight, "Ah, but spilled blood is so much more satisfying."

"Poison is for the faint of heart, I suppose," said Anthony, trying to recover from Shaw's scrutiny. The heavy odor of stale whiskey, spent tobacco, traces of opium smoke, and unwashed flesh accosted Shaw's antithesis, the obsessively tidy professor.

Anthony rose from the table and nervously set about retrieving his coat and hat, fished some money from his billfold and placed the bills down before me, babbling words to the effect that it was very late and there were appointments in the morning, and so on, and then he strode quickly out of the speak.

Shaw sat back wearing a self-satisfied grin, having properly unnerved Anthony Young. Shaw's behavior had sunk even further my previously low estimation of him. He had brazenly pushed his way into our discussion, commandeered it, and before very long became its critic.

After some minutes, Hunter stood up to leave, and not wanting to be left alone with Shaw, I settled the bill and walked home through the first snowfall of the season. Occasionally, I would turn to look over my shoulder, sensing that Shaw was following, but I could see him talking animatedly with Hunter as the two passed under a streetlamp a block distant from the door of the speakeasy. The man unsettled me.

One evening, a few weeks later, I ran into Daniel Cousins and Mark Wendt at Romany Marie's, and somewhere along the line, Mark talked about wanting to write a mystery novel. Daniel listened for a bit and then said, "You know, I think I need a plan, boys. A plan to write within the constraints of what is called these days a genre. Maybe mystery writing is the way." I told him about my talk with Anthony Young and suggested that he and Mark ask Anthony about the unique process of writing a mystery story.

The following evening, Anthony Young agreed to meet with me and Cousins and Wendt, at my request. He appeared to relish his role as teacher. He arrived with Trevor Hunter, which was just fine, too. Young always appeared quite free of professional envy, and had asked Hunter to join him for the evening and to share with the young writers his insights into the creation of mystery stories. As the Conan Doyle apostolate was the next best thing to Doyle himself, Trevor Hunter was warmly welcomed. And Hunter was quite charming and forthcoming. We engaged in a short discourse, and then, as the evening progressed and the noise of the cafe became intolerable for conversation, Anthony suggested we continue our talk in the comfort of his 9th Street brownstone.

And so our get-togethers continued over the next few months. We'd meet for dinner at Marie's and then we'd walk over to Anthony's house. We would freely, trustingly discuss ideas for plots. Cousins was always reticent, although he was very astute and offered the occasional suggestion for untangling unexpected snags in any scenario. We all enjoyed these sessions, and surprisingly, thanks to Anthony, we all left our egos at the door. The life of a writer is often lonely, but soon we became each other's sounding boards and this helped tremendously in our personal instruction. Even Anthony admitted that he was becoming a better technician in the art of mystery writing.

Things changed one sultry night in July of 1928.

Manhattan was a furnace, and the night we all met at Marie's, we took a table outside under the vines on the "back porch," as Marie liked to call the little courtyard. Other than a hanging lantern pooling light over our table, the area was swallowed up in shadows cast by the mulberry tree at the courtyard's center. We were the only customers remaining outside when we finished our meals, or so we thought.

Trevor Hunter had brought a bottle of gin he had distilled in his "lab," which we all assumed was a euphemism for a still in his bathtub. Marie didn't serve liquor - there were too many people who would have turned her in to the Feds to get rid of her "bohemian influence" from the neighborhood - a neighborhood that had long been aesthetically bohemian in nature. But tonight we were outside in the dark, not inside the cafe proper, and if the Feds decided to raid Marie's that night, which was unlikely, we'd smash the bottle on the brick pavers to get rid of the evidence.

We decided to remain there for our talk rather than going to Anthony's after we'd eaten. The air was cooler under the vines and under the canopy of the mulberry tree. There was a slatted wooden bench built around the tree's circumference and, above, supported between its limbs, a landing of wood, like a tree house, which was reached by means of a ladder.

We asked Marie for glasses and ice and we five sat back and talked, not about our writings, but about the business of writing: publishers, agents, lawyers, and all the compromises artists are expected to make.

I suppose the change in venue may have prompted a more relaxed discussion, along with the gin, which loosened our tongues, and the cooler evening air that served as balm to our feverish brows after the stifling heat of the day. It was on this night that Cousins decided to tell us about the theft of his work by Mycroft Publishing.

This was not exactly news to any of us. And although we didn't know all of the details before Cousins laid out the story - the names of the culprits involved - rumor had it that the dry spell Daniel Cousins was suffering and his fear of showing anybody his work were the result of his ineffectual accusations of plagiarism against a publisher. Hunter commented that although there were a number of unscrupulous people in the publishing world, it was unlikely to happen to Daniel again. "Anyway, Daniel," he assured him, "we are all friends here; you are safe with us. We are witnesses on your behalf, should anyone in future try to claim your efforts as their own." We all smiled and nodded encouragement.

It was Mark Wendt, upon hearing the names of publisher Jim Morrow and the accused plagiaristic author, Frederick Feldman, who dropped the bomb about the men's suspected affair. These new revelations were bandied about among us for a time like gossip at a ladies' garden party. Although I was not born yesterday, and the Lord knows no better than I the goings-on at boys' prep schools and universities and the shenanigans of Broadway chorus boys, Mark Wendt's new and lurid tidbit about the men's sexual peccadilloes appeared to actually release something in Cousins, although I cannot say just how or why he was set free. His spirits were raised, and I chalked it up to the idea that he now felt his claim of plagiarism justified; his accusation was proven at last, as if the men's deviant sexual behavior, their depravity, attested to their crime against him.

And then Daniel Cousins said savagely, "I could kill those fucking bastards!"

"Daniel!" I protested with a nervous laugh. His vehemence had startled me, albeit justified from his point of view.

"Yes, I could kill them – if only I could get away with it!"

"If only," repeated Anthony. "_If only!_ Those are words pregnant with possibility; words, too, heavy with regret. If only...."

"You should write a book, Daniel – a fiction book about this," said Wendt. "I mean fiction – the names are changed to protect the blah-blah-blah."

"You can make it a murder mystery, Daniel," said Anthony Young, encouraging him. "Yes, you <u>must</u> write it as a murder mystery."

"Yes! Murder, of course," said Mark Wendt. "Write it in the first person."

"Who gets killed?" asked Daniel Cousins.

"Oh, you kill the publisher and the writer, of course. Very satisfying for you. Revenge in absentia, so to speak," said Anthony.

"I'll bet there are a dozen possible twists on that one!" I said.

"Yes," agreed Anthony Young, "take your pick, boy: Writer kills plagiarist author or plagiarist author kills the writer of the original work. Whoever does what to whom winds up trying to prove his innocence."

"Or," interrupted Hunter, "there is the blackmail scheme that leads to murder. Decide who blackmails whom, of course. You have sex and passion and money and fame and greed and revenge – "

"Not to mention suspense," said Anthony Young.

"But, now that you have a theme, it's only a springboard, Daniel," I remember saying that to encourage him. And I remember feeling encouraged about my own work suddenly. If only I could find a story - perhaps something from my own life that could be the catalyst for a book. I knew it was out there, and I would find it, something that would excite me, ignite me, so I was feeling very generous toward my fellow writer this evening.

Daniel Cousins smiled a grateful, pathetic little smile that barely turned up his lips. "Yes," he said quietly, "it is a basis for a good story. I can see it. I think I could even do a good job of it. But, I might just go mad replaying in my head what these men did to me. But, if I killed them first, got my revenge, then I could write my story without going mad!"

"Yes, Daniel, and then after you've published your story, you do understand that the police will come and arrest you for murder?" said Anthony Young with a chuckle.

"Well," said Mark Wendt, "he'll sell more books if he's a notorious killer."

"Sometimes I'm not sure what's more important to me: a career as a successful author, or getting even with the bastards who screwed me over."

"Sure you do," a voice rang out from the dark regions of the courtyard, and I turned, thinking it was Marie or her husband, the chef, come out to us from the kitchen door. It was a familiar voice, with a booming sure-and-cocky ring to it. Stephen Shaw stepped out from the shadows like an apparition and walked toward us from behind the trunk of the mulberry tree. He stopped just short of total illumination from the hanging lantern and his hulking presence was disconcerting. Hamlet's Father's ghost came to mind with a frightening twist: This ghost of a forsaken netherworld was an errant soul clinging to the world of the living. Despite the heat of the night an icy chill ran through me.

"You'll never be free until you know retribution," he said.

Cousins, whose back was to the tree, stiffened and turned sharply at the sound of Shaw's voice. I could swear I saw the hair rise up on the back of his neck. Anthony Young's flaccid jowls quivered in a double-take.

Shaw stepped into the pool of light. "Whose cock do I have to suck to get a drink around here?"

"Nobody's I want to know, Shaw," Hunter chortled. "How long have you been playing with yourself out there in the dark, you damn pervert?"

"Long enough to know this man's got a hard-on he's got to tend to before he can set down to work." He patted Daniel's shoulder, and I watched him cringe and shrink under Shaw's hand.

Stephen Shaw grabbed a chair from a vacant table and in one sweep brought it to rest between Cousins and Young. Hunter filled his own glass with gin and pushed it across the table toward Shaw, who knocked it back in one fast swig. Shaw exhaled a loud grunt and smacked his lips, considered the empty glass as if assessing the quality of the liquor before passing it back to Hunter for another round.

Again, he knocked back the liquor, and then said: "How do you kill a man and not get caught?" I knew he was serious in spite of the mocking cackle he emitted before downing the dregs of the glass.

Breaking the heavy silence that had fallen over the table, Hunter said, "That's the rub."

"Yeah, well, if you haven't the balls to make them pay with their lives, why not make them pay from their pockets?"

"Blackmail?" I spurted out, unaware I had spoken my thoughts aloud.

"Sure, sure! You got the dirt on them queers, now, don't you, Daniel?"

"Forget it, Stephen," said Hunter. "Things rarely fare well for the blackmailer."

"Yeah, it's true. You have to have heart - and balls - to run a scheme like that, and our Daniel here hasn't got the heart or the balls for such a venture. Killing is better. But how to do it?"

"Have you ever killed a man, Shaw?" I asked, and almost immediately regretted the question.

What compelled me to speak? I didn't really want to hear his confession and know of his deeds; I wanted no part of Stephen Shaw, and I knew that any association with him would only lead to trouble. I wanted to bolt out of the courtyard. What had been a most pleasant evening had suddenly turned menacing with his arrival. But, I kept my seat, as if tied to it by invisible, inescapable bonds. Shaw looked me over, a cunning leer in place of a smile. He nodded, ambiguously. He was not about to reveal any of his secrets.

And then he turned his attention on Anthony Young, and I could see the history professor back away, imperceptibly, from Shaw's foul breath. I realized then how terrified he was of the man, and that try as he might to hold his ground under the scrutiny of Shaw's eyes, his fear did not abate. I heard his unconscious and sharp intake of air and the nearly inaudible little whinnying that escaped his lips.

Shaw heard it, too, for he laughed and turning his attention on his empty glass said, "Tony, Tony, Tony . . ."

"What's that all about?" spat out Young, spittle flying across the glaring light from the lantern, a rash instantly appearing over his collar, moving up like a tide along his jowls to his cheeks. He shifted in his seat and with a show of indignant objection stated, "What in God's name do you want, man!"

"Well, now, Tony, there's no need to get all hot and bothered. You, more than anyone here, can relate to the, uh . . . the raping Danny took - "

"Shut the hell up, you despicable thing!"

"But what have you ever done about it, I ask you, now?"

"I order you to stop!" yelled Young, bolting from his chair and sending it crashing into the table behind ours.

"Really, Shaw," said Hunter, "you're such a bully sometimes."

"I will not remain as long as this - this -"

"Sit down, Anthony," said Hunter with great authority. "Stephen, if you want to stay, show some respect."

"I have nothing but respect for Tony, here. He, more than anyone at this table, has known great success through his mystery novels, if that's the kind of book one wants to write, of course: a middling entertainment for the middling mind."

"That's a backhanded compliment, if ever I heard one," said Mark Wendt. "Odd, don't you think, that we're all gathered here tonight to learn how exactly to create what you call middling entertainment!"

Daniel Cousins snickered and said, "At least Tony doesn't get sued and brought to court for defamation like some muckrakers I can think of."

"All right, boys, I can see how you might want to defend the professor over there.

He's not a bad sort, that I know. And he's
stood up to me, so I have to credit him with
that, I suppose," said Shaw, nodding and
lighting a cigarette, smiling all the while.
He stuck out his hand to Anthony Young,
as a gesture of peace. Anthony looked at
it: the hairy wrist, the bulbous sinews, the
knotty knuckles, the blunted fingertips.
A more attractive claw was the talon of a
hawk. But, then, of course, in spite of the
dubious offer of peace, Shaw _was_ a hawk,
and Young was always intended to be his
prey.

Anthony Young turned away with a look of
disgust, retrieved his chair, and resumed
his place at the table. I offered him a
cigarette, which he took, and I lit it for
him, steadying his trembling hand as I held
the match.

Shaw's appearance had put a damper on the
evening, but not to give him the advantage
of having driven us off, we remained a few
minutes longer talking about nothing of
any consequence.

Throughout the summer we met weekly
at Marie's, and we remained in the cool
courtyard after dinner. Shaw invariably
would show up late in the evening, but now

he behaved quite civilly toward Anthony
Young.   There was no more baiting or
insinuations toward any of us. It was a
complete reversal, and I chalked up Stephen
Shaw's past offenses as having been caused
by drunkenness and his opium habit.

Anthony Young weathered Shaw's abrasive
edge. He avoided direct eye contact with the
man, and it made me wonder what it was that
Shaw knew about him that disturbed Young
so.   I couldn't help thinking about the
confrontation that first night we spent in
Marie's courtyard when Shaw busted in, and
the comment linking Cousins' predicament
with something about Young.   He had
referred to Cousins' suffering plagiarism
as "rape," and he had implied the same had
occurred to Young. Odd choice of words
at the time, but eventually I would learn
the truth behind them. In the meantime,
I watched as Shaw became more solicitous
toward Young, which struck me as out of
character.

By the end of August, I saw a marked
changed in Anthony Young's demeanor. It
was difficult to put a finger on any one
thing that was different about him, but he
appeared more in command of himself, more
assured of his place of importance in what

we began to call our "Murder Club." He was, after all, at the heart of our group, and he was more than generous with his help as we began to weave our individual mystery stories. Soon, this tidy professor, impeccably attired in Brooks Brothers, who never before now had taken a step out of his townhouse without newly shined shoes, the crease of his trousers sharply pressed, and wearing a vest over an immaculately and stiffly starched collar and bowtie, began arriving at our summer dinners wearing boat-neck poloshirts under his linen suits and, of all things, a boater atop his head.

In the spirit of appreciation, I suggested that a young woman must have entered Young's life, and was sorry to have embarrassed the man, for he blushed, as was his cross to bear in life, and it was Hunter who spoke and explained that "the new book Tony had put to bed at the end of July was considered by his publisher to be a notable work of brilliance."

"I am beside myself with envy, Tony," lauded Hunter. "It is the work of a genius!"

The old fussy maiden-aunt persona that was so much a part of one's initial impression of Anthony Young had been abandoned, but for a brief moment it shone through when he twitched his mouth with false modesty at the praise and replied that if he had done anything at all that was good, it was because of the assistance of Trevor Hunter, who supplied him with all the forensic and scientific data he had needed for crafting his book, as well as the weekly support of his fellow club members.

"But, we don't even know what the book is about, Tony," said Daniel Cousins. "You never shared anything about it."

"Ah, yes, but you all inspired me to write it. You see, I have become fearless thanks to you all, and I have left the series that was so popular, so lucrative, to approach in this new book a more visceral study of vengeance."

"Tell us about it, Tony; what's the story about?" I asked.

"What is it about ... what is it about? It's about a man who waits nearly twenty years to have his revenge on the schoolboys who caused his humiliation, and how the crime he commits serves to heal his crippling wounds and sets his spirit free."

"Redemption through revenge?" I asked.

"Revenge is a dish best served cold?" asked Daniel Cousins.

"It makes for the perfect murder," nodded Young. "And do you know why?"

"I suppose," said Mark Wendt, "that a crime committed in the heat of the moment is likely to get one caught. But twenty years after the injury, well . . ."

"Yes, that is so," agreed Young. "As Daniel said, it is best served cold. It is the distance in time that can make all the difference, especially if you, the killer, have had no contact with your victim, no dealings whatsoever over the years, so that you are never even remotely considered a suspect in the murder. But, most importantly, if your victim's transgression against you all those years ago was an act so heinous, so despicable that he wished to forget what he had done, to bury it, and so had never dared to share what he did with another living soul, then who would ever suspect a ghost from the distant past being responsible for murder? There would be no motive against you, because your victim was never culpable as having committed the crime for which you sought revenge!"

"It does sound like a perfect crime," said Daniel Cousins, and I could see the wheels turning in his head. For Daniel had been hard at work on his new book, the book we had discussed early in the summer about a plagiaristic publisher and his lover. Our weekly meetings were his only time away from his typewriter, on which he pounded in the evenings and on weekends when not at his copy-editing job at <u>The Saturday Evening Post</u>. These days Daniel had the look of a driven man. He was no longer the meek, depressed, and hopeless fellow of half a year ago, but one determined to succeed. Daniel always came to us with questions, and now I could see his book plot shifting and a new scenario developing before his mind's eye.

"Congratulations, Tony," said Shaw, appearing late as had become his habit. I always felt that his tardiness was deliberate, that he was always lurking somewhere nearby, waiting for the moment to arrive in the conversation when he could most influence the discussion, if not disrupt it altogether.

"It sounds like you finally put your story down on paper," he said, and a pall fell over the table.

As everyone remained mute, unable to move, Shaw said, "It's all right, we're all friends here. No one's going to let this leave the table."

Anthony Young gathered his wits and with resigned acceptance said in a quiet, even voice, "It is how an injustice can be avenged."

I watched as Trevor's eyes widened at Anthony's proclamation and then narrowed as he scrutinized him. Silently, he rose from his chair and left us. He did not return.

It was from this moment on that everything changed. We were no longer simply writers crafting fictitious tales of murderers and their victims. It was our knowledge of the veracity of Anthony Young's murder plot that made us accessories to his crime. Little did I realize where all this would lead over the months following this revelation. Little did I know then the effect it would have on an impressionable man like Daniel Cousins, and how Mark Wendt, blind-sided by love that was suddenly and violently ripped from him when the woman he had loved was run down by an automobile, would come to discover that all that was left for him to hold onto was his plan of revenge. Revenge he was about to enact.

And I was not immune. I was not above seeking retribution against the man who had sunk me into a mire of pornography in order to survive, which meant the ruination of my career should my authorship ever come to light. A braggart who couldn't keep his mouth shut. And so it came to pass that I put my plan in motion.

The whiskey was meant for him, not his partner.

I killed the wrong man, and the loathsome one, Harvey Price, who should be dead now, thrives, having inherited a fortune in his partner's insurance money.

But then, I thought I could get the right man through blackmail. Yes, Shaw planted the idea in my head one hot summer night: <u>Make him pay, if not with his life, then from his pocket.</u>

For a time I thought the blackmail money would somehow compensate, and the plan was working. All I had to say was that I knew he had poisoned his partner, and an autopsy would prove it. I was protected by the members of my Murder Club. They were my alibi, as we stood together for each other. Harvey Price never called my bluff; he just paid.

I have wondered: If, as intended, Harvey Price had downed the liquor and not left his full glass on the side-table to take a telephone call while at his club, and had he returned instead of bolting out with just a message to his partner sent in by a steward on a tray, claiming that something had come up, or, if his partner, John Mitchell, would not have given a fig about discarding a double shot of imported single-malt whiskey, would I have been confessing this? I don't know.

But, I killed the wrong man.

That is my sin.

I had sunk into a mind-numbing despair. It was winter, February, and I couldn't bear to stay in the apartment a moment longer. It was late afternoon. It had been snowing since early morning, and the cold, clean white of it covered the dirty streets and lent a strange comfort as I trekked through Washington Square. The air was still; the traffic on Fifth was hushed, and if one listened, one could hear the crackle of flakes as they landed on one's shoulders. The bare branches of the park's rain trees were encased in white. There was no one about. As I walked, the park lights came on. It was dusk, and everything glowed with a crystalline shimmer. I decided what I needed to do.

I walked the few blocks to 9th Street. I walked up the stoop of Anthony Young's brownstone and rang the bell. He was surprised to see me, of course. My visit was unexpected, but Tony didn't mind. I was just in time for tea, he said, as he led me into the beautiful drawing room where a fire was crackling in the grate.

I wasn't sure how to

"What!" I whined, "'I wasn't sure how to'— *what?* Is that all there is?"

"It tells us a lot. It tells us that this bunch of crazies killed a lot of people."

"Yes," nodded Mr. Benchley, "but it doesn't tell us where Soledad is, and that's our most pressing concern."

"We picked up Stephen Shaw. And although there is nothing to say that he was directly or even indirectly involved with the murders performed by Daniel Cousins or Ernest Stringer or even Anthony Young, we are holding him as a material witness. He may be able to tell us where Young is likely to be hiding."

"It will be too late, Detective!" said Mr. Benchley. "This man has murdered before and one more murder won't mean much to him. To him Soledad is expendable."

We turned to face an angry Harpo Marx who stormed noisily into the waiting room followed by a very determined Alexander Woollcott.

"If we don't get our hands on Anthony Young soon," continued Mr. Benchley, who threw a glance over at the new arrivals, "I know someone who will."

"Lemme at 'im!" hissed Harpo.

"Wait!" I said, before anyone could say another word. "I think I know how he'll try to get out of town."

"Bus, bridge, boat, train, they're all covered, Mrs.—"

"No! Looking at my clown friend over here reminded me!" I smacked the sheaf of papers I had just read from. "Ernest Stringer just told us the *how*."

Trevor Hunter's house can be seen left of the Arch on Washington Square.

Writers' treehouse in Romany Marie's back courtyard

Ernest Stringer's typewriter

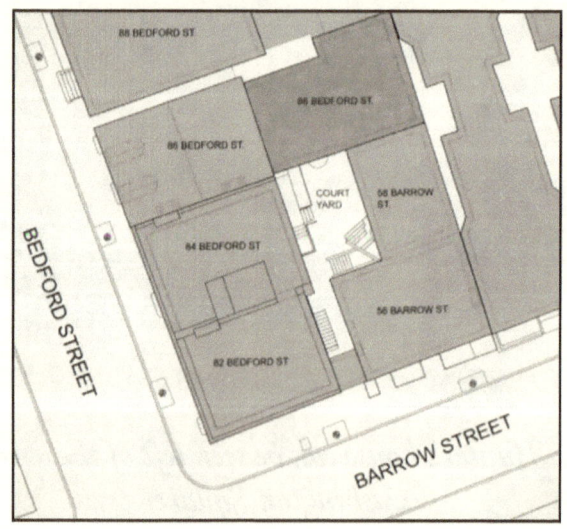

Chapter Fourteen

Advancing with a purple haze, and slashed with a pinprick of yellow light, dawn was breaking over the city. Buildings stood like dark sentinels against the brightening sky as our cars raced up the East River Drive to the 59th Street Bridge.

At first Detective Sparrow's squad car was in the lead as we crossed Manhattan, siren blaring, but once on the Drive, Harpo, impatient at the wheel of his new Caddy, pulled ahead of the line of three police vehicles. As we crossed over the bridge, his concentration on the road, we spoke little. Aleck was in the front passenger seat, Mr. Benchley and I, with Woodrow on my lap, in the back.

"Are you saying that Trevor Hunter had nothing to do with the murders of Ersatz and Wendt and Cousins?" asked Aleck.

"That's right, he didn't," I replied.

"And I don't believe he assisted the men in fulfilling their murderous vendettas against others," said Mr. Benchley.

"But the poisons in his laboratory!" objected Aleck.

"Just because he kept poisons doesn't mean he would use them to kill anybody," I said. "For goodness' sake, his father was a chemist and in the pharmaceutical manufacturing business; many of the vials there are part of his father's original lab. His mentor is Sir Arthur Conan Doyle, who has a poison stash of his own. Poisons are not always used to kill, you know. They are used in medicine, too."

"But, how—" began Aleck, and I preempted his question.

"Niles Pickering brought Anthony Young and Trevor Hunter together years ago. Since Trevor was the expert on all things lethal—poisons, rituals, and weaponry—as well as the forensic sciences, he shared his knowledge, which helped with the technical aspects of Young's mystery novels."

"But, how—" began Aleck again, and again I knew what he wanted to ask before he asked it.

"Good question, Aleck," I said. "You see, nobody knew about the laboratory. He kept the rooms on Barrow Street for his lab equipment and experiments, rather than having them in his townhouse on Washington Square. He camouflaged the lab's entry and kept it a secret because he knew the dangers of what he had there. He kept it secret from everybody except Anthony Young. He trusted his friend Tony."

"But—"

"No, he shouldn't have trusted him. The dates of the murders of the two surviving men of the students who tormented Young when he was at Harvard show that his were the first executions to be performed. Daniel Cousins must have gathered some confidence that he, too, could wreak revenge on his plagiarists. First he hangs Frederick Feldman, the author, and then he kills the man's lover, the publisher, Jim Morrow."

"I'll bet Cousins even typed the suicide note that was left when he killed Morrow," said Mr. Benchley.

"And then Ernest went about settling the score with Harvey Price—"

"But he didn't anticipate that a telephone call would take Price away from his cognac as well as from his club," said Mr. Benchley, "where he was having an after-dinner drink with his partner, John Mitchell. So Mitchell drops dead and Price receives a fortune in life insurance money."

I added, "Ersatz's last-ditch effort was to blackmail Price—even though the publisher didn't kill his partner—well, what jury would have believed

Price hadn't killed the man once Mitchell's body was exhumed to find the poison? An anonymous telephone call would have done him in. But the blackmail plan fizzled after a paltry payment of five thousand dollars to Ersatz because Price left the country, and Ersatz couldn't live with the knowledge that he'd killed an innocent man."

"Mark Wendt, now, he poisoned Welles at the Waldorf in retribution for his girlfriend's death by a hit-and-run," said Mr. Benchley. "That happened the day after Stringer died, you know?

"Maybe it was Wendt who posed as Trevor Hunter, wearing the deerstalker when he argued with Ersatz on the morning of his death, which conversation was overheard by Mrs. Vega. 'I'm going to the police,' was what Ersatz said, because he was riddled with guilt. Think about this: Ernest Stringer was left orphaned when his father killed his mother when he was very young. Can you imagine living with such a thing? He regretted what he did, I'll bet, not only for killing the wrong man, but for perpetuating the murderous legacy, a kind of madness, inherited from his father."

"Maybe it was Mark Wendt who slipped the poisoned allergy spray into Ersatz's pocket. Getting rid of Stringer gave Mark time to fulfill his mission to kill Welles."

"So," Aleck prefaced, waiting for another interruption. When there was only expectancy in our eyes, he continued: "Anthony Young, having grown brazen from two successful, let's say perfect, murders, tutored our three dead writers in how to perform the perfect crimes?"

"Yes," I said. "And he provided the poison, stolen from Trevor Hunter's laboratory."

"And Hunter claims he didn't know."

"If he suspected, I can't say. But how would he know about the murders of men hundreds of miles away from New York—and from each other—that were committed by Anthony Young? And Ernest Stringer killed the wrong man—few people knew about his pornography work and his gripe with Harvey Price. As for Cousins? Murder-suicide by the shamed men who screwed Daniel out of his work? And Wendt had yet to perform his deed of vengeance."

"But, Anthony Young killed the very men he was helping to achieve their crimes?" asked Aleck.

I said, "I think it was Wendt slipped the poison to Stringer."

"How can you be so sure?" asked Aleck.

"I'm not sure. Except that Mrs. Vega's description of 'Sherlock' was that of a tall, thin man. No limp. Hunter has a decided limp from a war wound. Cousins was short, Shaw, burly like a mean bear, and Anthony Young is a butterball. That leaves Mark Wendt—a tall, slim, onetime chorus boy and light on his feet."

"Then who killed Wendt?"

"Anthony Young killed Wendt and Cousins," I said. "After Stringer's poisoning brought attention to the club, Young had to make it appear that the club members were being targeted by some rejected and disgruntled author so that their crimes and his own would not be uncovered. It's also possible that Wendt and Cousins were beginning to break. Lots of weak links."

"But, you saw Trevor Hunter following Ersatz right before the bank robbery! How do you account for that?" said Aleck.

"Trevor Hunter told Detective Sparrow—when he awoke after surgery—that an hour before the bank heist, he'd received a frantic telephone call from Cherish Winter, wanting to know about the argument he'd just had with her man. He denied it, and he went out to track down Stringer. When he found him, Stringer accused Hunter of knowing all about the murders that the club members had committed. Hunter had his suspicions, of course. That's why he'd been gathering newsclippings about the deaths of people associated with his friends. Stringer was behaving oddly. He was incoherent, slurring his words, a symptom of poisoning that Hunter recognized. He was going to the police, he told Hunter, with the evidence he had, and when Stringer ran off Hunter followed him uptown on the subway. That's why I saw him following Stringer.

"When Stringer was shot, Hunter said he tried to help, but Stringer was already dead. Hunter got scared and he blended into the hysterical crowd, but only after taking the pages clutched in Stringer's hand. At the time, he didn't know what was in those papers."

"That makes him culpable," insisted Aleck. "And he destroyed evidence."

"But only Stringer was dead at the time," I replied, "and Hunter believed he may have poisoned himself. What Stringer wrote could be read as a confession of guilt, not unlike a suicide letter, you see? Hunter read Stringer's confession and realized his own culpability and the terrible consequences for his friends of the Murder Club. But he had murdered no one.

"He started an investigation of his own, based on the suspicions he had early on about his friend, Anthony Young, found out the names of the school-mates who had raped him, and learned the fate of two of them over the past year, one of whose wives was on trial for the murder of her husband by poison. He gathered news stories, built a case, and figured out what all the men of the club had been up to with their real-life murder schemes."

"Our Miss Cherish Winter lied to us," said Mr. Benchley. "She never mentioned her telephone conversation with Hunter, or the fact that when she had returned home, Mrs. Vega told her about the fight."

"She had her reasons. She really didn't know what was going on. I suppose she was trying to protect her man. Anyway, if she had told us about telephoning Hunter, we'd have been on the wrong path to finding the murderer."

Harpo veered off the ramp of the bridge and turned left, heading for Astoria Boulevard. The sirens behind us kept singing their song.

"How far away is this airstrip?" asked Aleck, as we zoomed past the factories lining the road, and then a series of storefront apartment buildings and residential side streets lined with new brick townhomes in the thousands.

"Ten more miles. Speed's Airstrip in College Point, near Whitestone," said Harpo. "Are you sure that's where Hunter keeps his aeroplane?"

"Yes, Harpo," said Mr. Benchley. "Detective Sparrow asked Hunter when Mrs. Parker figured Young would try to escape town by air. Hunter taught Young how to fly his biplane last year."

"It's where I keep my new plane, but I never saw either of them out there."

"You've just started flying, Harpo. Hunter hasn't been out flying since last summer."

"Wait till I get my hands on that Young!"

Detective Sparrow's squad car pulled around Harpo's to lead the way once again. We needed the siren to get through the gradually congesting intersections. Trolleys and trucks and cars were doing their morning scramble; children were crossing the roads to their schools. The sunlight was a direct and blinding beacon as we traveled east and onto the bridge crossing the inlet over Northern Boulevard; the marquee of the new Keith's-Albee Theater announced Bob Hope's appearance as we continued past the Flushing Bowling Green on Northern Boulevard. We passed the three-hundred-year-old Quaker Meeting House and then turned sharply left off the divided thoroughfare, past the campus whose sign read Flushing High School. It was all trees and big rambling Tudor houses until the scenery changed to open fields and the smell of low tide on Flushing Bay.

We drove onto a lonely road bordered with tall, waving marsh grass and nothing but sky above it. "Where the hell are we, Kansas? Looks like a Kansas wheatfield. If this is what a Kansas wheatfield looks like. I've never been to Kansas and its 'amber waves of grain,'" I babbled, nervously.

And then I saw the low structures up ahead, the hangars, and I knew we had arrived and that the showdown was about to happen. I was scared for Soledad.

"*Crap!*" yelled Harpo, and I bent my head to look out in the direction he indicated through the windshield. "That's *got* to be *him!*"

The sirens of the squad cars were cut, and Harpo hit the brakes so hard that I thought I'd fly out into the sky without any help from an aeroplane. Woodrow barked, sensing the urgency. As Harpo leaped from the car and ran to look up at the heavens along with the half-dozen cops following the progress of the biplane overhead, Woodrow escaped through the open car window.

For Harpo, there was only one thing to do, and his appeal to Detective Sparrow was not unheeded.

Harpo led his contingency of policemen to where his biplane rested off the tarmac. Woodrow, always ready to play, gave chase, assuming it was just another game. I called out to him, but he was having none of me, not when a football team was chasing the ball. I decided to let him have his fun. After all, there was no traffic and the field was wide open. But when Harpo mounted the cockpit of his aeroplane, Woodrow leaped onto the lower wing, barely three feet off the ground, and then, scrambling for a paw-hold, reached his front paws up for a grip on the fuselage.

No one paid Woodrow any mind, as one man repeatedly pulled down hard on the propeller and three others lifted the plane's tail. The propeller spun at last, and the engine engaged, so loud that no one could hear my calls, or hear the scratching of Woodrow's dangling hind paws seeking a grip on the sleek metal. As the plane started to lurch forward, I ran like a madwoman to retrieve my pup, who was dangling, unseen by Harpo, on the outside edge of the cockpit.

As Harpo turned the plane to taxi for takeoff, I had just about reached Woodrow, but not quite. I grabbed onto one of the crossbars connecting the upper-right wing to the lower, but the plane was charging ahead too quickly for me to step off.

"What!" shouted Harpo in the rear pilot's seat. The momentum prevented me from pulling my boy into my arms without risk of falling. All I could do was to bring up my foot to steady myself on the wing's connecting supports. Rather than slow down, Harpo waved at me to get in. I pushed up on Woodrow's rump, shoving him forcefully into the front seat.

I couldn't hear the screaming calls of the frantic men racing after the plane, for the noise of the motor. Nor did Harpo heed my ineffectual and barely audible little "whoops" as he accelerated down the runway. I had no choice but to climb into the forward cockpit and join Harpo for the ride.

We must have frightened him real good, because he was lifting one moment and bumping down hard the next before he raised the nose of the plane into the sky.

"Don't ask!" I shouted back to him. "It was a matter of death *now*, or death *later*. Dear God, please tell me you really know how to fly this contraption!"

I felt the sudden lift, and my legs went numb as my stomach fell into my feet. I looked down and saw the tiny figures of men and automobiles below, and nothing between me and the ground. And then my stomach leaped into my throat.

"Put on those goggles, and if you're going to be sick, lean out the side."

"Thanks. You're a prince," I shouted, and felt my bowels churn.

Woodrow's eyes narrowed against the wind—he was as happy as I've ever seen him.

The aeroplane dipped to the side and the motion sent a wave of nausea through me. We were flying over a curving waterway; to our left were little forms like stacks of children's building blocks interspersed with jagged lines that were crawling with—oh, my God! Automobiles!

The plane pitched to the right, and below was the silvery snake of the East River glittering in the morning sun. We followed the path and I could see ahead the broadening of land that was the island of Manhattan, its thousands of windows facing east reflecting the morning sun like the tiny mirrors of a glitter ball.

The Queensboro—59th Street—Bridge sprawled across the river, and beyond it, through a burnished haze, appeared Trevor Hunter's biplane.

Did Anthony Young have Soledad with him? Or had he done away with her? For he had a gun. The Winchester.

For a moment I let my speculations go as we approached the bridge we had just traveled over. *Would Harpo fly above it or beneath it?* We were approaching so fast that if he didn't act quickly, we'd hit its stanchions within seconds.

As soon as I found the breath to scream out to him, the air was sucked out of my lungs as he swooped down suddenly and the shadows of a hundred automobiles on a grated track flashed over my head. I would have swooned but for the expletives I needed to lash out at the maniac behind me at the controls.

But what controls? A couple of sticks, a couple of knobs was all that this ridiculous balsa-wood child's toy was provided with.

"You all right, Dottie? You don't look so good."

"There are easier ways to commit suicide," I shouted at the top of my voice. I never considered this torturous way to die when writing my poem, *Resumé*.

"You're safe in this."

"That's what they said about the *Titanic! We're in a kite, for God's sake! We're in a kite! And nobody is holding the string!*"

"More likely to die in an automobile than flying in a plane, you know."

"Cut the crap—you think you're Lindberg?" I screamed.

"Smooth sailing the rest of the way, now that we've caught Young's tail. He's heading for Jersey, I'll bet."

"Jersey?" I shouted back. "Why the hell's he want to go to New Jersey for? Nobody in his right mind wants to go to Jersey!"

"Beats me, but—"

Before he finished his sentence, Harpo swooped down low over the river and angled the wings sharply for a turn over Manhattan. I figured we were over 50th Street, as I could see the spire of St. Patrick's Cathedral dead ahead.

Although I felt a sickly, sinking feeling in my gut, I still experienced the fascination of the bird's-eye view of my hometown, and I wanted to laugh and cry from joy and from fear both at the same time. I looked at Woodrow. He was content and fearless. *Ahh*, to be a dog!

All right, I said to myself, *if I die, I die.* I surrender.

"Hold on," said Harpo. "Trust me," and he maneuvered a dizzying swoop down low over oncoming traffic, the plane's wings skirting the buildings flanking Lexington Avenue.

"*Ssshhhiiiiit!*" I screamed.

My life was in the hands of a crazy man! I took back my surrender. Dead ahead stood the stalwart symbol of American Industry, and it would not move aside for us to pass.

And then, Harpo yelled out, "What the—!" as we made our final approach over the tower from the east. "It's growing!"

"What?" I screeched, as Harpo tilted in a suddenly wide and fitful maneuver up and away from the tower. As we turned back to face the obstruction we saw that the Chrysler Building was indeed growing taller: A great spire was rising slowly above the dome!

I closed my eyes when my head flew back, for we were ascending sharply, but I couldn't resist peeking out to meet my Maker. And the vision was frightening until I understood that what I was looking at was a gargoyle—like a giant automobile hood ornament—that hung out from the tower.

It was then that I glimpsed Soledad's blue-chiffon scarf fluttering overhead, over the Chrysler Building tower, as the plane we were chasing crossed our path. I was blinded by the sunlight reflected on the building's bright steel façade.

We completed our rise and were turning, reeling up and over, my body pressed against the side of the cockpit. The beauty of the city with its new crowning jewel was mesmerizing and I was lost in ineffable wonder.

The situation forced Harpo to fly south, away from the building, before turning west. Harpo's maneuver to catch up with his quarry had proved futile and time had been wasted. Perhaps the southern route would be the way to catch up.

Crossing west over 34th Street, we passed over Herald Square, Macy's, the wedding cake of Pennsylvania Station, and then over the train tracks and the piers jutting out into the Hudson River.

And there they were, crossing our path once again. I could see there was trouble as the biplane sputtered and dipped suddenly.

In less than a minute we were on it. "They've stalled," said Harpo.

"Will they land in the river?"

"Not if Young knows what to do."

"Well?"

"Glide to a landing."

"But where?"

The plane's motor caught, and the biplane shot out ahead of us, but now on a northerly route along the Hudson. We passed over steamships and ocean liners being tugged in and out of port. A barge trudged upstream and people on piers waved as our planes flew past.

And then the sputter, the sudden dip of the plane's nose, before another recovery. "They're out of fuel," shouted Harpo.

We followed now, back over Manhattan island, keeping to the river, heading north, and there before us was the rectangle that was Central Park, its lakes blue from the reflected sky, the roads and bridal paths obscured by the russet leaves like bouquets tossed along the green meadows.

"They're landing!"

"Sheep Meadow!" yelled Harpo. "Do you have your gun?"

"What? What gun?" I screamed. "I don't carry a gun, you idiot!"

"All right, then, grab a croquet mallet, will you?"

"You nuts?"

Down, down came the biplane with Young and Soledad, skirting the top branches of trees and bouncing on the meadow in a bumpy landing. Sheep scattered in all directions. And I didn't have time to feel afraid as Harpo brought our aeroplane down and finally taxied it to sit nose-to-tail with theirs.

Soledad lifted the hem of her skirt and stepped onto the wing, smiling and waving at us and brandishing a little pearl-handled revolver. Harpo rushed over to help her down, but this amazing woman was triumphantly in charge, ordering Anthony Young out from the plane, and convincing Harpo that other than restraining Young, she would have no violence.

"Do you love me *now*, Sollie?"

"You are the cutest, most adorable, most annoyingly persistent man I have ever known, dear Harpo."

"Does that mean *yes?*"

"What do you think?"

A crowd was gathering from the surrounding paths and motorways. A reporter, on his way to photograph the Chrysler Building in the very act of surpassing the 40 Wall Street tower by several feet this morning with the surprise lifting of its one-hundred-twenty-five-foot spire, making it the tallest building in the world, received a front-page scoop for the afternoon edition: THE CAPTURE OF THE MURDER CLUB KILLER BY MYSTERY WRITER SOLEDAD SOLEIL.

Woodrow, like Harpo, had only one thing on his mind, so he ran across the meadow to romance his lady-sheepdog obsession, Eleanor, who would have none of his nonsense as she had a job to do, rounding up those pesky sheep. She chased him off.

The reporter posed Soledad and Harpo—who held Anthony Young by the collar—and then penciled an interview into his notebook:

> *Miss Soleil stated, "When the plane ran out of fuel, I pulled my little revolver—I always carry it—and told Mr. Young to give me his gun, and that I was taking over the controls. Louis Blériot, the*

famous French aviator, taught me how to fly, and told me what to do when things go wrong."

Sirens whined somewhere in the park, and as they got louder, I knew that the police had arrived. Five squad cars, and Mr. Benchley, driving Aleck in Harpo's new Caddy, arrived behind them.

Detective Sparrow walked through the expanse of meadow, his amusement evident and overriding the fact that he would have to, by law, ticket Harpo for landing his aeroplane in Central Park.

I watched Mr. Benchley sauntering over to me, his face a blank page. "Did you enjoy the ride?"

"There are easier ways to commit suicide. I think I'll stick around for a while."

 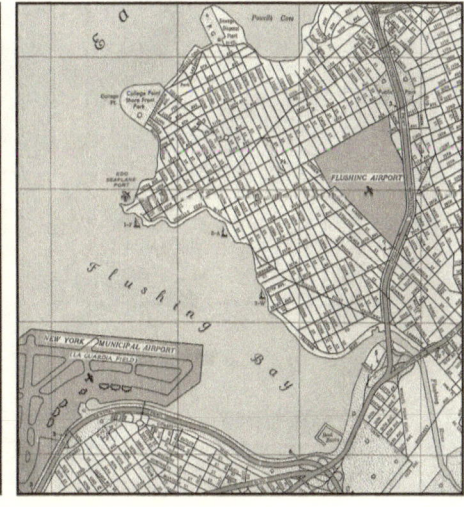

Louis Blériot, Soledad's flight instructor

The Queensboro Bridge—we went over and under.

From my bird's-eye view

The new Keith's Albee Theater in Flushing

The Final Chapter

"Gino," Aleck called out grandly, waving the restaurateur over to our table, "we need more antipasto!"

My gang had gathered at the speakeasy for a late dinner. Our turbulent morning had been followed by an afternoon of exhausted sleep, and then evening commitments. With us were Mr. Benchley, Ross and Jane, Edna Ferber, Frank Pierce Adams, Soledad, and Detective Nate Sparrow. The Marx Brothers were expected at any moment, the curtain of their Broadway show having come down fifteen minutes ago. Heywood Broun would arrive with them, I figured, having watched the show for the umpteenth time from the wings.

Aleck indicated the nearly empty antipasto dishes on the table before him. "Bring us more, and with extra *sopressata* and the *lugano* olives—and bread—don't forget more bread."

"Yes, Mr. Woollcott," said Gino, and as he walked from the table he mumbled something in Italian that made Sparrow, who was sitting next to me, chuckle.

"What did he say?" I asked, leaning in.

He whispered in my ear, "He's afraid he'll lose his best customer, after his belly explodes tonight."

"Yes," I replied, "Aleck has always attacked his food as if it's about to sprout wings and fly away."

Soledad was answering Ross's questions about the events of the morning, while FPA was jotting down her version of the flight across Manhattan and her disarming of Anthony Young for his morning column.

"It was quite simple, really. He hadn't a clue about how to bring the aeroplane down safely under the circumstances, and he had no idea that I knew how to fly. I could say I wrestled the weapon out of his hand, but it didn't happen that way. It was resting on his lap and when the plane went loop-de-loop it fell and he couldn't retrieve it. I pulled my gun from my purse and told him I was taking the plane down, and certainly not into the Hudson. So I didn't *really* disarm the poor fool."

"You disarm every poor damn fool," said Ross, cow-eyed.

"You better watch out, my dear friend, or your beautiful Jane will disarm you."

Jane grinned wickedly.

Perhaps I was tired; a blue funk overtook me. I suppose I sensed it coming. The change, that is. Everything was barreling along much too fast, much too nicely, and as I am basically a pessimist, I am also suspicious by nature. I was to be proven right two weeks later when the world shuddered to a stop.

But, sitting here this night with my gang at Gino Di Cenzo's restaurant, I felt a wave of dread. What appeared to be rising opportunities for my friends, those new ventures that promised them fame and fortune, I feared were about to split us apart.

Everything changes. I'm the first to say it. There are no happy endings.

Rumor has it that there is a plan to tear down whole blocks of the West 40s—which our favorite speakeasy, Tony Soma's, calls home—to build a complex of skyscrapers and a grand music hall. Another tycoon like Chrysler is behind it all, John D. Rockefeller. The march of progress will not be slowed.

But the lights on Broadway are as bright as ever. There are colored lights now. It is no longer the stark "White Way" of yesteryear. Sunlight at midnight. They flash and they chase and they tell you why Chevrolet is the only car to drive, and which cigarette is good for your throat, and which tablet to swallow for that upset tummy after an evening of too much fun. The news of the day continuously revolves around the Times Tower: L-I-N-D-B-E-R-G—F-L-I-E-S—D-E-T-R-O-I-T—T-O—C-A-P-E—H-O-R-N . . .

F-O-R-M-E-R—P-R-E-S-I-D-E-N-T—W-H—
T-A-F-T—D-I-E-S . . . G-A-L-L-A-N-T—F-O-X—
W-I-N-S—T-R-I-P-L-E—C-R-O-W-N . . .

Yes, the flashing lights are more garish and louder than carnival barkers hawking their rides and sideshows while hoping to lure you into their world of the fantastic. Even though our decade of speculation is over, there is one consolation. One can always find a few hours of fancy behind the spectacularly lit marquees that line the side streets off Times Square.

Times Square, Broadway, 42nd Street—these are the magical streets in a town filled with infinite possibilities, and I doubt that will ever change.

"Well, the case is solved, thanks to you, Mrs. Parker, and your wonderful friends," said Detective Sparrow, pulling me away from my ruminations.

"With nary a shot fired," said Mr. Benchley.

"A shot would have made fast work of my torment," I countered, dangling the last slice of Italian salami under the table for Woodrow to snatch.

"And a woman out West, Mary Connelly, the widow of one of the Harvard Four who tormented Anthony Young, is now free of all charges of murder in the death-by-poisoning of her husband," said Detective Sparrow, "thanks to all of you."

"I would have put my money on Shaw as the murderer," said Ross. He's a nasty piece of work."

"After reading Ersatz's version of events," said Aleck, "I would have, too. He certainly was the instigator, the puppeteer behind the scene."

"There's no proof that he actually did anything," said Detective Sparrow. "Young claims full credit for providing the poisons for the others to carry out their crimes."

"I suppose it's a good time to tell you that I've solved *another* case," I said.

"Oh?" everybody said, and I let a long, pregnant pause linger over the table before I continued.

"Your bank heist." I was enjoying the dramatic buildup.

"Well, that would be grand, if you did," said Detective Sparrow. I enjoyed the admiration that shone from his eyes. "We haven't gotten very far. The getaway car turned up clean of prints. It had been stolen, as I figured, and there are no suspects."

"Well, Detective, you should check out the Golden Pagoda Chinese restaurant across the street."

"What about it?"

"Their Peking Duck is excellent," said FPA.

"Not as good as a little place I go to in Chinatown," countered Aleck.

"I found out that they *don't deliver*," I said.

"Never did," said Detective Sparrow.

"The restaurant is right next-door to the bank, you see. So, I wondered why, just moments before the gunman emerged from the bank, I saw a Chinaman carrying a package as he walked out of there and then getting onto a delivery tricycle with a sign that reads, 'The Golden Pagoda Restaurant.' I think your getaway robbers and their car were merely decoys. The cash was literally 'delivered.'"

"On a delivery bike! You may have something there."

"Well, I'd love to have a little of the reward money, if you get it back."

"At the very least, I'll take you out to dinner, Mrs. Parker."

I looked around the table at my friends, and my eyes returned to his. "*Alone,*" I whispered. Natali Speranza smiled.

It really was a nice smile, but after a moment my attention was drawn to a study of my best friend, Mr. Benchley, who sat across the table from me, engaged in his chicken cacciatore. When he caught my eye, he put down his fork and threw me a winsome look. There followed a silent communication between us, free of banter and wisecracks and full of wistful sentiment that could never be voiced aloud.

Tomorrow morning he would be carried off on the Twentieth Century, bound for Hollywood. It would no longer be a matter of moving across the street to the Hotel Royalton—a scant dozen steps—for Mr. Benchley to avoid the conflict of work versus the company of our friends. It would be a matter of three thousand miles.

I thought, *This night should be a celebration heralding his success in his new career in motion pictures*, but for me it was a bittersweet parting of ways. We knew in our hearts, no matter how much we tried to reassure one another that we would see each other soon, that such would not be the case and things between us would never be the same. My champion, my brother, my "Fred"—*yes, the love of my life*—was going away from me and I would have to cope with that reality.

Our silent exchange was interrupted when Detective Sparrow addressed me. I furtively wiped away the tear that threatened to escape and betray me, as I turned my head to give my reply.

The End

The Winner

40 Wall Street takes second place.

Magical streets in a town filled with
infinite possibilities

Praise for *Dorothy Parker Mysteries*

Those of us who since childhood had wished there was a time machine that could let us experience and enjoy life in other periods, should read Agata Stanford's "Dorothy Parker Mysteries" series. They wonderfully recreate the atmosphere and spirit of the literary and artistic crowd at the Algonquin Round Table in the 1920s, and bring back to life the wit, habits, foibles, and escapades of Dorothy Parker, Robert Benchley, and Alexander Woollcott, as well as of the multitude of their friends and even their pets, both human and animal.

—*Anatole Konstantin*
Author of *A Red Boyhood: Growing Up Under Stalin*

Agata Stanford's "Dorothy Parker Mysteries" is destined to become a classic series. It's an addictive cocktail for the avid mystery reader. It has it all: murder, mystery, and Marx Brothers' mayhem. You'll see, once you've taken Manhattan with the Parker/Benchley crowd. Dorothy Parker wins! Move over, Nick and Nora.

—*Elizabeth Fuller*
Author of *Me and Jezebel*

Dorothy Parker and the Regulars of the Algonquin Hotel Round Table are alive and well in Agata Stanford's *The Broadway Murders*. Descriptions are fantastic in this who-dunnit as Stanford writes very colorfully. This is an adult's picture book, too, which in the end turned out to be pretty terrific.

—*Terri Ann Armstrong*
Author of "Medieval Menace" for *Suspense Magazine*

If you like murder mysteries, the fast-paced action, witty conversation, and glib repartee of the flapper era, you will love Agata Stanford's recreation of the atmosphere of the crowd at the Algonquin Round Table in the 1920s.

—*Mr. Tomato*
for *TheThreeTomatoes.com*

Dorothy is presented with wit and sarcasm sprinkled with tremendous insight. The life she lived is believably recreated, including the escapades of the Marx Brothers, the late nights of theater and dinners, even the famous speakeasy they drank at; all serve as backdrop to the investigation. The writing style affects the breezy language and popular slang to further transport you to that era when jazz artists and flappers coined modern terms. It is a heady mix and an escapist pleasure.

—*A.F. Heart*
for *Mysteries and Musings*

About the Author

Agata Stanford is an actress, director, and playwright who grew up in New York City. While attending the School of Performing Arts, she'd often walk past the Algonquin Hotel, which sparked her early interest in the legendary Algonquin Round Table.